W9-AXG-479

Quinn

By Sally Mandel

Change of Heart
Quinn

Delacorte Press / New York

Published by
Delacorte Press
1 Dag Hammarskjold Plaza
New York, N.Y. 10017

Lyrics from "Hit the Road Jack" by Percy Mayfield. Copyright 1961 Tangerine Music, Inc. Reprinted by permission.

Lyrics from "Yesterday" by John Lennon and Paul McCartney. Copyright © 1965 Northern Songs Limited. All rights for the U.S.A., Mexico, and the Philippines controlled by Maclen Music, Inc. Used by permission. All rights reserved.

Lines from "Easter 1916" from COLLECTED POEMS of William Butler Yeats (Copyright 1924 by Macmillan Publishing Co., Inc., renewed 1952 by Bertha Georgie Yeats). Lines from "He Gives His Beloved Rhymes" from COLLECTED POEMS by William Butler Yeats (New York: Macmillan, 1956). Reprinted by permission of Macmillan Publishing Co., Inc. and A. P. Watt Ltd., London.

Copyright © 1982 by S.E.M. Productions, Inc.

All rights reserved. No part of this book may be reproduced or transmitted in any form or by any means, electronic or mechanical, including photocopying, recording or by any information storage and retrieval system, without the written permission of the Publisher, except where permitted by law.

Manufactured in the United States of America

First printing

Designed by Richard Oriolo

Library of Congress Cataloging in Publication Data

Mandel, Sally.
Quinn.
I. Title.
PS3563.A446Q5 813′.54 81-15269
ISBN 0-440-07205-0 AACR2

For Barry
with my love

My gratitude to Peter Lampack for his perspicacity and hard work, to the Writers Room, which is my Shangri-la, and to Maureen Madden Marlowe for herself

Chapter 1

The November wind picked up a wad of paper, whipped it past the stone buildings and out the other side of the library steps, leaving the central quadrangle litter-free. The grass, freeze-dried a month ago by Halloween frost, hid under a crust of brown leaves. The old maple trees that lined the interior walkways of the campus were bare, branches stretched against the pale sky, stark and clean. Knots of students hustled along the sidewalk, oblivious to the austere beauty of the place, chattering, laughing, dropping books, clutching jackets tightly against the chill.

Quinn Mallory raced across the campus with her battered suitcase, darting past the slower students. Her auburn hair flew against her cheeks. Her red sweater was a bright splash of color, like a winter cardinal startling against the subdued landscape. She emerged at the far end of the quadrangle, bounced down a flight of marble steps, and came to a halt at the tall wrought-iron gates of the college's formal entrance. Panting to catch her breath, she watched an elderly Volkswagen bus drive up to the gate and stop. Its brakes protested with a metallic screech, temporarily drowning out the Shirelles as they professed, full volume, "Baby it's you."

Stanley Markowitz pushed his mass of tangled black curls through the window. "Been waiting long?" he asked.

Quinn grinned at him, swung her suitcase onto the backseat, and climbed in. "Hours," she answered, still gasping. "What kind of limousine service is this, anyhow? Oh, God, I'm dying."

Stanley persuaded the bus into first gear and they shuddered past the gate onto the main road. Vanessa—Van—Huntington, who sat next to Stanley, turned around to scrutinize Quinn's cheeks which were steamy red from exertion. "We wouldn't have left without you, you know," Van said.

"What?" Quinn yelled. John Lennon and Paul McCartney were wailing "I wanna hold your hand."

Van snapped off the radio. "I *said* we wouldn't have left without you."

"I was afraid I might hold you up."

"Where's your jacket?"

"I don't need it," Quinn said.

Van looked at Stanley. "There's something wrong with her. It's forty degrees out and she doesn't need a coat."

"Comes from all those years at St. Theresa's, watching our breath in class," Quinn said. "They never turned on the heat until Sister Superior declared winter, which usually wasn't until December fifteenth." She stretched luxuriously. "Let's hear it for vacation. Come on, come on." She raised her hands to summon applause from the front seat.

"Yay, Thanksgiving," Van said.

Stanley glowered at them. "I'm happy for you both. I only pray this thing has a coronary so we never get to Boston."

"Stanley's nervous." Van gave him a gentle smile, and he took his hand off the wheel to tug on a strand of her long dark hair.

"Not a coronary exactly," Quinn said, listening to the engine wheeze into fourth gear. "Nervous breakdown, maybe. Your caburetor's screwed up. Before you make another trip, you've *got* to let me work on the wheel alignment."

"Yes, doctor. Anything you say, doctor," Stanley said.

Quinn settled back into her favorite corner against the left-hand door and thought about home. She always enjoyed the trip from school to Medham. Not long, cramped hours that caused her body to ache, yet time enough for decompression. As they picked up speed she could feel herself shedding burdens—term papers, exams, after-school jobs—preoccupations that evaporated behind her like the exhaust from Stanley's bus. Instead, her mind was cheered with images of home: the faces of her parents, the cozy comfort of the house on Gardner Street that awaited her two hours down the road. She smiled. It was lovely to be taken care of every now and then. Tomorrow morning Quinn would awaken to the smell of fresh-baked muffins and black coffee as her mother quietly entered her room with the tray. They would sit on the bed and enjoy their first-morning-home breakfast together, gossiping and catching up. Just thinking about it made her feel drowsy and warm.

Suddenly Stanley pressed hard on the accelerator and roared past a city bus that hobbled along near the curb.

"Go get 'em, tiger! Ah, there's life in the old nag yet," he said.

"That bus was not moving," Quinn remarked.

"It was," Stanley protested. "I distinctly saw the back wheel move. Vanessa, defend your chariot."

She craned her neck to look out the back window. "Sorry, honey. That's a dead bus."

Stanley's eyes in the rearview mirror were tragic—huge and brown. Quinn stuck out her tongue at them and they sparkled.

"Know what I'm going to do tonight?" Quinn said. "Set my alarm for six A.M. so I can turn it off, roll over, and go right back to sleep."

"Why don't you just sleep?" Van asked.

"Didn't you ever do that? I thought everybody did."

"It seems like I always had to get up for *shul* on weekends," Stanley said. "Maybe if your daddy promises to get me into Harvard Med School I'll give him a treat and take him to Temple Emanuel on Saturday."

"Oh, sure," Van said.

"Right!" Stanley exclaimed heartily, pulling onto the eastbound ramp of the Massachusetts Turnpike. "Who's for Burlington, Vermont?"

"No, no, my darling," Van said. "Straight on to Beacon Hill."

Stanley glanced at her. "The closer you get to Boston, the more you sound like Mummy and Daddy."

"*Oy vay*," Van replied. She had the inflection wrong so that the expression came out sounding prim and stiff. Stanley and Quinn laughed.

"You think we'll have turnips?" Stanley asked. "I always wanted to see a turnip in the flesh."

"You never had turnips on Thanksgiving?" Quinn asked. "Sacrilege. What did you eat in Brooklyn?"

"Turkey with stuffing and potato pudding and noodle pudding and *kasha varnishkes* and potato pancakes. And a nice bowl of chicken soup with a couple of matzoh balls lurking on the bottom. Real sinkers."

"The Indians shared maize with the Pilgrims, not matzoh balls," Van said.

"In Flatbush we didn't have Indians. Chassidim, yes. Indians, no."

Quinn examined Van's profile. In repose her friend's features were classically long, rather somber. Stanley liked to call her his Modified Modigliani. But when she smiled, particularly at him, the angular lines of her face lifted and two faint dimples appeared beside her mouth, making her seem vulnerable and girlish.

"Hey, Mallory," Stanley said. "What would your parents do if you brought home a Jewish boyfriend?"

"Enroll me in a convent."

"Oh, you'd make a great nun," Van laughed.

"It's never been mentioned," Quinn continued, "but I think they'd *appreciate* a Catholic, preferably Irish. Preferably from County Kerry, except not one of those heathen Calhouns."

"Did they give your boyfriends a rough time?" Van asked.

"Mom never gives anybody a rough time, except for my father, and he always deserves it." Quinn scratched her nose, remembering. "Tommy Flanagan was the only one who counted, and they thought he was the second coming of St. Patrick. Until he dumped me, of course, and then my father nearly lynched him."

"Hey!" Van exclaimed suddenly. "Aren't you going to see him this vacation?"

Quinn nodded.

"Oh *ho*, romance is in the air," Stanley said.

"Don't get all worked up," Quinn muttered. "I'm going to his engagement party. Actually, I'm going to Margery O'Malley's engagement party. Tommy Flanagan just happens to be the person she's marrying. Otherwise I'd drop dead before I'd show up."

Van peered at her. "Your freckles just got darker. You

must really hate him." Quinn rolled her eyes. "No, really," Van insisted. "Look, Stan. Isn't that amazing?"

Stanley obligingly twisted his head around to view Quinn's freckles. "Topographical map of Ireland, right there," he said. "How come Tommy Flannelman dumped you?"

"Flanagan. I told you. He was a shit. The only potential Marvin the Magnificent I have ever known, and he turned out to be El Creep."

"Oh, Lord, Marvin again," Van said. "I don't like to disillusion you, dearest, but there's no such thing as the perfect man."

"I resent that," Stanley said.

"Marvin will be perfect," Quinn protested. "Body beautiful and mind *extraordinaire*. Four-oh average, of course. Poetic soul. Man of my dreams. Although," she added, "if he turns up at Margery's party, he won't have a four-oh. I'll be the only one there who goes to college. But he could still be brilliant. Tommy was."

"How come he didn't go to college, then?" Stanley asked.

"Thought it was a waste of time. He got a full scholarship to B.U., the jerk. Can you believe anything so ridiculous?"

"What's he doing now?" Van asked.

"He works at a bank. He's doing all right, I guess, but I haven't seen him in three years." She watched out the window as the Berkshire foothills smoothed out into long, flat fields. "Maybe I should have been a nun," she murmured to herself, and fell silent. Holiday traffic was beginning to crowd the turnpike. The van clattered into the left lane to overtake a slow-moving caravan of cars. A campaign poster, remnant of the election three weeks ago, whizzed past: *Vote for Moore in '64.*

Suddenly Stanley boomed out in a hearty, man-to-man voice, "Well, stuck in the rough, were you, eh, Dr. Huntington? Guess I'd have used my seven wood or my widge."

"Wedge!" Van howled. "Oh, Lord, it's hopeless. The wedge is for sand traps. He'd probably use his five iron in the rough."

"Five iron," Stanley echoed morosely. "Can't we talk about stickball? I bet you didn't know one time I hit three sewers. I mean, what's a hole in one compared to three sewers on Avenue J?"

"What?" Van and Quinn said in unison.

"You know," Stanley explained. "Those manholes in the street. If you hit the ball past two, you were a champ, but three was Hall of Fame. Izzy Pinkowitz was a three-sewer man too. Me, and Izzy, and Jackie Halpern, of course."

Van shook her head. "I don't think Father would relate to sewers."

"Aw, shucks," Stanley said regretfully. "Better refresh my memory on putts." His face brightened and he adopted a heavy Yiddish accent. "*Oy*, a Jewish voyd. I'll explain 'im all about my *putz*."

"Oh, Stanley, for heaven's sake, they're not going to eat you," Van said.

"Were they really so awful the last time?" Quinn asked.

"I was a perfect gentleman. They hated me."

"They did not," Van protested. "They just never saw anybody in jeans, an army shirt, and a black silk vest."

"You're kidding," Quinn said.

"It was from my grandfather's tuxedo, and I wore it out of respect for your parents," Stanley said. "They hated me. They still hate me. Why are we doing this mad thing?" He swerved the car as if to make a U-turn.

Quinn reached into her sweater pocket and held out a

metal object. "I brought you a lucky charm, so now you don't have to be so nervous." Stanley took his hand off the wheel and examined it. From heavy wire Quinn had fashioned a Star of David with a cross in the center. "I'm going to buy you a chain for it, but I just finished it this morning. This way, see, you've got all the big guns on your side."

"I'm going to keep it with me every second," Stanley said. "Thanks, babe."

"May I see?" Van examined it. "It's wonderful. Would you maybe make me one someday?"

"Sure." Quinn thought about the pile of rejects that had accumulated on her desk as she puzzled over the talisman. It had taken two weeks to get it right.

Van stretched out a hand to touch Stanley's cheek. "Well, there's nothing my parents can do about the way I feel," she said.

Stanley grabbed her fingers and began kissing them ferociously. "I can take all kinds of abuse as long as I get to sneak into your bedroom and ravage your body," he said.

Quinn studied Van's flushed profile and remembered the night she had watched her friends saying good night in the shadows beside the dormitory entrance. They were crushed together, their mouths locked, parting briefly only to join again. Quinn had caught a glimpse of their faces as they stared at each other in wonder. They had looked awed.

Margery's party flashed into her head, a shimmering question mark. Marvin, she thought, where are you? It's time. It's time.

Medham was part of the blighted area of Boston situated halfway between the central city and the suburbs.

In April the trees wore a hopeful tender green veil, but they soon blackened with soot from the nearby shoe factory where John Mallory worked. In summertime the tiny front lawns were overgrown with weeds, and in September the leaves made no final dazzling display of predeath defiance; rather, they just curled into defeated husks and fell to earth beside the shabby wood-frame houses, most of which, like the Mallorys', were divided into two sections and shared with another family. Now, in late November, the ground was a bleak crust of brown with an occasional splotch of frozen slush.

Quinn waved good-bye to Stanley and Van and marched up the steps. Before she could ring the bell, John Mallory opened the door and grasped her in a tight hug, suitcase and all.

"Daddy, I've missed you," she murmured against his bony shoulder. "Hey, you're squishing me to death." She held him away from her and smiled into his face. For a fair-skinned man his whiskers were very dark, as were his eyebrows. Quinn had always thought the coarse auburn hair, a shade darker than her own, and the hazel eyes under dark brows made him unusually handsome.

As always, the house had a faint smell of the lemon oil her mother used to polish the piano.

"Where's Mom?" she asked.

"In the kitchen." John set her valise on the bottom step of the staircase.

"Naturally," Quinn said, and started off down the hall.

"Is that you, dear?" a voice called.

"No," Quinn answered. Ann Mallory met her at the kitchen door, and the two embraced.

"If it isn't my girl, who is it, then?" Ann asked her.

"Um, Moll Magee."

"God forbid," John said. His lifetime devotion to William Butler Yeats had resulted in a family habit of referring to the poet's wild and tragic characters as if they lived just down the block.

John went to the stove, lifted the lid off a large simmering pot, and grabbed a potato with calloused fingers.

"Sit down, John," Ann said. "You'll burn yourself." Elbowing him out of the way, she began ladling out the stew. John carried two bowls to the table and started back for more, but Quinn intercepted him.

"Since when are you so gallant?" she asked, taking the dishes from his hands.

"Since your mother's been feeling poorly."

"Mom?" Quinn inquired.

"I got overtired working on the bazaar for St. Theresa's. Your father's being silly. Not that I mind him waiting on himself now and then."

"She's going to see Dr. Marshall next week," John said to Quinn.

"I'm not," Ann retorted.

"Ten thirty Tuesday morning. If I have to drag you by the toes."

"Such a fuss over nothing, John," she said, giving him a light flick with her dish towel. "Besides, I have a heavy schedule the beginning of the week."

"Since your mother got promoted to administrative assistant, she thinks she runs the college," John said to Quinn.

"She'd be good at it."

"I'm the only person in the history department without a degree," Ann protested. "I work hard because I don't know enough."

"By the time you're finished with these research

projects, you'll know more than any of 'em," John muttered. "And be worn out, too."

Ann turned to roll her eyes at her daughter. Quinn had been busy inspecting her, probing for signs of illness. There were none. Ann moved efficiently about the kitchen, as always. Relieved, Quinn plunked down at the round oak table in the corner. The caned seat felt comfortably familiar beneath her. She kept her eyes on her mother.

"This chair always was a perfect fit for my ass."

Ann turned to flash Quinn a look of reproach. Quinn stared back with eyes twinkling and recited along with her, "Oh, Quinn, honestly . . ."

Then they both laughed and Quinn said, "Now I *know* I'm home."

Quinn watched Ann sit down, taste the stew, wrinkle her nose critically, and reach for the pepper grinder. She had curly dark hair, creamy freckled skin, and blue eyes. Quinn's were blue as well, but bright and clear, filled with sparkling prisms of light. Ann's were darker, deep-sea blue, shadowed. Quinn enjoyed looking at her, though today she thought her mother did seem a little tired. Maybe it was the dying winter sunlight against her mother's soft cheeks. Ann looked up, smiling, and Quinn decided the pallor was only in her imagination.

"You heard about Margery? She's engaged. To Tommy Flanagan, of all people."

Quinn held up three fingers and wagged them at her. "Once by mail, once by phone, and now in person."

"Oh, did I really? I must be getting old. And surely Margery would tell you in *her* letters."

"She surely would. Besides, you know I've got the party tonight."

"Yes, of course."

"You trying to tell me something, Mom?"

Before Ann could answer, John muttered, "The O'Malleys will rue the day they allowed that boy in the family."

"I'm sure he's perfectly nice now. Susan O'Malley's delighted," Ann said.

"Susan O'Malley would think Adolf Hitler was perfectly nice."

"That was four years ago, Jake," Quinn protested, reverting to her childhood habit of addressing her parents by their first names, or in John's case by his nickname. It had pleased her to think of them as comrades. "We were just kids, for Christ's sake," she continued.

"Don't swear, dear," Ann said.

"You must hear a lot of cursing up at B.C., Mom. When are you going to get used to it?"

"She chews them out too, don't think she doesn't," John said. "And Tom Flanagan behaved like a dog. You know, I found out from Father Riley that the Flanagans were first cousins to the O'Roarkes. Not the Dublin O'Roarkes, the farmers. My great-grandfather on the Madden side got fleeced by old man O'Roarke when he bought that pitiful little shed near the river. Took all his savings and the damn thing nearly floated away in the spring floods. Worthless, it was."

Quinn tipped her bowl to capture the last spoonful of stew and sang with an exaggerated brogue, "The thing about John Mallory, y'see, the man never carries a grudge. Sure, and not past the sixth or seventh generation."

Ann laughed.

"*He had done most bitter wrong/ To some who are near my heart*," John said. His eyes were crinkled at the corners.

Quinn leaned back, balancing her chair on its hind legs. "I bet everybody'll be at Margery's tonight. All the old gang."

"I think I heard Noreen's cousin from Quincy is up," Ann said. "You remember, dear, the tall good-looking one."

Quinn grimaced.

"She remembers," John said.

"Is there anyone special at school?" Ann's voice was casual.

"No. I really don't have time."

"Of course you have time. Every young girl has time."

"There's the cafeteria job and the work at the garage. I see a lot of Gus Lenowski. We spend many a weekend together changing points and plugs."

Ann looked closely at her daughter. "He's . . . older, isn't he?"

"Ancient. Forty if he's a day. There isn't anybody, Mother. I'll probably go to my deathbed a virgin."

Ann set her soup spoon down abruptly.

"Besides, you've been a career lady for two years now. How come you're still putting the pressure on me to get married?"

"Was I?"

"You were," John said. "There'll be plenty of time for all that after graduation. Let her concentrate on her studies." He turned to Quinn. "Make Phi Beta Kappa yet?"

"Speaking of pressure," Quinn said, "don't I always do all right?"

"All right? What's that?"

She made a face at him.

"Leave her alone, John," Ann said. "She just got here, for heaven's sake."

"That's all right, Mom. I wouldn't recognize him if he wasn't surly."

"I'm the most even-tempered person in this house," John said. Quinn hooted.

"Did you bring home something nice to wear to the party, dear?" Ann asked Quinn.

"I have a nice greasy sweat shirt with matching cut-offs . . ."

"Jesus Mary!" John interrupted with mock horror. "You'll do your mother in, girl. You know she has a weak heart."

"Margery getting married. It's hard to believe," Ann remarked.

"Seems just the other night she came in here crying and carrying on, poor lass," John said.

They all sat quietly for a moment, remembering. Several years ago when she and Quinn were still in high school, Margery had appeared at the front door late one night, asking for Ann. She refused to tell Quinn what was wrong, only insisted through her tears that she must talk to Ann, until finally Quinn got her mother out of bed. She and Margery sat in the kitchen with the door closed for almost two hours while Quinn and John tried to concentrate on Marlon Brando in *Viva Zapata*. Days later Margery confided in Quinn that she was pregnant. She miscarried soon afterward, and, as far as Quinn knew, the O'Malley family never found out.

Troubled people had always turned to Ann Mallory, and it was only during their unburdenings that the kitchen door was kept closed. Quinn would go to her room or sit by the television with the volume turned way up so that she wouldn't be tempted to eavesdrop. As a child she had felt uneasy about those sessions. On the one hand, she was proud that people valued Ann's advice. On the other hand, she sometimes wished it had been possible to hoard her mother's special comforting gifts. Some things were hard to share with the general public.

"I don't suppose you'll tell me what it was all about?" John asked. As Ann looked at him he held up his hands. "No, never mind. Forget I asked."

Everyone knew that with Ann a secret remained a secret. Quinn shoved back her chair and began collecting dishes.

Ann started to rise. "Yes, you'd better get a move on if you're going to make it to the party by six."

"Sit down, Ann," John ordered. "I'll do it."

Quinn stared at him as he stacked the plates and carried them to the sink.

"Your shower," Ann prompted.

"Yeah, thanks, okay. Stew was great, Mom." On her way out she planted a hasty kiss on her mother's cheek.

They listened to her clatter up the stairs.

"It's nice to have noise," Ann said.

John, up to his elbows in soapsuds, grinned at her from across the kitchen. "You betcha," he said.

Quinn dressed carefully. Just in case Magnificent Marvin shows up, she told herself. Why did it seem as if two weeks ago she'd been primping in front of this same mirror for the sake of Tommy Flanagan's admiring smile? She supposed it was the absence of any important person ever since. Besides, she was sixteen when she fell for Tommy and eighteen when it was all over. Everything gets exaggerated during those years. Her hormones must have been making her crazy. She brushed her hair energetically, pleased at how the light caught its waves. It shone against her shoulders, and her blue sweater matched her eyes. Tommy was probably ugly. Maybe even fat. What the hell.

The party was in full swing when she arrived. Susan

Kelly shouted, "Hey, there's Quinn!" But immediately she was pressed up against Jim Donohue. He handed her a papercupful of beer.

"How's our co-ed? Still learning how to be better than us poor working slobs?"

"Now tell me, Jim, how in the world could I ever be better than you?"

He gave her a squeeze. "You're still pretty cute, Freckles. For an intellectual."

It took her fifteen minutes to shove through the crowd to the happy couple. She managed to swallow another cup of beer on her way. When she spotted Tommy's curly head beside the window, she gulped down a third. He watched her approach, and she caught his quick appraisal of her face and body. Margery, busy with her mother, didn't notice.

"Hi," Quinn said, smiling into the smoky eyes that had bewitched her way back in seventh grade when she'd had to pitch a no-hitter to make him know she was alive.

Tommy returned her smile, dipped his head for a chaste kiss. Then Margery interrupted her conversation with Mrs. O'Malley long enough to hug Quinn. Margery had an aureole of wild, frizzy brown hair that had always dismayed her. Since the boy-crazy days of junior high she had experimented with every remedy: expensive conditioners touted by Italian countesses with sleek dark tresses; creams sold exclusively in the ghetto drugstores of Roxbury—she had even talked Quinn into ironing it the night of the Junior Prom, but the result was always a disappointing thatch that was as brittle as hay, or singed kinks that exuded alarming wafts of Eau de Bonfire with every movement of her head. Quinn concluded that Tommy's attentions must have given Margery confidence. Tonight her hair, left to its own devices, was a pillow of tangled curls. Her face was a perfect heart shape, her eyes were golden brown, and Quinn thought she had never looked prettier.

"I'm so glad you're here," Margery was saying. "But we won't be able to get two words in tonight. When am I going to see you?"

"I'll be around till Sunday," Quinn said.

"Terrific. I've got so much to tell you." Margery gave Tommy a mischievous look. "Come on, Mom, we'd better find those ashtrays or we'll have a new pattern in the rug."

Margery's mother said hello, then looked from Quinn to Tommy with undisguised anxiety. But Margery escorted her toward the kitchen.

Left alone with him, Quinn said, "Congratulations. You couldn't have done better."

"I'm a lucky son of a bitch," he said. The gray eyes watched her closely. "How are you, Quinn?"

"Never better. I hear you're a banker now."

"Yeah."

"You like it?"

"Beats college."

"Now, how would you know?"

"You going to start on that?" he asked.

She stared at him in silence for a moment, wondering if she had just found out why he hadn't shown up that last Saturday night. "I bet Margery's much too easy on you," she said finally.

"Yup. She seems to think I'm acceptable in my present flawed state."

"Everybody can use improvement," Quinn said.

"Some of us are hopeless." He reached out a long arm to grab two more cupfuls of beer from a passing tray.

He handed one to Quinn. "Are you working on anybody at school?"

Quinn felt herself growing flustered and took a swallow from her cup. "No."

"I can't believe that. There must be all kinds of guys who need motivating. Better grades, more touchdowns—"

"Is that what you think I do?" she interrupted. "Go around like some missionary bettering people's characters?"

She realized immediately that her tone was far too intense for his cheerful banter. She looked down into the nearly empty paper cup, and Tommy touched her shoulder lightly.

"Hey, I was just teasing."

"And all this time I thought it was because I wouldn't go to bed with you." Infuriatingly, her eyes began to fill with tears.

"Quinn, what in hell did I say?"

She shook her head. "Sometimes I think that was my first mistake. I actually believed all that eyewash about going straight to hell."

"You're still pissed off at me," he said. His voice was quietly incredulous.

"You broke my heart, you bastard."

"Hey, listen, that was kid stuff. I never meant—" A lone tear trickled down her cheek and he broke off miserably, "Jesus."

"Margery makes you happy, doesn't she?" Quinn asked.

"Yes."

"She'll be good to you. She'll make your bed and wash your socks and have your babies and never demand a thing." He opened his mouth to protest, but she didn't let him speak. "I'm not putting that down."

"Like hell."

"She's the best-natured, kindest person on earth, and you'd just better be nice to her forever." Quinn glanced toward the kitchen and saw Susan O'Malley staring at them. "I'm going to mingle. It's good to see you, Tommy. All the best." She kissed his cheek and turned to lose herself in the crush.

At Thanksgiving dinner, and for the remainder of the vacation, Quinn's parents thought she seemed quieter than usual. Instead of pursuing her customary frantic schedule of visiting and parties, the front door banging with incessant entrances and departures, she mostly stayed at home, reading magazines and tinkering with her father's car. On Sunday afternoon Stanley and Van stopped by to pick her up.

Stanley waited until she had finished waving goodbye to Ann and John from the back window of the bus. "So, how was it?" he asked.

"Fine. What about yours?"

"Your mother is so pretty," Van said.

"You don't look anything like her," Stanley commented.

"Gee, thanks," Quinn said. "You're both alive, so it couldn't have been too bad."

"Yeah, but you should see *them*," Stanley said gleefully, "lying in a pool of blood on the pale white carpet, hatchets sticking out of their backs."

"Stanley was wonderful," Van said. "They couldn't find a thing the matter with him."

"Drove them nuts. I could feel them inspecting my nails. I wonder why they didn't ask me for a urine specimen."

"Oh, Stanley," Van said.

"Who knows, they might have detected some rare

disease found only among those of the Jewish persuasion. Fatal, of course, preferably within the hour."

"They're coming along," Van said firmly, and turned around to ask Quinn, "Was Marvin at the party?"

"Not that I noticed. It was very crowded. Did you do anything special?"

"Wait a minute," Stanley said. "What about Flannelmouth? Has he reformed?"

"Hard to tell. Did you pass the golf test?"

"God damn it, what happened at the party?" Stanley bellowed.

"Nothing. I said 'hello' and he said 'hello' and we shot the breeze for a while and that was that. I think he'll be extremely happy with Margery." Her voice was even. Van peered into her face, and Quinn smiled back sweetly. After that she fell silent, watching out the window.

Finally Stanley complained about the unnaturally low noise level in the backseat, and Van said, "Tell her about the Great Freudian Slip."

"You tell her."

"Oh, no, I'm much too humiliated."

"We're all sitting at the table looking like a Norman Rockwell painting," Stanley related, "and Mrs. Huntington gives me this tight little smile, hands me a thimbleful of coffee, and says, 'Stanley, wouldn't you like another piece of this lovely chocolate kike?' "

"She didn't! I don't believe you," Quinn howled.

Van shook her head. "Do you think maybe I was adopted?"

"That got a rise out of her," Stanley said, referring to Quinn. But she had already slipped back into her reverie. "Mallory, what in *hell* is going on with you?"

"Nothing. I'm thinking." It had begun to snow, and

Quinn watched the fine dry powder whirl into fanciful shapes beside the road as the bus roared past.

"Yes, but what about?" Van asked.

"Just working on Marvin, that's all."

"That's all," Van echoed.

"If he wasn't at the party, where'd you meet him?" Stanley asked.

"I didn't. But I'm going to. Soon. Now leave me alone. I'm plotting."

Van shrugged at Stanley. For the rest of the trip all conversation was confined to the front seat.

Chapter 2

"We're late," Van said, her arms loaded with books. She watched Quinn's disheveled figure emerge from beneath the jacked-up truck—battered sneakers first, then overalls, and finally the grease-streaked face. Bright tendrils poked out from beneath an oversize plaid handkerchief tied around her head.

"You look like a chimney sweep." Van took a small step backward, unconsciously avoiding the possibility of besmirching her skirt.

"Chim chim cheroo," Quinn replied. "Thanks for bringing my stuff." She stepped out of the overalls, undid the handkerchief, and shook her hair. "Gus!" she yelled into the shadowy recesses of the garage.

"Christ, Mallory," Gus answered. "You trying to bust my eardrums or what? Hello, Vanessa."

"I didn't see you, sneaking up on those little cat feet," Quinn said, cleaning her hands with a rag. Gus looked down at his size thirteen work boots.

Quinn nodded at the truck. "She's okay now, but they ought to give that maniac a nice safe desk job. He's hell on transmissions."

"What about number 63? I need her by Friday."

Quinn groaned. "I can't, Gus, really. I've got a Religion final."

"Listen, nobody else has your way with shock absorbers," he said. "You'll get your A anyway."

"Come off it, cheapskate. You just don't want to hire a union mechanic." She tossed him the rag. "Can't it wait until the weekend?"

"For you it'll wait."

"Deal," she said. Van glanced pointedly at her watch. "Okay, I'm coming."

As they headed for the door Gus called, "Hey, good luck in Religion! If you don't know the answer, pray!" He reached through the window of the truck and started the engine, nodding as it roared into life.

The two figures raced along the campus walk, Quinn slightly ahead of Van, their breath exploding in icy clouds. Despite her long legs Van struggled to keep up with Quinn's unrestrained gallop.

"We're not *that* late," she gasped.

"Have to check the mail before class."

"You've got a break after English. My God, you're making me perspire."

"It's good for you. Cleans the pores," Quinn said.

"But I don't *like* to perspire." Van slowed to a trot as Stanley intercepted them.

"Hello, ladies," he said, draping an arm across Van's shoulder. He and Van were almost the same height, but Stanley's bulk and lumbering gait made him seem bigger. Quinn was shorter than either of them and bobbed up and down next to Stanley's shoulder.

"What's with you, ants-in-the-pants?" he asked.

"Gotta check the mail. Save me a seat?"

"They probably haven't even sorted it yet," Van said.

"Thanks for bringing me my books. See you in a minute," Quinn said, and she dashed off toward the student union, hair flying.

"Forgot her vitamins this morning," Stanley muttered. Van snuggled against him as they made their way toward McLane Hall.

By the time Quinn slipped through the doors, Dr. Buxby was well into his lecture. Van signaled to her, and the professor stopped in midsentence to watch Quinn navigate the long legs of the Robinson twins and plop down next to Van.

"Uh, Miss Mallory, are you quite comfortable now?" he asked.

Quinn nodded, unperturbed. "Yes, thank you." Her cheeks were flushed from the brisk air and exercise rather than from embarrassment. "Sorry I'm late."

The classroom was a small amphitheater with fifty seats rising in graduated tiers. Dr. Buxby paced back and forth at the front. He wore his three-piece pinstriped suit with the red paisley handkerchief poking out of the breast pocket in three perfect points.

"We're, uh, sorry too, Miss Mallory, because I am certain you would have enjoyed Mr. Ingraham's, uh, remarks regarding Catherine Earnshaw."

"Pithy, I'm sure," Quinn said.

"Excuse me?" The professor cocked his head at her.

"Miss Mallory has a lisp," drawled a voice toward the front of the room.

There was a ripple of laughter as Quinn sought out the shaggy head and angular body of Will Ingraham, who sat, or rather, lolled, in his seat, long legs stretched out comfortably into the aisle.

"Correct me if I misquote you, Mr. Ingraham," the professor said, then addressed himself to Quinn. "Mr.

Ingraham, uh, defends Catherine's behavior, viewing her, uh, passionate refusal to, shall we say, renounce Heathcliff as an act of, uh, courage, a symbolic revolution, if you will, against the rigid hypocrisy of her time." He paused to let his words resonate, then glanced at Will again. "Do I catch your drift, Mr. Ingraham?"

"More or less," Will said.

"Well, Miss Mallory?"

"I'm sorry I mythed it," Quinn replied.

Dr. Buxby paused to let the snickers subside, then went on, "You don't mean to say you concur with Mr. Ingraham's assessment."

"On the contrary," Quinn said.

Van put her chin in her hand. "Oh, Lord, here we go again."

"Catherine Earnshaw was no revolutionary. She was anything *but* a free spirit. She lived under the absolute tyranny of her glands." Out of the corner of her eye Quinn caught sight of Will Ingraham's legs as he very deliberately crossed one booted foot over the other. He inclined his head in her direction as if loath to miss a single syllable. She smiled in admiration at his gift for communicating such profound rearview arrogance with such minimal effort.

"She vacillates between her sexual passion for Heathcliff," Quinn continued, "and her greed for prestige and money as exemplified by what's-his-name, Edgar."

"I assume that Miss Mallory prefers the virtuous Jane Eyre," Will said, no emphasis on the word "virtuous."

"Jane refuses to compromise her belief in what's right for anybody, even the man she loves." She felt her voice rising.

"So she abandons Rochester because she's too weak to buck polite society. Nice lady," he said.

"That is *not* what I said." Quinn leaned forward now, fist clenched. "You're missing the point. People just can't do what they damn well please. They have to set up standards for themselves and have the guts to live by them."

Will turned around now and looked at her. His eyes were blue, lids almost half-mast, lazy. "That sounds like something Jane would say."

Quinn glared at him. "Thank you," she said. Will shook his head slightly, as if to say he thought she was getting pretty worked up about all this. "Well," she sputtered, "I'm not saying I don't believe in freedom. Everybody should have freedom, especially to love. . . ."

"That's a relief," Will said with a quick grin.

There was a murmur of laughter, and Quinn stared at him furiously. "You are very smug."

He tilted his head to her in apology. "Sorry," he said. "Cheap shot."

"Children, children," Buxby said, clearly delighted with the exchange. "Let's not allow our, uh, literary enthusiasm to create factionalism in the classroom, pleased as I am that our, uh, assignments have made such a, shall we say, personal impact. We shall confine ourselves to the issues at hand. Now, Mr. Hartley, I want you to, uh, contrast for us, if you will, the imagery in the two novels."

The rest of the hour Quinn found her mind drifting. She watched out of the corner of her eye as Stanley's hand fell casually to Van's knee and crept halfway up her thigh. Van's face seemed impassive, but Quinn noted the flush on the usually pale cheek. When the bell rang at last, jolting her from her daydreams, Quinn waved Van and Stanley off, promising to meet them at dinnertime. She dawdled collecting her books. Suddenly she realized that she was delaying until Will Ingraham had left the classroom. She'd had no intention of walking down the corridor with that complacent smile burning a hole in her back.

Chapter 3

Quinn's room in the women's dormitory was moderately neat, due to the day's cleaning binge. Each month, exactly twenty-four hours before her period arrived, Quinn became ferociously tidy. She folded clothes, straightened drawers, sorted socks, dusted surfaces with maniacal energy. The urge disappeared the following day, not to return for another four weeks. By the time she was fifteen, she had learned to take full advantage of her compulsion or the piles of books, clothes, souvenirs, and half-eaten Hostess Twinkies would collect underfoot until the next time around.

She had livened up her cubicle with warm colors—a bright patchwork quilt on the narrow bed, a second-hand rocking chair that she had fitted with yellow pillows, and beside the chair a straw basket that held three giant paper flowers—red, yellow, and orange. On the linoleum floor were three bath mats from Woolworth's bargain table—again, red, yellow, and orange. The walls were decorated with posters: John Kennedy barefoot on a Cape Cod beach; Ike and Tina Turner in concert; and a travel poster of County Kerry, Ireland. All were unframed but carefully attached with hidden circles of masking tape.

At the bottom left-hand corner of the Kennedy poster drooped a wilted white carnation, taped there to commemorate the first anniversary of his death.

Quinn sat at her desk by the window, ostensibly committing to memory the postulations of *Totem and Taboo*. Her right foot tapped rhythmically against the floor as she absorbed the marked-up pages.

Perched precariously on the edge of the desk was a portrait of her parents. Their features, fuzzy and idealized, faded into one another with varying shades of beige—except for the eyes, both pairs identically blue there, although, of course, her father's were actually hazel. Quinn had gazed at the picture so often she imagined she had blurred the outline of their faces by staring at them so much.

Her yellow Magic Marker squeaked as she highlighted another paragraph. All but five sentences were illuminated with the bold transparent track. Sighing, she tossed the book on the desk and stretched. Her eyes shifted to the drawer. She stared at it and then, after a quick glance over her shoulder, opened it cautiously. She removed an envelope, extracted from it two typewritten sheets that were stapled together, and began to read.

Quinn was halfway down the first page when Van entered the room. She approached the desk unnoticed and reached down curiously to examine the papers that appeared so absorbing. Quinn jumped up with an exclamation, stuffed the pages into the envelope, and held it behind her back.

"Excuse me. I didn't mean to startle you," Van said. "What's that?"

Quinn's face had begun to redden, but she summoned enough composure to slide the envelope back into her desk. "Nothing," she said casually, closing the drawer. "You just surprised me, that's all."

"Letter from home?" Van pressed.

"Yeah."

Van peered closely into the flushed face. "I don't believe you."

Quinn watched Van's eyes fix on the drawer.

"You wouldn't," Quinn said.

Van's body was stiff and she held her breath.

"You're much too inhibited, Vanessa."

Van lunged for the drawer and yanked it open. Quinn yelped and grabbed at it, but Van had got there first. She backed away, holding the letter above her head. Quinn stretched desperately, but Van was just tall enough. She waved the envelope back and forth out of reach.

"I don't believe you did that. I'll never trust you again," Quinn protested. "It's a federal offense, interfering with the mail."

"I'm not going to read it. I just want to see who it's from." Van peered at the return address. "Chris Hartley? Hey, is this what the recent mailbox obsession is all about?"

Quinn slumped down at her desk, defeated.

"I want to read it. May I?"

Quinn looked at her balefully, then shrugged. Van began to skim the pages. She made no comment, only raised her eyes once to glance at her friend's defiant face. When she had finished, she sat still for a moment, then said, "Are you going to report this?"

"What for?"

Van dangled the letter gingerly between two fingers as if it were on fire. "This is one sick boy."

"Oh, that's not his own stuff. He copied it all from secondary sources."

"Which, an Abnormal Psych textbook or The College Man's Rape Manual?"

"Mostly the *Kama Sutra*, I think," Quinn said.

Van sat down on the bed. "You mind telling me what's going on?"

"Yeah, I do. But since you bullied your way into it, I guess I might as well. That letter was commissioned."

"Commissioned," Van repeated dully.

"Look, I'm going to be twenty-one years old in a few weeks and I'm probably the only virgin in the senior class."

"That may well be true."

"I can't *graduate* like this."

"What would people think?" Van said.

Quinn continued, her voice extravagantly patient, as if she were talking to a feebleminded child. "I don't want just *anybody* to do it, do I? It has to be the right person."

"Chris Hartley is applying for the position of your deflowerer?"

Quinn nodded.

"You're crazy," Van said.

"I knew you'd say that, which is exactly why I didn't tell you. And if you mention this to a living soul I will personally remove your toenails."

Van shook her head. "What're the conditions of this contest, or whatever it is?"

"Well, the rules called for something original," Quinn answered. "I hope the other guys read the instructions at least."

"Just how many *are* there?"

Quinn reached for her Religion notebook and flipped it open to the last lecture's notes. Silently she pointed to the list she had penciled in the margin. The names and their descriptions had been heavily embellished with doodles, but Van could still make them out.

CHRIS H.: maternal instinct
JERRY L.: body beautiful
PHIL S.: wiseass
MYRON S.: intellect
JACK W.: good jokes
BOB K.: gentle soul

Van looked at Quinn in silence for a moment. Then she said, "Did you ever consider availing yourself of the free student-counseling service?"

"Are you kidding? What would I do with a shrink?"

"It might help."

"Help what? I don't need help. I need Marvin the Magnificent. I'm going to get him."

"But Quinn . . ." Van's forehead was wrinkled with the effort to explain. "It's kind of . . . bizarre, don't you think? To go about it this way?"

"I think it's eminently practical."

"I wish you all the luck in the world."

"You have no faith."

"Can't you see? It's like . . . coupling by computer. Mail-order sex. You've got this thing about control, and it isn't something you *can* control. Or ought to, anyway. People fall in love by accident."

"I don't."

"I really get the feeling you're involved in a classical search for the ideal father figure."

"Oh, *can* it, Freud, for God's sake. Quit analyzing me."

Van fell silent.

"Until you butted into this I was having a lot of fun," Quinn said. Van looked so pained that Quinn's face softened and she held her hand out placatingly. "Hey, listen, it's just that it's time for me now. It'd be okay if we could put Stanley through the mimeograph machine, but there's no way. Can't I have someone, too?"

Van held her hair coiled into a twisted mass on the top of her head. Now she sighed and released it, letting it fall silky and dark past her shoulders. She stood up, headed slowly for the door, and turned to look at Quinn. "Listen, you'll keep me posted?"

Quinn nodded.

Van hesitated for a moment, then said good night and closed the door carefully behind her.

Chapter 4

Jerry Landring's room was a mess. Every conceivable surface was littered with something—football uniforms, soccer uniforms, sweat shirts, sneakers with cleats, sneakers without cleats, helmets, kneepads, and jockstraps. At the moment the chaotic atmosphere of the place was augmented by the presence of six young men who sat or flopped wherever space permitted. Jerry stood barefoot on his rumpled bed and scratched on a chalkboard that hung shoulder-high from a tired-looking nail. The others watched intently as a pattern resembling a tennis tournament scoreboard appeared. Six names were listed on the left-hand side: *Bob*, *Chris*, *Jack*, *Myron*, *Phil*, *Jerry*. From a bracket directly to the right of the names two lines projected, upon which were written the names *Chris* and *Jerry*. Then, from another bracket, one line extended, where Jerry now drew a large question mark.

"So," he said, finishing off the question mark with an emphatic dot.

"I took mine right out of the *Kama Sutra*. I don't know why she didn't like it," Jack said.

"Oh, *no*. You didn't tell me that," Chris Hartley moaned. He sat on the floor beside the bed with his hands clenched around bent knees. "*I* used some stuff from the *Kama Sutra.*"

"Not very subtle, guys," Phil remarked from his perch on the windowsill.

"She should only know how subtle my prick is."

"Shut up, Jack," Chris said. His voice was brittle, and there was a sudden silence.

Finally Jerry said cheerfully, "Don't despair, Chris. It's fifty-fifty now."

Chris looked up at Jerry's athletic body and handsome face. "How much longer is she going to keep us waiting?" he asked anxiously.

"The Virgin Quinn will no doubt take her own sweet time," remarked an amused voice. Everyone turned to see Will Ingraham leaning against the doorframe. "Jesus, Jerry, this place looks like an armpit."

"Smells like one, too," Jack muttered.

"So who's going to win the Irish Sweepstakes?" Will asked, nodding toward the chalkboard.

"I'm ecstatic to report that Mr. Chris Hartley and yours truly," Jerry said with a small bow, "have attained the status of semifinalists." He pronounced *semi* as if it were *sem-eye*. "In a few short days one of us will be the proud possessor of the gold medal."

"How do you know it's gold?" Jack asked.

"Maybe you'll get a brass ring instead," Phil remarked.

Chris shot Phil a malevolent glance and said, "I just want to know why it's taking her so Goddamn long. . . ."

"Maybe a light went on in that weird head and she decided to back out," Will suggested.

"She wouldn't!" Chris exclaimed.

"No, probably not," Will said. "She set the rules, she'll go through with it if the winner brings along his pet boa constrictor."

"If Chris wins, he's got one built in," Jack said.

Everyone laughed, even Chris. When he was pleased, the tense line of his jaw relented, softening into a child-like curve.

"Good luck," Will said. "Especially to the winner." He disappeared from the doorway. Phil's high-pitched version of Catherine Earnshaw's ghost floated down the hall after him: "Oh, Heeeeea-th-cliff . . ."

Chris got up quickly and left the room. When he finally caught up with Will, Chris grabbed his arm a little too hard.

Will spun around, frowning. "What the hell are you—"

"Sorry," Chris panted. "Jesus, you're fast. . . . Look, this is a little embarrassing . . . there's a favor. See . . ." he stopped to take a breath and patted Will's arm tentatively where he had fastened on to it. "You okay?"

Will nodded, curiosity replacing his irritation.

"You're good in English," Chris went on. "I mean, you really have a mind. Original. Could you . . . I mean, I'd pay you. I gave Quinn Mallory this thing and it's no good, and I know Jerry's going to win if I don't hustle." Will looked puzzled, and Chris shook his head in frustration. "Look, I'll give you fifty bucks to do something really great for her. But it has to be right away. Tonight . . ."

Will interrupted him. "Hey, listen, Chris, I can't do that."

"Please. Jerry doesn't give a damn. She's just another piece of ass to him. I really care. I never even dared ask her out and then I got her letter about the contest, and I've really got a shot at it . . ."

"I'm sorry. No."

"Oh, come on," Chris pleaded. His mouth smiled, but he had taken hold of Will's arm again.

"Sorry," Will repeated, prying himself loose. He started off down the hall and heard Chris's voice following him.

"Oh, come on, Ingraham. It's only a game. . . ."

Chapter 5

Will gazed out the window of the bus as it rattled up North Main. Once past the center of town the street became pitted, the trees sparse and stunted. Battered garbage cans vomited their frozen contents over the sidewalks like grotesque cornucopias. The city, once one of western New England's prospering textile centers, had begun its decline when the mills moved to South Carolina. Then Springfield, its flourishing neighbor, dealt the fatal blow by siphoning off most of its remaining industries.

Will rubbed his gloved hands together. Even the temperature inside the bus seemed to drop five degrees as they hit the North End ghetto. He glanced at the other passengers and noted that, as always by Myrtle Avenue, he was the only white person aboard. He stood, joints stiff with cold, and rang the bell. The bus shuddered up against the curb and expelled him through the back doors onto the littered sidewalk.

Harvey's school was only a block away, but Will stood at the bus stop trying to conjure up a tantalizing —and inexpensive—afternoon for the boy. He stamped his frozen feet—what a lousy day to experiment with spontaneity. Besides, for the first time in three years of weekly visits with this special little brother, he was late.

Harvey Jackson had been searched out and assigned to Will by the college in what now seemed an ill-fated investment in culture clash. Take a black kid to lunch, pitch him a softball across the lush campus athletic fields, buy him a mug handsomely embossed with the school seal, and send him home to the rats and filth. Soon the novelty of playing social worker wore off, and one by one the volunteers opted for an afternoon working out at the track or guzzling beer at the student union rather than shattering their spinal columns on a North End bus. The program was officially canceled in letters citing academic pressures, signed personally by the president of the college and sent to each ghetto participant. Some of the notices reached their destination, some were stolen from broken mailboxes along with the welfare checks, and one was delivered, read, and incinerated over the gas stove of a weary woman with four young boys and no husband.

But Will had made it to Harvey's shabby apartment house before the letter did. Sometime during the first months of the Big Brother program, the seven-year-old child had taken up residence in an area of Will's brain that was reserved for permanent tenants. The inhabitants there were few: Will's grandfather; his brother, Sam; Marianne, his childhood friend and the sister of his soul until her car had crashed more than a year ago; the inspiring Edward French of the Red Falls Central High School English department; and now Harvey Jackson. Once one gained admittance to this guarded sector, eviction was impossible, so far even by reason of death. Certainly not by edict of a college administrator's pronouncement that Will could quit chasing off to the North Side Elementary School every Thursday afternoon.

Clusters of children began to spill around the corner, their noisy chatter jolting Will from his preoccupation. He headed toward the school, a curious sight—lanky young man with the western stride and sunstreaked hair loping upstream against the surge of laughing black faces.

Harvey, ten years old now, but small for his age, was leaning against the building. The dark eyes registered recognition at the sight of Will, but nothing else.

"Sorry I'm late," Will said, touching the boy's thin shoulder briefly.

"That's okay," Harvey said.

Will peered into the expressionless face. "You pissed off at me?"

Harvey looked up at him, surprised. "No, man. What for?"

Will saw that it was true. The boy wasn't angry at his tardiness, only resigned. Disappointment was to be expected, along with crushed dreams, brutality, and betrayal. Will drew the wiry figure close to him, suddenly understanding today's reluctance to meet the boy at all. Only six months until graduation, and Will had yet to broach the issue of their upcoming separation.

Will gazed down at the soft mound of frizzy hair trotting beside him about heart-high. "Give me a lesson in tough, Harve," he said.

"Whatchoo talkin' 'bout, man?" Half a dozen boys sprinted past them, a few turning to wave at Harvey and shoot him a look of envy. "Hey, Joe, Tony," he said with a stiff nod, but Will saw the pride in his face and felt the narrow back straighten a fraction.

With an effort Will cut short his speculation about

Harvey's Thursday next year this time. "What's new?" he asked.

"Nothin'. Where we goin'?"

"Downtown. The mall, where it's warm. School?"

"It's okay."

"Got your grades this week, didn't you?"

"Yeah."

"Come on, Harve."

The small face tilted up to show a hint of mischief and defiance. "Two B's. Two C's."

"Not bad, but haven't you got five courses?"

"Yeah, well . . ."

"Well?"

"And one D."

"In what?"

"Music."

"That's hard to figure."

"Aw, that old faggot don't know nothin'. He's into all that fancy junk you can't even *move* to. We gotta do a report on one of those old dudes he's so crazy about. Moe-zart or one of them . . ."

"Mote-zart," Will said.

But Harvey went on, his voice cracking with preadolescent outrage. "That Mr. Ballister don't even know who The Kickers is. *Shit*."

"Yeah?" Will tried in vain to remember who The Kickers might be.

It was cold waiting for the bus. They swung their arms and stomped their feet to keep the circulation going. Mercifully the downtown bus appeared before too long, and as Will boosted Harvey up the steps he said, "Hey, Harve, you ever hear of Prokofiev?"

Harvey flopped down into a seat that perched atop the bus's only operative heater. "That a disease?"

"A composer. Died about ten years ago."

"Yeah, I guess maybe I heard of him."

"We're going to the library first. They've got a record we can listen to."

"What kind?" Harvey asked suspiciously.

"It's about this wolf and a kid named Peter. The wolf swallows a duck, and Peter goes after him . . ."

Harvey's body was motionless. Will glanced sideways at the solemn face and kept talking, inclining his head toward the boy until he felt the soft brush of Harvey's hair against his cheek.

After dinner Will returned Harvey to the North End on the same drafty bus he'd ridden from campus. As always, Harvey refused Will's company up the four flights to his dismal apartment. Instead, they stood in the space just inside the doorway, out of the icy wind. A naked light bulb illuminated six decades of obscenities carved into the peeling walls, and Will supposed that, as usual, the rough scribbles would remain in his mind all evening. Perhaps archeologists in centuries to come would preserve those crumbling surfaces and exhibit them in museums along with the caveman's primitive sketches on his dank clay walls. Scratching their heads, future generations could ponder the significance of *off the pigs* and *Wilma eats white cock.*

Harvey's eyes peered up at Will through a veil of black, curly lashes, and Will knew that what might appear to be furtiveness was actually hooded misery. Will struggled with the dilemma that always tormented him when Thursdays came to an end: to let the boy erect his walls against the world, Will included, or reach out and touch him, hold on to him for another moment, allowing Will some last image other than graffiti to warm him on the long bus ride home. One evening Will had weakened, cupped Harvey's chin with his palm, and said, "I'll miss you." The boy's eyes filled, the lower lip quivered, and he flung himself through the door and up the stairs. Will had heard him stumble on the first landing, probably blinded by his tears.

So tonight he gave the boy a grin and a rough jab to the shoulder. Let him be, let him construct his defenses against the angry, exhausted voices that awaited him four flights up.

"See you next week," Will said, then gave Harvey a shove into the narrow hallway.

"Yeah," Harvey murmured. Then both of them moved quickly away from the point of separation.

Will was restless sitting on the bus's molded plastic seat that was so cold in winter and so sticky hot in the summer. If this was what being a parent was all about, screw it, he thought. Even the most minute decisions seemed momentous. Tonight, for instance, when Harvey had pleaded for pizza. Will had wanted to feed him something nutritious that he wasn't likely to get at home. But Harvey had persevered, and Will tried to assuage his guilt by ordering extra mushrooms and green peppers for whatever vitamins that might have survived the freeze-dry process. Occasionally Will had stood firm at dinnertime, and watched his silent charge munch resentfully on broiled chicken while hiding his peas under the mashed potatoes. At those times Will chastised himself for withholding the pleasures of junk food from a life so devoid of indulgences. Pizza or poultry, malnutrition or malcontent—for Will every alternative promised inevitable guilt. Screw it, screw it.

Will gazed at the flashing colors of the downtown

department stores. He longed for the undisturbed darkness that sped past the window of his father's pickup truck on the way home from, say, a Friday night basketball game at the high school. Perhaps the memory of that black sky masked many unexamined complexities. He used to enjoy thinking of his childhood as a series of gentle contours. Over the years, however, out of a natural introspective impulse, he gradually acknowledged the jagged peaks and depths that growing up had required. Tonight's anguish over Harvey's dinner menu troubled him. It heralded a future full of rough edges, no less treacherous and painful than those of the past. Up until now there had always been the unchallenged assumptions: Will the teacher, Will the father. Maybe the time had come to apply the relentless probings of self-examination to the concept of himself as an instructor and champion of the young. A guilt-free career in computer programming might suit. He would be riding the crest of progress. And bachelorhood, of course, or, at the very least, vasectomy.

The bus began to wheeze and whine, signaling the ascent up College Hill Road. Will stood, grateful to be moving, making a familiar resolution to quit thinking so much. He shook his head to clear it. A beer would help.

The late-night emptiness of the student union made the place seem strange. Will realized that in almost four years he had never noticed that the windows were framed with carved columns and that the walls were wainscoted in oak. Hardly the sort of place to withstand the incessant tumult of ravenous undergraduates. It might have been the drawing room of a nineteenth-century country estate. Will decided to make a point of coming here at this hour more often. The ambience pleased him.

He sat down with his beer and a bag of peanuts at one of the heavy round tables near the door. He had just stretched his legs out on an extra chair when something shiny caught his attention. The hallway outside was dark, so that the lighted phone booth opposite the entrance drew his eyes like a beacon. Inside sat a young woman. Her face was hidden by a curtain of red-gold hair. Will watched until she turned her face toward the glass doors. It was Quinn Mallory. As if illuminated by spotlight, every feature was dramatized, framed by the soft black of the deserted corridor. Her eyes glistened so brightly that Will wondered if she was crying. He looked down at the foam in his glass, reluctant to intrude on her private grief. But almost immediately he found himself watching her again. She spoke briefly into the receiver and gazed back at Will unresponsively. After a moment she spoke again, forced a smile as if to reassure the invisible listener, and hung up. She sat for a moment with her hands lying limp in her lap. Her chin quivered slightly, but then she stood up and opened the door. Her glance met Will's. Unsure whether to smile at her, or even to acknowledge her, he just stared back silently. She turned away, and he was left wondering if she'd seen him at all.

"Hey, Ingraham, gimme a break, willya? I've got a French exam tomorrow."

Will looked up at the student bartender. "Sorry. Jesus, it's ten thirty." He drained his glass, slipped the unopened bag of peanuts into his jacket pocket, and walked out into the cold. The girl's image seemed to be burned into the air in front of his face. He blinked to make it go away.

Will found Jerry Landring lying in bed leafing through an antique issue of *Playboy* magazine.

"Did you ever get your decision?" he asked from the doorway.

"What?" Jerry mumbled, irritated at the interruption.

"Quinn Mallory."

"Oh, that," he said. "She axed us both."

Will stood quietly for a moment. Finally he murmured, "Appropriate imagery," and strode down the corridor to his own room.

Chapter 6

As the bell rang, Dr. Buxby's oration faded into the clamor of notebooks slamming shut, pens dropping, coats zipping. Van, felled by a virus, languished at the infirmary with Stanley in attendance, and Quinn hurried out of the classroom alone. Preoccupied with obligations, she wove her way quickly through the throng of slower students. There was her last-minute commitment to fix a motorbike for Gus. Then there was cafeteria duty and another class, with just enough time, if she really hustled, to deliver fresh orange juice to Van. Quinn thought it was a miracle that they managed to cure anybody in the infirmary with the kind of vitamin-deficient slop they spooned into their helpless patients. Poor Van had looked so peaked and miserable last night. Quinn flew down the corridor, organizing her immediate future, when suddenly a hand closed around her arm and brought her to a halt. Will Ingraham pulled her toward the wall, out of the stampede. His face was weary. Quinn looked up at him curiously.

"I hope I'm not too late to apply," he said. He held out a plain white envelope.

For a moment Quinn looked baffled, but then she reddened. "Oh . . . *that*. Well . . ." she stammered, feeling the color climb all the way to her forehead. She took the envelope automatically, but when Will released it, it dropped to the floor with a plop and slid away from their feet. Quinn said, "Oh," and stared at it dazedly. When she raised her eyes again, Will was halfway down the hall. He turned, gave her a friendly wave, and disappeared out the door at the far end.

That evening Quinn moved restlessly about her room, shedding clothes. Every few moments, she glanced at the white rectangle on her desk. Then she averted her eyes and took off something else, tossing the discarded items onto her bed in a heap. Finally, down to a pair of cotton bikini underpants, she pulled a T-shirt inscribed with "Property of Alpha Delta Phi" over her head and snatched the envelope angrily off the desk. Then she settled cross-legged on her bed and stared at her name printed on the front with a black felt-tip pen. The letters were square, neat, but not fastidiously formed. The dot above the *i* was sloppy. It looked like the accent for a French word. Quinn wondered if the contents were printed in the same strong, relaxed letters. Maybe it was script. She held the envelope up to the light, but the paper was too opaque.

She tried to remember Will's face in the hallway this morning. He'd smiled at her, but there had been something odd about his expression. Challenge, perhaps? No, nothing that strong. Something almost tender, like apology.

She should have let the damn thing lie there. But what if someone had picked it up and read it? God only knew what was inside. She could always destroy it. Or give it back. She pictured herself meeting with Will on Monday morning and returning the envelope to him unopened. That was the thing to do. After all, he hadn't been invited to participate in this thing.

She stared at it again, and turned it over to confirm what she already knew. It wasn't sealed.

Suddenly she was almost ripping the enclosed page in her haste to unfold it. A surprise—it was typewritten. She ran her eyes rapidly over the page, then began at the top and read again, slowly. After that she let the paper slide to the floor, stared blankly at her knees, and muttered, "Oh, shit."

Quinn opened Van's door softly, crept in, and sat on the edge of the bed. Van was asleep, breathing noisily through the debris left over from her bout with the flu.

"Van . . ." she whispered. There was no answer. "Van, are you up?" Van stirred in her sleep. Quinn grabbed a foot and began to shake it gently.

After a moment Van opened her eyes a slit. "Pardon?" she mumbled.

"I'm sorry. I couldn't help it."

"Anything the matter?" Van sat up halfway. Her stuffy nose made the words sound like *adythig the badder*. She fingered the neck of her long-sleeved flannel nightgown.

"Don't worry, you're respectable," Quinn said. "I've got something to show you. I tried not to. I mean, you've got this awful plague and everything, but I couldn't stand it."

"Go turn on the light. No, not that one, you'll blind me. The desk."

Quinn switched on the desk lamp, twisting the shade away from Van's puffy, reddened eyes. "You look awful," she said, perching at the foot of the bed again.

"I'll look worse in the morning. I heard you came to see me at the infirmary."

"Yeah, I broke the world sprinting record bringing

you orange juice and Janice Friedman was in your bed."

"Thanks for the thought, but am I ever glad to be out. What're they?"

"Applications," Quinn answered.

"I thought they were all in."

"Yeah, well, one was unsolicited. This is Jerry's." She held up a page by one corner and then released it deliberately so that it fell on the bed. "Your basic list of references, all his happy customers, who, by the way, include thirty percent of the women's dormitory. Did you know he screwed Barbara Tyson?"

"He says."

"Yeah." Quinn hesitated.

"And the other?" Van asked, eyeing the remaining page on Quinn's lap.

"Sure you want to hear it?" Quinn teased.

"You woke me up, for God's sake. Besides, I'll admit to a certain prurient curiosity."

"Listen," Quinn said, and began to read:

In bygone days, the swain must prove his mettle
To win and wed the kingdom's fairest lass;
Sadistic kings' or fate's requirements set 'til
the dragon fell, expiring, 'pon its ass.
The contest lives again, O campus princess,
The prize: fair Irish gem, O gleaming jewel.
From awesome trial this fierce knight never winces,
Such dares for William merely fire the fuel.
His athlete's grace, youth, modesty, high IQ,
To love's sweet challenge like the sun will rise;
With hands persuading, soft words (maybe haiku)
He'll coax his maid's bright laughter, giggles, sighs.
And, soul inspired, lean body tightly sprung,
He'll sate love's prime demand—and make it fun.

Van stared at Quinn in silence for a moment. "Who?" she asked finally.

"Will Ingraham."

Van's eyes widened. "Uh oh."

"Yeah."

"What are you going to do?"

"I don't know."

"Serves you right."

"It's even iambic pentameter, the bastard." Quinn looked at Van's smiling face. "Don't smirk at me, you . . . postnasal drip."

Van reached for a Kleenex and tried to blow her nose with ladylike discretion. After several unproductive sniffs into the tissue, Quinn said impatiently, "Damn it, just blow, will you? I won't listen." Quinn stared vacantly at the elegant Bachrach portrait of the Huntingtons that stood on Van's desk.

"All right, then," Van said. "Why don't you just tell him he's too late?"

"It's a winner."

"But he wasn't invited."

Quinn fell silent, then got up and switched off the light. "Thanks for listening. You'd better get some rest."

Van smiled into the darkness. "Sleep tight."

Quinn heard the delight in her friend's voice. "Oh, shut up," she said, and closed the door behind her.

Quinn was delayed in the garage on Saturday and had to hurry in order to pick up her mail before kitchen duty. Racing across the campus, she suddenly spotted Will ahead of her. He was walking with a girl—a pretty sophomore Quinn recognized from the cafeteria line. They were taking their time despite the frosty air. Quinn stopped short, intending to make a quick detour, but instead found herself staring curiously as Will bowed his head to better hear his companion. Then he laughed, threw his arm around her shoulders, and gave her a squeeze. What could that dark-eyed little underclassman have possibly said to elicit such appreciation from the cool Will Ingraham? She wrenched her eyes away from the couple and trailed behind them, determinedly forcing her feet to a slower pace. Finally they disappeared into Lenox Hall. She broke into a trot until the cold air whipped the image of Will and the girl out of her mind.

On Sunday, Van and Quinn sat in the dining room lingering over their desserts. It was Quinn's day off from her cafeteria job, and usually she enjoyed relaxing through her lunch. But today she felt impatient. Van's mealtime ritual had begun to grate on her. Each slice of turkey got carved into morsels of identical size to be transported to Van's mouth, one piece at a time, with the same compact gesture. She chewed each bite carefully, jaws meeting in a slow, relentless rhythm. After every two swallows she took a sip of milk. By the time she had finished her meat and started to subdivide the beets, Quinn had already cleaned her plate. She tried not to watch as the second of two forkfuls of beets disappeared down Van's throat. When Van reached for her glass, Quinn felt a shriek bulging under her larynx. She forced herself to stare out the window until the lump dissolved, but her foot was rapping out a tarantella under the table.

After she had gulped down the last spoonful of chocolate ice cream, Quinn wailed, "Oh, no. I forgot to taste that. I was looking forward to it all the way through the turkey and I don't remember any of it." She craned her neck around the sunny dining room, hoping to spy an untouched abandoned dessert.

Van disrupted her ritual to ask, "Something on your mind, dear?"

Quinn shot her a venomous look.

"My thought is that you really want to do this thing," Van declared.

"What thing?" Quinn asked. The tapping foot was now audible over the dining room clatter.

"The Noble Sir William thing."

"Oh, come off it."

"You don't have any obligation to go through with—"

"It's a matter of ethics," Quinn interrupted.

Van broke out laughing.

"God damn it." Quinn wadded up her napkin and tossed it onto her tray.

"Has anybody ever pointed out that you've got a problem with control?"

"Yes, Vanessa, ad nauseam. Why don't you just quit Fine Arts and be a shrink?"

"You'd make a great case study. Really, this whole contest thing is fascinating. You've set up all these controls as precedents for *losing* control. I mean orgasm, of course—"

"On second thought," Quinn interrupted irritably, "better stick with Fine Arts."

They sat in silence for a moment. Quinn's freckles had grown perceptibly darker. "You're mad at me," Van said.

"It's just that you are constantly psychoanalyzing everybody."

"Not everybody. Just you." Van tried out an apologetic smile. "I'm sorry. I'll stop. Well, I *can't* stop, but I'll keep it behind closed mouth."

"Much appreciated."

"Do you think it's a sin? Sex, for you, I mean."

Quinn shook her head slowly. "I'll tell you one thing," she said, "eternal damnation's gotta be more interesting than virginity."

Van laughed, and they finished their coffee amid speculation regarding Jerry Landring's alleged conquests, two of whom were sitting together at a table near the window.

Monday morning, Quinn lingered at the garage until finally Gus asked her if she was feeling all right. When she arrived at Lit class, she slid into a seat at the back of the room nearest the door and tried to concentrate on Dr. Buxby's remarks concerning Jane Austen. Her attention strayed around the room, and came to rest on the back of Will Ingraham's head. His hair was light brown with pale, sunny streaks. Amazing, really, for the beginning of December. It waved slightly, particularly at the neck, where it curled over the back of his collar. She wondered if it was coarse or soft. It looked soft, even though it seemed very thick.

"Miss Quinn Mallory?"

Her eyes flew to Dr. Buxby's face. Everyone seemed to be waiting for her to say something. "I'm . . . sorry, I guess . . . I didn't hear the question," she stammered.

Dr. Buxby frowned at her and snapped, "Mr. Ackley."

During Ackley's response Will turned to look at Quinn. She felt his gaze and stared straight ahead. When the bell rang, she bolted from her seat, down the corridor, and out the heavy wooden door onto the quadrangle.

Although in fact she managed to avoid him, her imagination found him everywhere. Lying on her back beneath a crippled truck on Tuesday, she concocted reasons for him to appear at Gus's tiny glassed-in office. Maybe Will needed a job. Maybe he wanted to borrow a special tool to fix something in his room, like . . . She stopped hammering on the muffler line and invented. Like his emergency generator. Surely he had a generator stowed away in his closet just in case the lights went out while he was studying for a crucial exam.

Gus's feet appeared, two sturdy shadows in the slice of light beyond the truck's underside. "Your friend's here," he said.

Quinn heard pounding in her ears.

"She's got your books."

Quinn scrambled out and blinked at Van in the sudden brightness.

"It's a good thing I happened to stop by your room," Van said. "You left everything on the bed. Aren't you going to Religion?"

"Yeah." Quinn reached for a clean rag. "I guess I just forgot them. Thanks." She took the books from Van.

Van stared at Quinn's smudged jeans. "Aren't you going to change?"

"She forgot her overalls, too," Gus said. He turned to Quinn. "You losing your grip, or what?"

She didn't answer.

"Got a lot on her mind," Van said quietly. Quinn grabbed her friend by the elbow and pulled her toward the door.

Quinn sat through the Religion lecture without hearing the completion of a single sentence. When the bell rang, she nodded a dazed good-bye to Van and walked out of the classroom like a somnambulist.

Will sat under a tree beside the massive stone steps that led to the library entrance. He leaned back against the tree trunk with one knee bent to support his book, a slim volume that absorbed his attention completely. Watching him, Quinn wondered if she had forgotten the mechanics of breathing. As she approached she tried to tell herself that she could still turn and walk the other way. But she knew she couldn't; there was this giant invisible hand pressing hard against the small of her back, propelling her toward him.

Will glanced up, and for a moment she thought he didn't recognize her. Then the vague, dreamy look lifted from his face and he gave her one of his strange half-smiles.

"All right. You win," Quinn said. Until this moment she'd had no idea what she would say to him. Her words seemed to float up into the branches of the tree and hover there. She felt as if she could follow them, she was so light and giddy.

"Thank you."

She waited for him to say more, but he just looked at her. Finally she stammered, "I'll be around this weekend. Next weekend." She stopped for a moment, trying to pull herself together. "Saturday night, this coming Saturday night."

"I know the one you mean."

She inspected his face to see if he was teasing her, but he seemed earnest enough. "Is that okay?"

He nodded.

"Seven?"

"Fine. Shall I pick you up?"

"No!" Quinn burst out. "No, I'll come to you . . . to your room."

"All right," he said.

She looked at his leg stretched along the frozen ground. "Aren't you cold?" she asked him.

"Yes."

Again, she waited for more, but he just continued to watch her patiently. She knew that her face had gone deep pink. "Well . . . see you then. Thanks . . ." She turned and started walking toward the library. Thanks for what? she thought. Thanks for turning my brain into rice pudding? She resisted a powerful impulse to run, but halfway up the steps she tripped anyway, barely catching herself. She could feel Will's eyes on her still, and cursed fiercely.

Once inside the ornate marble entrance she began to gasp like a drowning person surfacing for a final lungful of air. Then she started laughing and finally had to go to the ladies' room to splash cold water on her face before she could stop.

Chapter 7

Over the next few days she distracted herself with responsibilities, real and manufactured. For a baffled but delighted Gus she did a record number of brake jobs, repaired five snow tires, and performed a miracle on a particularly wayward exhaust system. She worked extra hours at the cafeteria. She researched a term paper for Poli Sci that wasn't due for four weeks. She exhausted herself, hoping to fall asleep every night without a thought in her head.

But as she lay waiting for unconsciousness, Will Ingraham's voice whispered in her ear, his face stared from the darkness—tender, enigmatic, apologetic face. She imagined his body, muscular and lean. Seduction scenes from countless movies played across the window shade. Will was Kirk Douglas in *Spartacus* watching her bathe naked in a lake like the lovely, sensuous Jean Simmons. Quinn was Deborah Kerr lying in the sand. The surf pounded as Burt Lancaster took her in his arms for a passionate kiss. She was Phaedra to Anthony Perkins's Hippolytus, twisting together in the firelight in an ecstasy of forbidden lust.

She flopped on her side and pulled the pillow over her head. There was time to back out. Even now. She didn't have to go through with it. But what to do about that sensation between her legs? Every time she thought about Saturday, she began to tingle. Her breasts felt as if they were stretching against the fabric of her T-shirt, turning her nipples to hard little knobs. Sister Maria Theresa always said you could tell a sinful movie if you had to cross your legs to watch it. Well, thinking about Will Ingraham made her cross her legs. Oh, Saturday. Maybe she would die before it ever got here. *Please.*

Please what? Quinn asked herself. Please *yes*, she'd die, or please *no*, she'd live to bed down with this potential Marvin the Magnificent? Fifty-fifty, she decided. Even Stephen between *nothankyou* and *yesokayIwantto.*

She lifted the pillow off her face. Liar, she thought with a sigh. The ratio was a whole lot more like twenty-eighty.

Van walked into Quinn's room at six o'clock on Saturday evening and said, "What's this, a garage sale?" She picked her way through the piles of discarded shirts, sweaters, and dresses that were heaped on the floor.

"I look awful," Quinn wailed. "I tried Vamp. I tried Sweet Young Thing, Nubile, and Urban Sophisticate . . . oh, the hell with it." She yanked a jersey off over her head and flung it onto the bed in disgust.

"What's the difference? You're only going to take it all off anyway," Van said.

"Jesus Christ," Quinn breathed, holding her hand to her heart. She closed her eyes, reached into her closet, and said, "Okay, whatever it is, I'm wearing it." She extracted a flowered blouse and slipped it on, tucking it into a pair of bleached-out jeans. Then she donned her ski jacket, brushed her hair, and stood staring at Van with wide eyes. Van reached into her pocket for a faded party noisemaker which she held to her mouth and blew. With a feeble wheezing sound it uncurled into a paper snake.

Quinn giggled.

"Well, I felt there ought to be some kind of formal send-off," Van said. "The walls of Jericho and everything. . . ."

Quinn gave Van a quick kiss on the cheek and marched past her and out the door.

Chapter 8

This was the first year of up-to-midnight visiting hours in the men's dormitory. In fact, it was rumored that next fall one of the women's residences would become co-ed for seniors. It was a far cry from St. Theresa's, and Quinn still felt awkward walking along the corridors of Will's building.

She stood in front of his room contemplating the pattern scratched in the peeling gray paint of the door. A fence, perhaps. No, more like a reclining skyscraper, or a jet plane taking off. Soft flute music piped away inside, but the sound was not comforting enough to neutralize her sudden longing to flee. The exit sign beckoned from the stairway at the other end of the hall. Her right sneaker tapped against the linoleum floor—dot-dot-dot, dash-dash-dash, dot-dot-dot—in unconscious imitation of the SOS code she had absorbed from Late Show World War II movies.

The music whispered again, soothing siren song. He was probably stretched out on the bed, deep into somebody's poetry, she thought. His eyes got a funny cloudy look when he read that stuff. Out by the tree, in front of the library, they'd appeared bright blue, when all along she had thought they were gray. Tommy's were gray.

Maybe she'd got them confused. All at once the need to know seemed urgent. She knocked on the door.

"Come in."

Quinn poked her head into the room. He sat in a chair by the window, his shaggy hair golden in the light of his reading lamp.

"Hi," he said with that weird half-smile. Blue eyes. Lazy, summery blue eyes.

YesokayIwantto, she thought. One hundred percent. She stepped inside and waited for him to tell her what to do.

He got up, reached her in two long strides, and drew her farther toward the center of the room. "Want something to eat? We could go to Lou's."

She shook her head. "I'm not hungry," she said, much louder than she had intended.

"Sit," he said, gesturing at the worn recliner. He pulled out his desk chair and sat reversed, one leg stretched out on either side. He wore a dark turtleneck jersey, jeans, and moccasins. He crossed his arms on the chair back, rested his chin there, and regarded her curiously.

"Is this music all right, or do you prefer jazz?"

"It's pretty. What is it?"

"Bach. Rampal playing Bach."

"I don't know anything about classical music," Quinn said.

"Then you're missing something."

"I can sing you any song from the top ten, 1959 to '63," she said, looking straight at him for the first time.

"What happened to '64?"

"I lost track after the assassination."

"Why?"

"I guess it just didn't seem important enough to bother with."

They watched one another in silence, but after a few seconds Quinn grew uneasy and began to toy with the pen that lay on Will's notebook beside the chair. She moved the point around and around inside one of the rings. Will observed the motion and began to smile. She flushed and dropped the pen as if it had stabbed her fingers.

"You don't have to go through with this, you know," Will said gently.

"Yes. I do have to."

"Whose rules?"

"Mine."

"Don't you ever bend them a little?"

"I committed myself and I'll go through with it."

"How noble," he said.

"Thank you." Her words were stiff.

"But not very sexy."

"Screw you," she said.

"That's much better."

She stared at him. Her freckles were turning darker by the second.

"You know," he went on, "I almost called to tell you to forget it."

"Well, why didn't you, then?" she asked.

"I decided you would never do anything you didn't really want to do."

"I haven't done anything yet," she retorted.

"No. And it's looking less likely every minute."

"I'd really like to know exactly why you did this," she said. "I mean, you're not an easy person to figure out. You don't grin, you smile. You don't laugh, you chuckle. You don't talk, you watch. Why the hell did you write that poem?"

He just looked back at her.

"It's for damn sure you don't like me very much. Was

it just the challenge?" Her body, already impatient at sitting still, was leaning forward, perched on the edge of the chair. Intermittently her left toe hammered the floor, acknowledging Bach's counterpoint.

Will ran long fingers through his hair. It was a weary gesture. "I'll admit there was some of that in the beginning. But then I started to think about you, and watch you, and besides . . ."

"Besides what?"

"I knew you wanted it."

"You arrogant bastard," she murmured.

He raised his eyebrows at her.

"I could walk right out of here—" she said.

"But you won't."

She headed for the door. "Watch me."

He stood as she passed him, and caught her by the waist. As she struggled he said her name softly, several times. Quinn looked up at him through tears of mortification and rage.

"Let me go," she pleaded.

"Not yet."

She tugged at his arms, but he held her fast. "Go flex your iambic pentameter someplace else," she said.

He was silent until she stopped moving.

"Quinn," he said again. "Listen to me. I want you. I want to make love to you." Her body was rigid. "This isn't how it should have been. I wish to Christ I'd asked you out months ago. Sent you flowers. Took you for walks. All that."

The burning sensation was beginning in Quinn's body, centering between her legs and radiating outward, tingling through her limbs. Will felt the tension along her spine where his hand rested, but she no longer tried to pull away.

"There's no rule that says it can't be done in reverse," she said.

"Rules again." He touched the back of her neck and lifted his fingers through her hair.

Quinn felt weak. "The . . . flowers and the . . . walk. Can come later."

He drew her over to the bed, sat down, and pulled her onto his lap. Her eyes seemed a very clean blue. He could not imagine her capable of evasion or falsehood, not with those eyes.

"You promised to show me," she said.

He kissed her carefully. His mouth felt softer than it looked, with lips that were curious rather than tentative, exploring hers in their own good time. He held her away from him and began to unbutton the flowered blouse. Again he was in no rush. She kept her eyes on his face. His lashes were dark against his cheeks as he watched his hands making her naked.

"Stand up," he said. The blouse slipped off her shoulders. He unzipped her jeans and slid them off with her underpants. He kissed her breasts.

The power of Quinn's arousal seemed to be melting her body from the inside out. She clasped her hands behind Will's neck, clinging to keep herself from falling. Her legs had turned to hot liquid. Will reached behind her knees and lifted her onto the bed. As she watched him undress, the space on the blanket between them seemed like desolate terrain. She was deserted, everywhere abandoned, all the pieces of her hungry for more touching. When his bare chest finally brushed against her, she cried out, feeling the emptiness fill with fire.

She lay next to him, one arm stretched across his stomach. His body hair was pale and soft, and the light from the reading lamp in the corner made minute rainbows in it.

"You think I'll get the hang of it?"

He turned his head on the pillow to smile at her. "I'd say there's hope."

"Have you done that a lot?"

"What's a lot?" He picked up a tendril of hair from behind her right ear and began twisting it. Shivers scurried down her back.

"With a lot of different people, I mean."

"Never under these circumstances, I assure you."

"Do you have any brothers or sisters?"

"One brother. Why?"

"Older or younger?"

"Younger. What is this?"

"I want to know what you think. What you had for breakfast. Everything."

"No, you don't."

She lifted herself up on one elbow and stared into his face. "Oh, yes. Everything."

"You can't."

"Why not?"

"Some things have to stay inside."

"Why?"

"Because nobody wants their guts on display."

"I don't mind. You want to see mine?"

"No. You should be allowed the privacy of your own intestines."

"I'm an only child, I was spoiled rotten, my family's poor, I don't believe in capital punishment, I don't have any phobias but I hate the idea of a bat getting stuck in my hair. Or a bird. My idol used to be John Wayne but now it's Ted Manning because I'm going to have my own TV news show exactly like his and interview everybody who's anybody. I went to a Catholic school and I don't think it screwed me up much . . . Hey," she said, and stopped abruptly. "You aren't listening to me."

"Yes, mostly."

"You aren't even *interested* in my guts."

His eyes fell appreciatively to the soft curve of her stomach. "I'm sure they're beautiful, as guts go."

"Don't condescend to me, you complacent—"

"Wait, wait . . ." He put a hand on her cheek, cooling it. "I was floating. I'm sorry. I feel so Goddamn good."

She glared at him for another second, then mischief twitched at the corners of her mouth. "What do you suppose old Buxby would say if he could see us now?"

Will kept his voice dry and clipped. "Rather barbaric. Rather, uh, primitive. If you catch my drift."

Quinn laughed and bent her head to kiss him. It began as an appreciative, friendly kiss, but soon became greedy. She fell back against the pillow.

"You know, the mythology is all wrong."

"What?" he asked, stroking her hair.

"You didn't take anything away from me. I didn't lose anything. It's like being filled up with . . . with beautiful things. Being showered with presents . . . shit, I can't say it."

"You do all right."

"But Will . . ." She looked pained.

"What is it?"

"Well, sex is great and everything. I really like it a lot . . ."

"But?"

"First I've got to go to the bathroom, and then if I don't get some dinner I'm going to wither up and die right here in your bed. When do we eat?"

Chapter 9

Quinn and Will plunged into the frozen night outside the dormitory. After the warmth of Will's drowsy room each breath felt like the inhalation of something solid that filled their throats and lungs with microscopic icicles. The streetlights lining the sidewalk were great hazy globes, a parade of winter moons. Will put his hands over his ears.

"My brains are freezing," he said.

Quinn laughed, took his hand, and tugged him across the grass. It crunched underfoot, each blade stiffened by frost.

"Aren't you cold?" Will asked, eyeing Quinn's open jacket with concern.

"How could I be cold after what we just did?" She held his palm to her face so he could feel the warm skin. With the toe of her sneaker, she drew a scalloped pattern in the frost.

A figure stopped under a light across the expanse of grass. "Ingraham, that you?" it shouted.

"Henry?" Will called back.

"Yeah! Got the History notes?"

"On my desk!"

Henry stood still, watching them approach.

"He's trying to figure out who you are," Will whispered.

"Quinn Mallory here!" Quinn shouted.

"Great!" Henry waved at them and walked into the darkness. "Good night, Heathcliff! 'Night, Cathy!"

"Will, you think everyone on campus knows what we've been up to?" Quinn whispered. "That we just . . . that you just . . . that I'm not . . ." She hopped a little, making quotation marks in the crystallized grass.

"In the dark from fifty yards?"

"Yeah, but I'm screaming it. Can't you hear me? Tonight I am a woman!" Her toe traced an exclamation point. The ground was slippery, and she had to grab Will's arm to keep from falling over.

Will smiled at the jubilation he saw on her face. "Nice. Quaint. Very turn-of-the-century."

"Personally, I prefer 'I have just been' "—she dropped her voice to a stage whisper—" 'fucked.' " Then, in her normal voice, she continued, "But they don't let you scream that around here."

"Where'd a little convent girl like you learn to talk like that?"

"I said 'fuck' in front of Ann once. My mom. And she smacked me across the face. It's a perfectly good English word. Chaucer used it, Shakespeare used it, and if it's good enough for them, it's good enough for Mallory. Besides, there's no substitute. Is there?"

Will ran through the euphemisms in his head. "No. Except maybe 'grumpled.' "

"I've just been grumpled!" she shouted. Then she peered at him. "You made that up," she accused. He grinned.

Quinn dragged on his arm, bringing him to a halt. "Look." She pointed at the footsteps trailing off behind them. "Are there people who analyze footprints? You know, like handwriting?"

"Sure," Will said. "Pedographists. My aunt was one." Quinn looked up at him, fascinated. He returned her gaze sideways through half-open eyes.

The light dawned. "You turkey," she said. "I think I'll just trip you up." She poked her foot out in front of him.

"I wouldn't be at all surprised," Will said.

Lou's was an oasis of warmth. Faces glowed in the soft light of the jukebox while Diana Ross's smoky Motown sound undulated and throbbed. *Baby, baby, where did our love go?* The booths were crammed with students drinking beer, consuming hamburgers the size of grapefruit and Lou Rizzo's heavily embellished pizzas. Quinn and Will squeezed their way to the bar, ordered cheeseburgers, fries, and a pitcher of beer. Will began to talk about Professor Buxby.

"The man's a true pedant," Will was saying. Quinn reached out a finger and ran it along the line of his nose, across his lips, and down under his chin. "Don't accuse *me* of not paying attention," Will complained.

"I am. Our Buxby, a true pedographist. You're craggy."

Will shook his head. Quinn's neighbor at the bar got up and headed for the jukebox, leaving an empty stool.

"Thank God," she murmured. "I have to cross my legs." After a moment she looked up at him plaintively. "It doesn't help."

"What?"

"In your experience," Quinn said, "have you ever encountered a nymphomaniac?"

"Nadine Kowalsky in seventh grade."

"How did you know?"

"My brother told me." Will's eyes were half-mast again.

"I think I'm one."

"The Catholic kind are always the worst."

"I wish we were back there in your bed." She stuffed three french fries into her mouth and chewed thoughtfully.

"You just got started late."

She offered him the catsup bottle. "You gonna help me ketchup?"

He leaned over to give her a kiss. He smelled deliciously of beer and salty potatoes. "Don't do that," Quinn cried, pressing her knees together hard.

On their way out they met Stanley and Van at the door. Will held the door for them as everyone said hurried hellos. Then Quinn ducked out under Will's arm, turning to catch Van staring at her through the steamy glass pane. Her face was pursed with obstructed curiosity. Quinn flashed her a quick goofy grin. A debauched grin, Van told Stanley later over her whiskey sour.

Quinn lay in bed that night, trying to assess the evening. She had expected to feel changed, as if something momentous had happened. She wasn't disappointed. At first it had been quite painful with him inside her. He seemed much too big. There was a burning, stretching sensation. But Will was gentle. He eased himself in and out of her slowly, carefully, until the time came when she only wanted that particular pain to go on and on, until her body arched toward his and her legs wrapped around his hips, urging him into her again and again. She didn't think she had had an orgasm. She was confident that she would recognize one when it occurred, but in the meantime, the excitement of Will's naked body against her naked body and of part of him buried so deep inside her, well, it hardly made sleep come easily. She smiled into the darkness. There was a scuff mark on the ceiling directly above her pillow, put there by a high-flying Statistics textbook in a moment of midterm exasperation. The splotch was invisible in the dark, of course, but she often imagined it there and pretended it was the footprint of an angel who guarded her sleep. Tonight she could see only the face and body of William Ingraham. Some angel.

The nuns at St. Theresa's had warned her about sex, pointing their white fingers and whispering warnings about "going the way of Mary Frances DeFalco," poor Mary Frances, who compensated for her flat chest and buckteeth by dispensing favors from the backseat of her brother's Chevy. Well, Quinn had finally accomplished the unmentionable, and despite all predictions had not fallen under the wheels of a truck on the way back from Lou's, nor had she become crippled or blind, nor even, she was confident, pregnant.

She stretched, aware of the texture of the sheets against her bare legs. The things her body knew how to do—amazing. She would never get to sleep. Not tonight.

Fifteen seconds later Van poked her head through the door and whispered, "You awake?" There was no answer. Quinn lay on her back with arms flung out to either side in a posture extravagantly relaxed, like a sleeping child. The blanket had been kicked off onto the floor. Van retrieved it and gingerly covered her friend's bare legs. She studied Quinn carefully, but was unable to determine a thing from the quiescent face. She left the room, tiptoed down the hall, and resigned herself to postponing the questions until morning.

Chapter 10

Will kept drifting in and out of his dream, not sure whether it was a good one and worth continuing. When it began, he and Marianne were on a large wooden raft that looked as if it might have been constructed by Thor Heyerdahl. Seagulls swooped overhead, and great mountains of turquoise water swelled beneath them. Marianne was explaining something unintelligible and sad, and Will was crying. When he half awoke from this section of the dream, his throat felt tight with a kind of nostalgic grief he sometimes felt when he remembered some perfect moment that was forever lost to the past.

He sank back into sleep, but now the wooden raft had become a haphazard structure beside a river that was too narrow to be the Salmon and too wide to be the creek that ran along behind the house back home. Fragrant smoke emerged from a hole in the roof, and Will was drawn inside. A naked girl sat cross-legged in the dirt. Her skin was golden in the firelight. Her hair was the color of the flames that she stirred with a long stick. She looked at him solemnly, then dropped the stick and held out her arms.

In the morning Will woke up feeling luxuriously warm

and snug, but when he tried to recapture the dream, he could see only the water of the river rushing over dark stones.

There had been no romantic episodes in his life since Marianne's accident nearly two years ago. Her death had siphoned off his vitality, as if he had lost a Siamese twin who had been attached to him in many crucial places. His brain no longer hummed and clicked. His heart was indifferent, continuing to beat out of a sense of obligation rather than joy. His perceptions were dulled by dispirited nerve fibers. That first year Will had marveled that he didn't actually limp from the crippling effects of losing her.

As he lay thinking about Marianne with her quiet voice and serene intelligence, it occurred to him that what he had anticipated was someday meeting a similar woman who would plug in the holes and revitalize the parts that had died with her. What he had not expected was Quinn. Thinking of them both was like trying to compare pearls with sapphires. Will had spent the first quarter of his life with Marianne. He had only just begun to know Quinn. How could it be that he was already wondering about the children he and Quinn would produce? Would they be redheads? Would they be fiery and extroverted, or contemplative and withdrawn? Where would this new family live, in the valley near Will's school, or would they build a place far up in the mountains?

These speculations seemed an affront to Marianne's memory. But despite the guilt, Will was powerless to snuff them out. Quinn was not gradually healing his wounds. She was cauterizing them.

Will thrashed his legs, trying to untangle himself from the wreckage of his sheets. He felt as if these past two weeks he and Quinn had been living in a glass bubble. They floated just off the ground, rotating lazily together in their luminous sphere. Any separation—for class, for Quinn's jobs, to say good night—seemed excruciating, as if the bubble were being shattered by a cruel thrust from the ice-cold winter reality outside.

Harvey Jackson was the first guest to be invited into their world. Today, he and Quinn would meet. Will sat up on the edge of his bed and tried to generate some enthusiasm for getting dressed. He would just as soon lie around and dream all day. Besides, he was beginning to feel some uneasiness about how Harvey and Quinn would get along. It would be nice if they could get acquainted without him; he wasn't sure he wanted to watch.

On the bus to the North End, Quinn itemized her plans for the afternoon. "We'll take him to the movies. No, that's not social enough. We can't get to know each other. Let's go bowling. That's it. Perfect. Kids like bowling. Then we'll take him for fish fry. It tastes good and it's even got some vitamins."

Will looked out the window. Fat, wet snowflakes fell against the pavement and melted on impact. If he were outside, he would stick out his tongue and catch them.

"Okay?" Quinn said.

Will imagined the sweet bite of the crystals in his mouth.

"Will!"

He turned his head to look at her. His eyes were cloudy.

"Anybody home?" she asked. Will blinked. "We're taking him bowling. Okay?"

"Fine." His eyes began to drift toward the window again. Quinn put her hand on his chin and brought his face around. "Oh, no, you don't." She kissed him lightly, and then once again not so lightly. His mouth responded and finally his eyes. He initiated the next one.

"Do you think it's an obsession with us? Sex?" she asked.

"No question about it." With the bus window behind her, she was a blaze of colors against the snowy blur. Looking into her eyes was like leaning over the edge of his canoe—bright blue Clearwater River, deep pools among the rocks. He felt like diving in.

"Maybe it's just the physical thing," she was saying.

"Possible." Absently, he took her fingers and blew on them, although they weren't particularly cold.

"Aren't you worried about it?" she persisted.

"Why?"

"Well, what if we're not compatible? I mean besides in bed."

"Could be."

"Will, you're a pain in the ass."

He slid a hand between the legs of her blue jeans. Quinn shot a quick look at the hulking black man in the seat across the aisle. "My hand's cold," Will explained.

"If we're not compatible, we have to do something about it. Fix it. *N'est-ce pas?*"

"Absolutely." His fingers moved against the tight denim fabric. She leaned her head on his shoulder, making every effort not to squirm.

"I know we'll be okay, though. We have this basic thing in common."

"Is that so?" Will said.

"Yeah, haven't you noticed? Our pubic hair matches."

Will laughed and tugged on her ear with his free hand.

They reached the North Side Elementary School in time to see Harvey explode from the doorway. He hopped down the steps with a quick and agile body and an expression lit with anticipation. When he caught sight of Quinn, however, his face fell. Almost instantaneously, disappointment darkened into hooded suspicion. He folded his arms and leaned back against the railing by the stairs. He kept his eyes averted.

"Is that Harvey, over by the steps?" Quinn asked.

Will nodded. He knew Harvey had spotted them as they rounded the corner from the bus stop.

"Looks pretty tough," she whispered.

"Tough as chocolate mousse. Hey! Harvey!" Will beckoned to the boy. As if the effort were almost more than he could muster, Harvey straightened up and ambled slowly toward them, arms still crossed on his chest.

"Uh-oh," Quinn murmured.

Will reached out a hand and drew Harvey close. "I think I mentioned I'd be bringing a friend today."

"I forgot," Harvey said with eyes trained on a bottlecap beside his foot.

"Harvey Jackson, this is Quinn Mallory."

Quinn extended her hand. "I'm pleased to meet you."

Harvey touched her fingers briefly and stuffed his fist back into his pocket. He shot Will a look of accusation.

"Come on, we're going to do something special." Will draped an arm around each of them as they started toward the bus stop.

"How'd you like to go bowling?" Quinn asked him.

"What for?"

"For fun," Will said. "Don't be such a curmudgeon, Harve." He gave the frizzy hair a swipe.

"Don't use them fancy words with me, man," Harvey muttered.

Will held up his hand placatingly. "Okay, okay."

During the ride to the bowling alley Quinn chattered about fourth grade at St. Theresa's. Her teacher, Sister

Mary-Margaret, was so pious and soft-spoken that it was hard to remember she was even in the classroom. Quinn did forget one day, and during a whispered conversation with Margery at the next desk, took God's name in vain. Miraculously the pale seraphic nun appeared at Quinn's side, whipped a thick wooden ruler out of her habit, and rapped Quinn's hand with a snap that could be heard all the way to Salem.

"Wicked elbow action. She would have made a great tennis player." Quinn looked hopefully at Harvey, but the boy continued to stare out the window in silence. She mouthed at Will, *Your turn.*

The bowling alley was crowded. Quinn guessed that most of the white people were Italian, since the place straddled the border between the black ghetto and the Italian blue-collar neighborhood.

"I been at one of these once," Harvey said.

"When was that?" Will asked.

"I dunno. Last year maybe. With Leroy . . . you know, Ma's . . . ." His voice trailed off.

"I think I remember you telling me."

"It was bigger than this, lots more lanes. Cleaner, too." He kicked at a paper cup that had missed the trash can.

They rented shoes and bowling balls and set off for the far lane. Quinn was grateful at not having to share a scoring table; the other bowlers' stares seemed openly hostile.

Will went first. He took two long steps, sent the ball rolling smoothly down the alley, and picked off all but two pins. His next roll toppled them for a spare.

"Yay!" Quinn yelled. She smiled at Harvey.

"You go next," he grumbled.

Quinn approached the line with an erratic skipping motion and flung the ball onto the lane with a clunk. It teetered at the edge of the gutter, then rolled slowly down the alley in a slow curve and knocked over all the pins.

"Holy shit! Did you see that?" she hooted.

Will applauded, and Harvey said, "They don't even have a soda machine around here."

Over hamburgers he asked Quinn if St. Theresa's was a Catholic school.

"Yes," Quinn said. So he'd been listening after all.

"Are you one?"

"Well, yeah, I guess so. I don't think you ever stop being one even if you never go to mass."

"Like Jews?"

"Sort of."

"Can't they throw you out if you do somethin' the Pope don't like?"

She nodded. "Excommunication."

"That don't sound like democracy to me."

"Most religions aren't very democratic."

Harvey kept up a steady battery of kicks against the frame under his seat. "There ain't no way I can see where the bill of rights, and all that America stuff, can mix with Catholics."

Will's eyes were dancing. "Harvey's into American history this year."

"I guess so," Quinn said, impressed.

On the way back to campus she sagged limply in her seat and moaned. "I felt like I just spent the afternoon trying to melt an iceberg by breathing on it."

"I didn't think he'd be so tough. You were terrific." He kissed her on the cheek.

"I was a terrific failure."

"The iceberg will melt eventually."

"That's what they told those good folks on the *Titanic*."

He laughed. "Christmas is coming. We'll try again after vacation."

"I don't know, Will. Maybe we're being cruel. He gets so little of you as it is."

"You're a bonus. He just doesn't know it yet."

"Uh huh," Quinn said dubiously. "Anyway, he sure as hell is a smart little monster."

Chapter 11

Quinn took the evening train home for Christmas vacation, paying three dollars over the bus fare out of enthusiasm for the festive spirit she knew would prevail, particularly in those cars closest to the bar. Will hoisted her luggage onto the rack, then, after a quick kiss, stepped off the train to stand on the platform. She smiled at him through the window. There was sadness in her face, and he remembered her image captured in the light of the telephone booth, before he had written his sonnet. She had smiled then, too, for the benefit of the voice on the other end of the wire. The train sighed, sending a billow of steam around Will's ankles. Quinn's smile broadened, and she mouthed the words at him, *You . . . look . . . like . . . an angel.* He shook his head. She began flapping her arms, playing charades. "Bird?" he shouted, but the wheels began to move, and soon she disappeared into the train's cloudy breath, grinning and shaking her head.

Always leave 'em laughing, Will thought. He walked down the platform feeling as if Quinn had ridden off with the train station's wattage allotment; the Christmas decorations were suddenly shabby and dim.

As the train neared Springfield, Quinn's thoughts

fastened on that same telephone call. John had told her the tests showed that Ann had something called lupus erythematosus. Quinn detected the alarm in his voice, but when she suggested hopping the next bus home, he'd sounded positively dismayed. It wasn't necessary. Ann would be upset about Quinn's missing classes. And there was the money. Everything would be all right, she'd see.

Quinn had spent the next morning in the medical school library. What she found under systemic lupus erythematosus was not reassuring. The definition resounded with obscure medical terminology. Tracking down any detailed clarification of the causes of renal failure proved futile. She knew what remission meant.

During subsequent telephone conversations her parents stubbornly resisted further discussion of Ann's condition. With God's help, Ann would come through fine, John said.

But what if . . . ? Quinn thought. Christmas lights blurred into dazzling streaks against the darkness outside the window. The sight was mesmerizing. The rhythmic click of the wheels against the track said: *what if she, what if she, what if she?*

"All right," Quinn said aloud, startling her seat companion. The young man was burdened with a full-size cello case that he was trying to balance on his lap. He stared at her.

"Talking to myself," she explained.

"Well, don't let me interrupt," he said.

Quinn turned her face back to the window and came to terms with the immediate future. She would cross-examine her parents, she would talk to the doctors herself and ask all the questions that needed asking; she would be brave. And now, having plotted her course, she would reward herself and think about William Hamilton Ingraham. A wild adventure it had been, wild enough to fill Quinn's days and nights and crowd out apprehensions about Ann. When Quinn wasn't with Will, she was obsessed with images of him: the fierce look of his face while he studied; the way he pulled his shirt over his head in a graceful gesture that left his hair all tousled; the texture of his skin under her fingers; the smooth long muscles of his back. He had the body of a swimmer or a dancer, nothing bulky about it, just spare and beautiful. She loved to watch him move about the room when he was naked—bending, leaning, stretching to pull down the window shade.

Now the clicking wheels were saying: *want him, I want him, I want him.* She pressed her knees together and glanced nervously at the cellist. The throbbing sensation had taken up permanent residence between her legs. She remembered Will's response to her anxious suggestion that she was oversexed.

"Probably," he had said with a laugh. "Let's take advantage of it before it goes away."

Half an hour outside of Boston, Quinn's seatmate uncased his instrument and positioned it in the aisle where he could manipulate his bow without impaling anyone. Softly he began playing Christmas carols. Someone toward the front of the car began to sing along, and soon other voices joined in. They worked their way through *The First Noel*, *Good King Wenceslas*, and *We Wish You a Merry Christmas. Oh Little Town of Bethlehem* was a failure, drifting off into improvised lyrics and laughter, but *Angels We Have Heard on High* got regular repetition, with the *gloria*s eliciting enthusiastic if inaccurate harmonizing. Will would have enjoyed all this, Quinn thought, particularly the cellist, who with his slight body and pale unkempt curls resembled a solemn, none too sanitary angel. As the train pulled into South Station he began to play *Silent Night*. The passengers sang, softly at first. Someone a few seats behind Quinn had a lovely baritone voice. With the swell of the music—*Sleep in heavenly peace*—Quinn felt her eyes sting. As she gazed around the car she saw that there were tears in several pairs of eyes besides her own.

John met her at the platform. He took one of her suitcases and threw his other arm around her shoulders as they walked out of the station. There was a fine filtering of snow coming down.

"Nine-oh-five, right on time," John said. "How was the trip?"

"Okay," Quinn answered.

John shoved aside the spare tire and miscellaneous tools to make room for Quinn's luggage in the trunk. Then he tossed her the keys. As a passenger John was only comfortable with Quinn at the wheel. She drove just as he did—aggressively, skillfully, and fast. She pulled out onto Boylston Street.

"How's Mom?"

"Fine."

Quinn glanced sideways at him. "You bullshitting me, Jake?"

"You'll see for yourself. You don't need to get all stirred up."

"Well, I am."

"Don't be. You'll worry your mother."

"I'll bet *she's* worried."

"She doesn't complain."

"Of course she doesn't. She's a Goddamn saint. I'll feel better about it once I've talked with her doctor."

"What for?"

"For information."

"We'll see." His voice was curt.

Quinn decided to lay off for the moment. Why start the vacation with a full-scale battle? "Where'd you get the tree this year?"

"Finnegan's."

Quinn smiled. Michael Finnegan sold the shapeliest, healthiest evergreens in Medham, which were removed in the dead of night from the estates and cemeteries of wealthy suburban communities. As a public service, Michael Finnegan explained, to thin out the overgrowth.

When they pulled up in front of the house, Quinn could see holiday lights blinking through the living room window. Four inches of new snow coated the roof. She turned off the engine and sat looking down Gardner Street. At Christmastime, Medham lost its tawdriness and began to sparkle. Snow was necessary for the metamorphosis, but in Quinn's memory there had been only one Christmas when the neighborhood wasn't covered with white.

She turned to tell John she couldn't imagine spending Christmas in Arizona, but he had gotten out to fetch her suitcases. He tapped on the window.

"Lock up and come on in. Your mother's pining to see you."

On her way up the steps Quinn swallowed hard and tried to prepare herself for how her mother might look. But Ann really did seem all right. She was wearing her bright blue wool dress and her face had a healthy flush. Quinn hugged her with relief.

Then they all sat in the kitchen drinking cocoa and eating Christmas cookies. As always, Quinn chose the star-shaped ones with the green icing first. She studied her mother.

"You've lost a little weight, Mom."

Ann nodded. "About time, too." Ann was forever trying out new diets, hoping to trim off ten or fifteen pounds, but it had always been difficult with Quinn and John around. They consumed enormous quantities of food and burned it all away while Ann despaired, nibbling on carrot sticks and holding steady at 142 pounds.

"Chic, but I don't know. . . ." Her mother's trim new figure would take some getting used to. Quinn popped another cookie into her mouth. "How do you feel?"

"All my aches and pains have disappeared just in time for Christmas."

"Are you in remission?"

Ann and John glanced at one another.

"Listen, you two. I'm not seven years old. You brought me up to be tough. Tell me."

"Lupus is an inflammatory connective-tissue disorder," Ann explained, "an autoimmune disease. It usually occurs in younger women."

"What's an autoimmune disease?'

"It's when your body's immunity system gets its signals crossed and begins to attack itself."

"Can they give you anything for it?" Quinn asked.

"Cortisone."

"That's pretty potent stuff. Are there side effects?"

"Not that I've noticed."

"I'm grilling you, aren't I?"

Ann nodded. For the first time she looked tired.

"I'm sorry. I'll let you be. But I want to see Dr. Marshall this vacation."

"He sent us to a specialist, a fellow named Gunther at Mass General," John said.

"Okay, then I'll see Gunther."

"All right," Ann said. "You get your questions together, and maybe I'll have a few to add to the list. And now let's talk about something else."

"Fine," Quinn said. "The latest bulletin from campus is . . . tadadaDA . . . your daughter's got a boyfriend."

"Irish, I trust," John said through a mouthful of gingerbread Santa Claus.

"He's very cute."

"What's his name, dear?" Ann asked.

"Will. William Ingraham."

"Bloody British."

"As a matter of fact, his mother's Irish, but I should've just let you suffer, you old bigot. He's from Idaho."

"Where's that?" John asked, deadpan.

"Exactly what I said." Quinn grinned at him.

"What's he think of you?"

"All indications . . . well . . ." Infuriatingly, she felt herself begin to blush. "He thinks I'm . . . oh, look, the feeling's mutual. Let me tell you about the train trip." She was certain that a few more moments of self-conscious fumbling for words and she would confess it all.

They sat talking for nearly an hour before John and Ann said good night and went up to bed. Quinn carried her cocoa into the living room and sat down on the couch. The room was aglow with the particular radiance of Christmas lights. She remembered decorating the tree when her toddler arms could barely reach the lowest branches. The same string of lights, her favorites, glittered tonight, brightly colored glass cylinders in the shape of candles. Always after the tree had been trimmed—Quinn's messy wads of tinsel bestowed and the china crèche on its bed of angel's hair at the base—John would switch off the living room lights. Ann would be summoned and they'd all sit waiting together. After a few moments a clear liquid in the bulbs would begin to simmer, hesitantly at first, but soon the boughs were ablaze with bright bubbles, yellow, blue, green, and red.

It was a magical event. Tonight, sipping her cocoa and breathing the pungent scent of Scotch pine, she was haunted by the presence of all those other Christmases.

She had assumed that the holidays would always be like this. Obviously that was absurd. She would have her own family soon. Then she and Will would come back to Medham with a brood of their own to trim the tree. Of course, someday her parents would no longer be here. Of course, and yet here was a thought that had not occurred to her until just now. She didn't like it much.

Her impulse was to reach for Will's hand. Instead she twirled a strand of hair around her finger. Will Ingraham was habit-forming. It had snuck up on her, this creeping dependency. She wondered if he was thinking of her out in Godforsaken Idaho.

She took another sip of cocoa, but it had grown cold. She rose stiffly, switched off the decorations, and went upstairs to bed.

Chapter 12

The next morning, Christmas Eve day, Quinn and Ann hurried through their holiday chores. Quinn baked cookies while Ann wrapped gifts. The house was lively with the sound of rustling tissue paper and the pungent scents of ginger and cinnamon.

Quinn, finished at last, was on her way out of the kitchen when she caught Ann slipping her coat on by the front door.

"Where are you going?"

"Oh. Are you done already, dear?"

"What's in this?" Quinn picked up her mother's shopping bag and peered inside. "Ice skates? These are kids' ice skates."

Ann made no comment as she tied a scarf around her neck. Quinn looked closely into her face until Ann began to flush.

"You're going to Aunt Millie's!" Quinn exclaimed. "These are for Sean."

Ann nodded and took the shopping bag.

"You can't go all the way out there. It'll take you hours."

"I'll be back by three."

"Just before Daddy gets home."

"That's right." Ann opened the front door.

"He doesn't know about this, does he?" Quinn asked.

"If he asks, I'll tell him."

Quinn reached into the closet for her jacket. "Let me go instead."

"No. I don't want you dragged into your father's feuds. You stay home. There's plenty to do."

Quinn put her hand on her mother's arm. "You're already worn out. Let me at least come along and prop you up."

Ann gave her a long look, deliberating. "All right," she said finally. "Your father would skin me alive, but I'll be glad of your company."

Aunt Millie, John's eldest sister, had left Ireland after having made her reputation as a British sympathizer. John, like Ann, had come to America as a small child, leaving his big sister behind in Dublin. Still, the old country retained its power over John's loyalties, and the contempt and shame for what he regarded as Millie's treason were so great that he never even spoke of her to complain. Until the day that she had come into the house in Medham, Quinn was unaware that such a person as Aunt Millie existed.

She'd shown up one afternoon ten years before, introduced herself to Ann, and explained in a trembling voice that her husband had left her. There was a child, an infant, and she was destitute. Ann listened, then both women waited fearfully for John to arrive home from work. When he came into the living room and saw his sister there, he said only, "Get out of my house." There was a short silence, then Millie rose and left.

Over the years Ann had tried to intercede. Once she'd gone so far as to enlist the aid of the priest. But John declared, in Father Riley's presence, that he would prefer to burn in hell for eternity rather than set eyes on his turncoat sister again.

So Ann kept up her own sporadic communication with Millie, sending her whatever money she could spare along with castoffs from Quinn's closet. Quinn had always suspected that Ann was in communication with her sister-in-law, but until today had never caught her at it.

The trip to Aunt Millie's required two transfers, and each trolley was jammed with holiday crowds. Quinn held her mother's arm and battled the hordes to win a seat for her. They were silent most of the way, but when they left the train at Somerville, Quinn asked, "How often do you do this?"

"Christmastime. I'm late this year, what with being sick and all."

"What do you think Daddy would do if he found out?"

"I don't know," Ann said.

"Remember the time we went to see the rerun of *The Red Shoes*?"

Ann smiled. "A couple of sinners."

When Quinn was in fifth grade, Ann had taken her to the movies on a school day. They had sneaked, giggling, into the theater just after the film had begun, so the darkness would hide them. The next day Ann had written the teacher a note saying that Quinn had been "indisposed." It wasn't really a lie. She was not disposed to go to school. But they hadn't mentioned the adventure to John.

Aunt Millie lived in a fourth-floor walk-up apartment. Ann had to stop several times on the stairs to catch her breath. Quinn watched her worriedly, but knew it was no use trying to persuade her mother to stay downstairs while she delivered the gifts. They rang the bell and waited a few minutes before the door was opened by a worn-looking woman in a bathrobe. She seemed tearful, but Quinn soon realized that her eyes must always look that way, anxious and watery. Ann hugged her sister-in-law and then introduced Quinn. Aunt Millie stared at her with intense curiosity for a moment, then led them into a living room so dark that it took Quinn a moment to realize that there was a child standing in the far corner near the couch.

Sean, now eleven, was an ideal candidate for the Irish Tourist Board advertisements. He was red-haired, freckled, blue-eyed, and adorable. At this moment his hands were balled into fists, and the glances he shot his mother were full of youthful outrage.

"Hello, Sean," Ann said. "This is your cousin, Quinn. I won't tell you how much you've grown since last year. I used to hate hearing that from my old aunties."

Sean bobbed his head, and uncurled one fist to offer a grubby hand to Quinn. She shook it and was surprised at how calloused and rough it felt.

"I'll put this over here," Ann said, setting the shopping bag down beside a table upon which perched a tiny artificial tree that Ann had brought them several years ago. Sean glanced at the shopping bag, then at the door. Aunt Millie glared at him until he said, finally, "Thank you, Aunt Ann."

"I'm glad we got a chance to see you, dear, but I'll bet you've got a lot of things to tend to, what with vacation and everything."

Sean's face brightened. At his mother's nod he snatched his coat off the back of a chair and tried not to run across the living room. He stopped short at the door, turned to give Quinn and Ann a dazzling, heart-melting smile, mumbled, "Nice to see you," and left. They could hear him clattering down all four flights of stairs.

"He looks wonderful, Millie," Ann said as the older woman poured tea. "How's he doing now?"

"Oh, I don't know. He doesn't tell me what he's up to, of course. There's been no word from school, good or bad."

"There's plenty of mischief in those eyes, but no malice."

Quinn sipped her tea and watched her aunt closely, searching in vain for some hint of political treachery in the faded face that resembled John's only in its prominent cheekbones.

"I see him in Quinn," Millie said.

"Sean?"

"No, my brother."

"Yes, they do look alike."

For the first time Millie's expression lifted in a half-smile. "Are you as stubborn as he is?" she asked Quinn.

"I hope not," Quinn replied. After the remark had slipped out, she felt a curious sense of betrayal and decided to say nothing more about John to this woman who was, after all, a stranger.

"I worry about your coming out here, Ann," Millie continued. "He'd never forgive you. I shouldn't let you come, but I can't tell you how happy it makes me."

"You know, I'm not so sure he doesn't know about these visits of ours. The only times he doesn't question me about where I've been is when I've come here. I think it's his way of staying in touch with you."

The watery eyes brimmed over. "You look tired today," Millie said. "Are you well?"

Quinn glanced quickly at her mother, but Ann said, "Oh, I'm fine. The holidays are a little hectic."

"It doesn't make it easier, your trekking way out here."

"On the contrary, it's a nice break from the goings-on at home, isn't that right, dear?"

Quinn nodded obediently.

Aunt Millie asked Quinn a few obviously dutiful questions about college, but then began to talk to Ann about her job at the local pharmacy, her health difficulties, and her guilt over having so little time to supervise Sean. She poured it all out as if she never spoke to another soul. Ann asked a few quiet questions, but mostly just listened. Quinn realized that at this moment her mother belonged completely to Aunt Millie. The forward curve of her body, the intense gaze of her eyes, her murmurs of sympathy and understanding, all assured Aunt Millie that Ann was hers and hers alone.

All her life Quinn had taken this quality of her mother's for granted. Ann was always there to listen—to her, to John, to whatever stray showed up at their door in need of compassion. Until now, it had never occurred to Quinn that there might be a cost. She felt like putting her arms around her mother and saying, "Now, Aunt Millie, Mom is going to tell us about all the garbage *she's* been putting up with these past few months, and we're going to hang on her every word."

But Ann wasn't a talker, and who was Quinn to say that there wasn't gratification for her mother in lightening other people's problems? Still, Quinn worried. She was glad when Ann looked at her watch and announced that it was time to leave.

On the trip home they were lucky enough to find two seats together toward the back of the train, where there were fewer passengers.

"What did you think of your aunt?" Ann asked.

"She doesn't look very wicked to me. I was disappointed."

"She's a tragic soul, really. She was a brilliant student back in Dublin, but got herself all mixed up in a political mess and was never able to find her way out. It's an awful waste of human intelligence."

"Sean's a cute little number."

"He's been picked up for shoplifting. Can you imagine, at eleven? Poor little boy."

"At least this year he won't have to swipe a pair of skates."

"I don't think he takes things just because he needs them."

Quinn studied her mother for a moment, then said, "I love you a lot."

"You'd better. I'm your mother."

"That has nothing to do with it. God, it's hot in here." She shrugged off her jacket.

"There's an open window. Put your coat on," Ann protested.

"I'm boiling."

"You'll catch your death." Ann tugged at the collar, trying to lift it around Quinn's shoulders.

"Hey, you wanna fight?" Quinn asked, mugging at her. "You've got a mean right hook, I can attest to that."

Ann dropped the coat. "Don't remind me. You know I still feel terrible."

"Everybody's entitled to child brutality every now and then, especially if I'm the child."

"No, they're not."

Ann looked so solemn that Quinn was instantly remorseful. "Hey, Mom, I was only teasing you." She reached out to squeeze her mother's hand. "I was thirteen years old, and it's the only time you've ever laid a hand on me. I don't think a thirteen-year-old needs to say 'fuck.' "

Ann winced and tried not to look at the other passengers. "Nobody should strike a child," she said, then went on, musingly, "I want you to know the joy of having children."

"Right now?"

"Soon." Ann shook her head as if trying to clear it of troublesome thoughts. "Did you like my new cookie cutter?"

"The angel."

"Yes. Did you notice anything odd about her?"

Quinn laughed. "She's not very heavenly."

"I know it. At first I thought they were her wings, but then I realized . . . well, she's the most buxom angel I ever saw."

"Let's put extras in Father Riley's package."

Ann giggled. They made quick connections downtown, and got home with time to spare.

Every Christmas Eve, in accordance with family custom, Quinn and Ann delivered their holiday offerings around the neighborhood while John downed several pints of Christmas cheer at the Ancient Order of Hibernians. They would all converge at St. Theresa's for midnight mass. As Mallory lore dictated, John would barely squeak in before the procession, leaving Ann to heave sighs and wring her hands out of a conviction that this year he surely wouldn't make it.

It had also become a matter of tradition for Quinn to protest her part in the ritual. It rankled that she was required to tote cookies around the neighborhood and make polite conversation with the adults while her friends were celebrating in a more lively fashion at Reston's in Brookline.

Tonight, as Quinn reached for her jacket without complaint, Ann peered closely at her.

"Where's Margery?" Ann asked.

"I don't know. With the gang, I suppose."

"At Reston's?"

"I guess."

"You were with me all day. I think tonight it'd be fine if you spent some time with your friends."

"They'll be around tomorrow. Are you going to be warm enough? Here." She helped Ann on with her coat and tied a plaid scarf around her neck. Ann was not in the habit of being fussed over; her arms hung awkwardly at her sides while Quinn tucked the muffler around her neck.

"Thank you, dear," Ann said.

Quinn nodded and looked away. A lump had suddenly formed in her throat, and she did not trust her voice.

Ann moved to the foot of the stairs. "John Mallory! Don't you be late for mass!" she called.

" '*Fasten your hair with a golden pin/And bind up every wandering tress . . .*' " John crooned from the top of the banister.

"And don't show up drunk!" Quinn shouted, in full possession of her vocal chords again.

"God forbid," Ann murmured.

"Do you think once in a while he could give us a break with the Yeats? I mean, what's wrong with Emily Dickinson?"

"A lot," Ann replied.

Christmas Eve passed with the usual warm blur of carols and candlelight, followed by presents on Christmas morning and the inevitable letdown. But the next day Quinn still felt depressed and lonely. Her mother was at the grocery store. John was working. The Christmas tree was dying, and the house seemed as still as a mortuary. She longed for Will, but not with the usual bittersweet nostalgia. Today she had to speak with him the way she had to eat when she was starving. She dug through her wallet and determined that she could pay the busfare back to school and still manage a long-distance call. Her voice trembled as she asked the operator to connect her with Red Falls, Idaho. She heard the ring at his end and tried to imagine the room that held the Ingraham telephone. Blank space, as if he were living in a vacuum.

"Hello?" The voice was a woman's, older, probably Will's mother.

"Is Will there?" Quinn was disgusted to feel her cheeks reddening.

"No. He went out."

"Oh." Quinn was crushed.

"Uh . . . can I tell him who's calling?" The voice was reluctant, not wishing to pry. Quinn decided that she liked Mrs. Ingraham.

"Please tell him Quinn Mallory called from Massachusetts. Just to say hello. It's not important."

"Gwen Mallory," the voice repeated carefully.

"Quinn! Quinn!" She was almost shouting. Hadn't he even mentioned her? She had told her parents about Will before the snow had melted off her shoes that first night home.

"Quinn Mallory. I'll tell him."

"Sorry to trouble you," Quinn said.

"No trouble at all."

"Happy New Year." She might as well get her three minutes' worth.

"Yes. Happy New Year."

Both of them hung up simultaneously. Quinn felt irritable and low the rest of the afternoon. When John arrived home at four thirty, Quinn mentioned that she had called Idaho.

"You did what?" John said.

Quinn felt gooseflesh creep across the tops of her shoulders. "I called Idaho," she repeated slowly. There were three dollars in the drawer under the telephone, paying for the call plus some, but defiance made her silent.

"I'll send you the bill, lass." John's jaw muscles were hard at work under the day's growth of stubble.

"You do that." She snatched her jacket from the closet and left the house.

Quinn sloshed through the wet snow, unable to decide whether to scream with outrage or break into tears. A compromise resulted in an audible *Goddamn bastard* that came out like a sob. She hated him. All the hard work to make good grades and keep her scholarship, the extra jobs at the cafeteria and the college garage while her classmates played bridge or went to the movies, all of it went unacknowledged. He could take all that for granted and, what's more, assume that she would cheat him out of one lousy long-distance phone call. She should take back the Goddamn money and buy a bouquet of flowers for Ann.

She trod with clammy feet across Commonwealth Avenue and nearly slipped on the icy trolley track. Her parents used to argue about money. In fact, that had been the only habitual source of contention between them. Now and then the battles had gotten pretty wild. Every week her father would leave the household allowance on the kitchen table. It always seemed like pitifully little to Quinn, but Ann was a wizard at stretching dollars. She clipped coupons, frequented sales, and knew the exact prices of canned goods in every chain in the greater Boston area. One day Ann had asked John for an extra five dollars to buy a leg of lamb on sale at Buy-Wise. He accused her of extravagance—she could have set aside some of the weekly allotment for such a contingency. Quinn sat curled up in a ball on the living-room couch and tried not to listen as they shouted at one another. The sounding board in the piano shook and hummed when John slammed out the door. For three weeks the atmosphere was cold but cordial. For three weeks the household money accumulated in a pile on the kitchen table. Somehow Ann had managed to prepare filling meals without laying a finger on the money, though Quinn suspected a surreptitious raid on the Christmas Club fund. The Mallorys ate spaghetti, lasagna, ravioli, omelets, manicotti, and scrambled eggs amid polite requests to pass the salt. The stack of bills made an eloquent centerpiece. About ten days into the siege Quinn decided that she would never be dependent on a man for her survival.

When she got home, John was at the door to meet her.

"Sorry I was so tough on you," he said.

"It's all right," Quinn answered, but she avoided his eyes as she hung up her jacket.

"Things went wrong all day. Somebody got hurt at the plant and then the car froze over. Not that it's any excuse to take it out on you."

Quinn faced him now. "There's money for the call in the drawer."

"You keep it."

"No. I insist."

John swiped at her hair. "We're not going to fight about that, too, are we, lass?"

"All right. Let's use it to buy roses for Mom."

"Done. Hungry? Soup's on."

After dinner John wandered into the living room and snapped the television on to Ted Manning's program. Quinn had admired Ted Manning since she was twelve years old and had watched him take Senator Joseph McCarthy apart at a televised news conference. Manning had been the first media personality to cross-examine his subjects on national television, and within a year of the McCarthy interview he was hosting his own show. Quinn had observed carefully as Manning exposed the prominent clergyman's sympathy for the Ku Klux Klan, a film director's contempt for his actors, a federal judge's cozy relationship with organized crime. The interviews were always conducted with skill and dignity. Under Manning's persistent encouragement private personalities emerged from behind the press-agent cartoons. Quinn gave Manning credit for triggering her fascination with world affairs. She regarded him as a contemporary artist at work in the medium that had become the focus of modern communication.

As soon as she heard the introductory music to *On the Line*, she was beside her father. "Giving up Huntley/Brinkley without a battle?" she asked in amazement.

"I guess I can put up with this jerk once in a while."

Quinn planted a noisy kiss on his cheek and settled back to watch Ted Manning interview Robert F. Kennedy.

At the end Manning's suntanned face was earnest. ". . . remains to be seen," his voice resonated, "whether Senator Robert Kennedy will capture the support of his colleagues in Washington as effectively as he has captured the votes from his home state of New York." There was the barest emphasis on "home." The camera flashed to Kennedy's face. Manning's irony had not slipped past the senator, and he grinned appreciatively. As the closing credits played over the men's faces, Quinn sighed.

"He's wonderful," she said.

"His brother was. I haven't made up my mind about him yet."

"No, not Bobby. Ted Manning."

"Give me Chet and David every time."

Quinn reached out to switch off *Mr. Novak*. "Did you see how he got Kennedy to talk about his father's shenanigans? I can't wait to work with him."

"Ah, it's work *with* him now."

"You think I won't?"

"Sure, I think you'll do whatever you set out to do."

Quinn studied her hands. They were sturdy and freckled, with rounded fingertips and trim nails. Not elegant, but capable. "You know, sometimes I feel like some kind of freak. Maybe I shouldn't have been a girl."

"You're a damn pretty girl."

She dismissed the remark with a wave of her hand. "That's not it. I keep wondering if something is missing in me, or maybe I've got some extra weird kink that makes me want to . . . to accomplish." She shook her head. "It seems as though every other girl in my class is either getting married this summer or finding any old job while they *wait* to get married."

"You think that's how Cleopatra felt? Or Queen Elizabeth or Catherine the Great or Jane Austen—"

She interrupted him, exasperated. "Oh, come on, Daddy. I don't want to conquer Western Europe. I want to be normal."

"Well, then, what's normal."

"Mom."

"Okay. She's got a family and she works, too."

"Yeah, and look at the conniption fit you had."

"That's different," John said.

"Uh huh."

"All right, maybe I resisted it a little at first."

Quinn laughed. Then she thought for a moment and continued. "You were a real creep about Mom, but the thing is, you always made *me* feel like I could do anything the boys could do. I had it all figured out. And then I met this . . . person, and now I don't know what's happening. I've known him a few weeks, and I'm already getting these sappy ideas about slipping into my apron and cooking him pot roast and rice pudding."

John tugged gently on a lock of her hair. "You can have it all, honey," he said.

"You think so?"

"I know so."

She reached over to kiss his cheek again. "You're a pretty cool guy."

"Oh, yeah, I know that." He was already on his feet. "I'm ready for a beer. Want one?" Quinn smiled and shook her head. Her father was always uncomfortable with praise.

Alone, she leaned back with her arms crossed behind her head and remembered the time she had run for class president in sixth grade. Until that particular year she had always been elected without opposition. Everyone had been shocked when Morgan Donohue stood up and nominated herself to run against Quinn. There was no contest; Quinn won hands down. But Morgan's bitter, tear-streaked face had haunted Quinn and she'd brought her anguish home to John.

"You'll have to make your peace with being a winner," he had told her. "Oh, you can hide yourself under a rain barrel the rest of your life if you want to. But it looks like you're born to lead the pack, and you might as well learn to live with it. That means being tough enough to look into the loser's face."

It hadn't seemed so at the time, but the issues were a whole lot simpler then.

Chapter 13

Will flew East the morning after Quinn got back. He boarded a bus in Boston and spent the trip staring out the window. The landscape seemed flat; everything was the same leaden color, so that it was difficult to define exactly where the horizon began beyond the fields. Every now and then a grove of evergreens would flash past, but they seemed stunted compared to the towering pines back home. It was all so worn out, worn down, on this side of the country. Even the mountains were more like oversize hills with no edges to them.

As the bus neared Springfield, Will's spirits began to rise. Quinn should be here already. He would call her first thing, and maybe she could get away from her cafeteria job for a quick bite at the union. Suddenly he missed her more sharply than he had all during vacation. The bus had slowed to a maddening crawl.

It was growing dark when Will walked into his room. Without bothering to flick on the light, he tossed his suitcase onto the bed. In the gloom he hadn't noticed a sizable lump in the middle of his mattress. The lump yelped, and the suitcase toppled onto the floor.

A disheveled, bright pink face, then bare shoulders,

appeared over the bedspread. Will took a corner and pulled. Quinn was stark naked.

"Hi," she said.

Will laughed. He sat down on the edge of the bed to kiss her.

Quinn rubbed her hip. "You almost paralyzed me with that thing."

"Sorry. At least I got you where you're padded."

"Hey." She narrowed her eyes at him.

"I didn't say plump. I said padded." He stroked the spot that was already beginning to bruise. "I must say this is a fine how-do-you-do."

"How *do* you do?"

"I'm glad to see you." His hand began to wander across her belly and up between her breasts. He drew invisible circles around her nipples with his index finger.

"You going to take your clothes off?" she asked him.

"Don't you think we ought to get reacquainted first?"

"No."

She helped him undress. They didn't even bother to lock the door.

Afterward they lay facing one another with legs intertwined.

"You're very beautiful," she whispered.

"I know it." He touched his tongue to the tip of her nose.

"So how are things in the wild wild West?"

"Quiet."

"You must have loved it."

"Yup. How's your mother?"

"Was there a pile of snow? We had tons."

"A blizzard or two. How's your mother?"

"I don't know." Quinn dropped her eyes. "I called you."

"You missed me by five minutes. I called back but nobody answered."

"Why didn't you try again?"

"I did."

"I liked your mom," Quinn said. "She's not nosy, is she?"

"No."

"How come she didn't know my name?"

Will looked bewildered. "Why would she know it?"

"Well, didn't you talk about me at all?"

"No."

"Not to anybody?"

"Well, come to think of it, I did."

"Who?"

"Whom."

"You're such a pain in the ass, Will."

"To my old English teacher," he said.

"Does he teach Old English or is he old?"

"A little of both."

"What did he say about me?"

"I told him your name. What is this?"

"I thought about you all the time. I didn't like missing you. It was . . . unnerving."

"I thought about you, too."

Quinn was silent.

"What's the matter?" he asked.

"Nothing. Did you see Marianne's parents?"

"Yes, Christmas Eve."

"How are they?"

"Sad. Is that what's on your mind?"

All of a sudden Quinn began to cry. She tried to turn her face away, but Will cupped it between his hands.

"What's the trouble? Honey, tell me."

She could barely talk. "I don't know. I don't know," she choked. He held her, rocking her gently until her breathing calmed.

"People shouldn't die," she said finally.

"Marianne and your mother?"

Her chin began to quiver again, so, rather than try speaking, she just nodded her head. After a few moments she took a deep breath.

"Okay, that's it for theatrics. Let's find something to eat." She got up, extracted her clothes from their hiding place under the bed, and started dressing.

"Somebody ought to come by five times a day and drop slabs of raw meat outside your door," Will remarked.

"Fucking always makes me hungry," she said cheerfully. The tears had left faint trails along her cheeks. Otherwise he would never have known she had just been crying.

Over coffee in the union Quinn said, "I didn't even get to talk to Ann's jerky doctor."

"How do you know he's jerky, then?"

"Because I did speak with his nurse over the phone, and she's a horse's ass. If he hired *her*, then he must be one too. I couldn't even get an appointment. But I called Van, and her father's giving me the name of somebody I can see in Springfield. Doctor Horse's Ass will send this guy Ann's files. She ought to have another opinion anyway."

"You sound discouraged."

"I don't get discouraged."

"You don't *admit* you get discouraged."

"I won't let anything happen to my mother."

Will looked at her steadily until her face finally relaxed into a sheepish smile. "Anyhow, I'm working on it."

"I can see that," Will said.

They strolled back to her dormitory slowly, enjoying the physical sensations of being together. Quinn held his arm and rested her head against him. Their legs made contact as they walked.

On their way up the last hill Quinn said, "I made a decision over Christmas."

"Oh?"

"I'm going to work for Ted Manning."

Will stopped.

"I can't really say it was over Christmas. I mean, I told you I always knew I'd go to New York and work in television, with documentaries or news, something like that. I've written the first draft of my letter applying for a job. I want you to look at it."

Will was experiencing a peculiar restriction in his stomach, a withering sensation. He kept his body very still and concentrated on his insides. Everything was crinkling up. His organs were retracting into wisps of dried paper.

"Will?"

His expression of dreamy abstraction belied the process taking place inside him.

"You're not even listening!"

She's trying to get a handle on it, Will thought. Her mother's sick, and she's scared out of her wits, and she has to impose some control over her life. But by now he was hollow inside, and there was a cold breeze blowing through. Finally he said, "I didn't know you'd worked things out in such detail."

"Well, I got to watch Manning every night over vacation, and there're a few things I thought he could fix. I figured, what the hell, I'll send him a letter and see if I can get a foot in the door." She tugged at his arm. "Come on, if I'm cold, you must be freezing."

"Where do I fit?"

"Don't look so miserable. I didn't leave you out." She held his hand to her cheek. "You'll come to New York with me. There're kids in the city who are desperate to learn. They probably need teachers more than anywhere else. We can share an apartment, maybe find a place in Greenwich Village, or if that's too expensive, Stanley says there's some really nice areas in Brooklyn."

"I don't want to go to New York."

"Of course you don't. Now. But you don't know anything *about* it." She began stamping her feet to keep warm.

"Neither do you."

"I've been there once. That's more than you."

"I haven't the slightest inclination to live there. Not for one day or one hour."

"Oh, Will, give it a chance. It might even be great."

"New York is not my idea of great."

He started toward the entrance of the women's dormitory. Students were still arriving in taxis with their suitcases. There was laughter and the jubilant shouts of reunion.

Hurrying along behind Will, Quinn said, "I thought you'd be pleased."

"You thought wrong. Don't include me in your schemes when you don't have any idea how I feel."

"But, Will—"

"I won't live in a place like that. Ever."

They had stopped in front of the building. His face seemed far away, high above her head where she couldn't reach. She wished it wouldn't be absurd to stand on the fender of the nearest car. Anything to put her face within range of those eyes that seemed to be floating in extraterrestrial space.

"I think you're being very close-minded," she said.

"You thought I'd just tag along after you," he said. "Well, no, I'll be back home where I can breathe. This *college* is too Goddamn overpopulated for me."

"Some reunion," she said finally, and headed for the door. He didn't try to stop her.

Will stood still, waiting for his equilibrium to return. It was as if their hot words had set them whirling around the sidewalk. He thought of the centrifuge machine that tests the astronaut's tolerance for speed. Strapped in a capsule, he spins around the chamber at the end of a long arm, velocity intensifying until his face is distorted as if it were soft clay. Well, the mad ride was over now, leaving Will disoriented and sick to his stomach.

He chided himself for the depth of his shock and anger. Hadn't she confided her goals to him from the beginning? Her sense of purpose had impressed him. But sometime between then and now he had allowed himself to forget the look on her face while she was describing her future. Somewhere along the way he had begun setting up house with Quinn in Idaho, just as she was hustling him off to their cozy apartment in Greenwich Village. What right had he to strike out at her?

He walked down the hill, oblivious to the greetings of other students. He wondered if he could coach his imagination to associate Quinn with Manhattan, like skyscrapers and Checker cabs. If the connection became automatic enough, perhaps eventually he would despise her with the same intensity that he despised the noise and filth of the city.

He remembered the look on her face when she emerged from under his bedspread this afternoon, all rosy and pleased with herself. He had a long way to go before he reached despise.

Chapter 14

Quinn sat alone in her room for about five minutes before she was on her feet again. She slipped into her jacket, brushed furiously at her cheeks, and vowed to waste not one more tear on William Hamilton Ingraham.

The night air was bracing. As she neared the garage she began to feel better. The side door stood ajar, but Gus was nowhere to be seen. Quinn grabbed her overalls from the wall hook and headed for a truck she had been overhauling. Lying beneath its metal entrails, she began to dissect the argument. A thorough soul-search convinced her that she had not deliberately usurped Will's choices; truly, she had expected him to be pleased. But by the time she had replaced the shock absorbers, she decided that perhaps she had made a few assumptions. Will had overreacted, but maybe he was scared. From now on she would approach the subject of their future with more tact. Will's mind, with its imaginative meanderings, could invent impediments where none existed. She always told him he thought too much.

She slid out from under the truck and hurried toward Gus's office. Will's dorm had already closed to women visitors, but she could still call him. She stripped off her overalls, and as she turned to hang them next to Gus's she heard a rustle behind her. She whirled around, but too late. An arm grabbed her around the neck, pinning her to a bulky body. Rough fingers covered her mouth. The reek of nicotine was sickening.

A gruff voice said, "I've got a knife. I'll use it if you yell."

Quinn stopped struggling and willed her body to remain still. There was tension in the thick arm at her throat. It was vibrating with what she hoped was indecision, or fear.

"Where's the cashbox?" He gave her neck a cruel squeeze. Sweat formed on her forehead, then the hand lifted slightly, testing, and finally released her mouth.

Quinn whispered in a voice she didn't recognize, "There is no cashbox."

"This is a garage, isn't it? There's gotta be cash." He was angry. The steel arm stiffened again.

"Not public. For the college." It was hard to speak with the vise twisting against her larynx.

"Fucking bitch," the voice muttered. "No cash, no cash. You bitch." The free hand slipped beneath her sweater and touched the bare skin of her stomach. Quinn felt her knees begin to give way. She made an involuntary sound like a moan. Instantly the hand clamped over her mouth. The arm cut off her breath until she began to see sparkles against Gus's overalls. She was staring at them where they hung on the wall, as if they would suddenly, magically be filled with the friend who belonged inside the baggy folds.

The man shoved his pelvis against her. His erection was stiff against her right buttock. She closed her eyes and tried to think. She hadn't actually felt a knife. Should she take the aggressive tack, bite that hand, hard, and try to make a run for it? He was very strong. Also, he had shut the side door.

Suddenly the hand eased again and she felt the salty taste of blood on her mouth.

"Get down on the floor. Take off your clothes first."

Somewhere in Quinn's brain there were cells that continued to function despite her terror. "Listen. Listen to me," she said, in a monotonous voice that she hoped was unthreatening. She could sense hesitation in the shift of the body behind her.

Out of nowhere a wild thought appeared in her head. It was a risk, undeniably, but there wasn't a whole lot of time for detailed analysis. She spoke quickly. "I'm sick. I have this thing. It's up to you." She had never heard the strange voice that was speaking now, but at least he was listening. "It's up to you," she repeated, trying to hang on to the soothing monotone. "Messy. It's a messy thing. Stomach. It's chronic, my stomach. Diarrhea. Lots of diarrhea. No control at all. Very messy, a real problem." Suddenly she felt the impulse to laugh. She forced the hysteria down and gulped. "It gets my clothes. My clothes are a mess, my bed, everything . . ."

"If you turn around, I'll kill you," the voice snarled. He released her, giving her a rough push. On his way out he drew his arm across Gus's desk and swept everything onto the floor. She never saw his face.

She fell to her knees beside Gus's desk and began to cry. "Thank you. Oh, Jesus, oh, God, thank you, thank you, thank you, thank you." After a few minutes she brushed herself off and began crawling around on the floor to pick up the papers and debris. It took her a while to remember that she ought to leave it all just as it was.

Gus strode into the office, saw her on the floor, and said, "Hey, Mallory, whadya do, shove a bulldozer across my desk?" She turned her face to him. Her cheeks were tearstained and smudged, but it was her look of fear and helplessness that most stunned him. He called the police, and they sat waiting together, on the edge of the desk, hand in hand. Soon the town police arrived to take Quinn to the station. Gus stood for a moment watching the flashing red light of the patrol car recede into the darkness. If his cursed insomnia was fated to make an appearance, at least it could have propelled him to the garage in time to spare Quinn. He walked into the garage, ripped a loose door off one of the campus vans, and slammed it against the floor.

Despite Quinn's protestations that at no time had she glimpsed the man's face, she was required to stare at hundreds of faces in a macabre photograph album labeled "Known Sex Offenders." She reported to Sergeant Collins, who seemed to be in charge, her conviction that the man's primary interest was cash. Any rape intentions were either incidental or a reaction to the frustration of finding no money.

A patrolman asked her if she had "done anything to invite a sexual attack."

"Oh, sure," she retorted, "I said to him, 'Gee, I feel so bad that there isn't any money for you to steal. How about I try to make it up to you?' Then I climbed up on the desk and did this cute little dance . . ."

Her voice had risen half an octave, recapturing the attention of the distracted sergeant. Collins was small and sinewy like her father.

"Cut it out," he said. Quinn wasn't sure whether he was addressing her or the patrolman, but they both fell silent. After two more albums she was escorted home in a patrol car.

She took a long shower. Too tired to dry her hair, she

just covered her pillow with a clean towel and climbed into bed. Suddenly she began to cry again, but this time she welcomed the tears as if they were cleansing the suffocating smell of nicotine from her nostrils, and washing the ugly incident out of her life for good.

Chapter 15

When she woke the next morning, instead of tumbling out of bed the moment her eyes opened, Quinn lay still and thought. The fight with Will seemed real enough, but not the events that followed. If God were going to send her a brainstorm to elude rape, surely it wouldn't take the form of diarrhea.

She tried to get up, but the room seemed to be revolving around her bed, slowly at first, except each time she moved, the tempo accelerated as though she were the center post of a merry-go-round. She leaned back against her pillow gingerly. Suddenly she was frozen and her body began to tremble. Her teeth chattered, her arms and legs quaked. And yet a moment later she felt as if she were being boiled alive and had to kick off her blankets. The movement made her groan. Every part of her ached. Wherever her flesh came in contact with the sheets, she felt bruised.

She closed her eyes and hoped that whatever was happening would pass. Ordinarily Quinn did not acknowledge the authority of pain. She never bothered with Novocain at the dentist's office. Scrapes and bruises, even broken fingers, were an inconvenience to be ignored. She never got colds. Now, this morning, she wasn't convinced she could even make it to the infirmary. Another bout of chills struck her. She tried to force her limbs to be still, but they disobeyed. Frightened and crying now, she hauled herself out of bed. With the room spinning she found a dime in her desk drawer and groped her way down the hall to the telephone. The first time she tried to insert the coin into the slot, her shaking fingers dropped it, but finally she managed to complete the call.

It wasn't difficult to persuade the person on the other end to wake Will. She knew she must sound desperate.

"Hello?"

Just the sound of his voice started her crying again. "Will? It's me. I'm . . . I can't . . ."

"What's happened?"

"I'm sick, I guess. It's so stupid. I can't seem to walk very well. Will you help me get to the infirmary?"

"Can you make it to the lobby?"

"I think so."

"I'll be right there."

Quinn crept back to her room by steadying herself with one hand against the wall. She pulled on a pair of jeans and a sweat shirt and cautiously made her way to the elevator. She didn't have to wait long for Will. He was red-faced and breathing hard.

"What happened to you, Quinn?" He was staring at the tendrils of sweat-soaked hair around her face. Her freckles looked gray against the white cheeks.

"Got sick. I'm sorry, I never had to do this . . . call somebody. I feel so dumb."

He lifted her from the chair, put his arm around her waist, and half carried her to the infirmary.

He sat with her while the nurse took her temperature. "How much is it?" he asked.

"Hundred and three point six," the nurse answered. "Into bed, young lady."

"May I stay?" he asked.

"Visiting hours are two to four."

"Please come back," Quinn said. Her eyes had filled again at the thought of his leaving. She was pretty sure that she had spilled more tears these past twenty-four hours than in all her life up to yesterday.

She slept through the morning. By the time Will showed up at her bedside, her temperature had dropped to a hundred degrees and she was feeling much better.

He sat down in the chair next to her bed. "You okay?"

"Yeah. I've got great recuperative powers. Will, I'm sorry about last night."

"Me, too. I was a churl."

"If you were a churl, I was a troll."

"A perfect match." He took her hand and examined it. She had freckles on the backs but none on the creamy skin of her palms. He tried to remember if her feet were similar. "I didn't want to hear what you were saying."

"I know."

"What's that bruise?" He pointed to her throat.

Quinn averted her eyes.

"Is it a bruise? Or . . ." He looked embarrassed. Quinn knew what he was thinking and started to laugh.

"I didn't exactly have a hot date . . . oh, God . . ." The laughter was getting out of hand. She knew that soon she would be crying again, so she took a few deep breaths and told him about the intruder in the garage.

Will pulled the neck of her nightgown aside.

"Looks like a Rorschach, doesn't it?" she said.

All of the muscles in his face had gone rigid. "Do they know who he is?"

"Please, don't get angry now. Just be calm and nice."

He understood at once. She needed his restraint, almost like a child whose tiny body cannot contain the fury of a temper tantrum. He remembered Marianne's little sister flying apart over some four-year-old disappointment. As rage overwhelmed her, her eyes had dilated with fear. She threw herself on the ground, pounding her arms and legs against the grass. Marianne had picked her up, ignoring the screams of protest and dodging the flailing limbs as best she could, and held the child tightly against her own quiet body. She talked soothingly, making repetitive comforting noises until finally, the tempest over, the little girl wiped her tears with the back of her fist and scampered off to play again.

"It's all over," Will said. "I'm going to sit here holding your hand forever, so everyone will think we're furniture. We'll be here in the year 2000, a couple of fossils stuck together."

"I love you."

Neither of them had ever said it before. He examined her face closely for a moment and then leaned over to kiss her.

Then he gazed at her, thinking that surely the pain circling his own neck had already manifested itself into hideous livid bruises like hers. It dawned on him that whatever happened to her had just as certainly happened to him. There was no escape.

Chapter 16

There was to be an all-campus costume party that Saturday night. Quinn and Will made a pact not to divulge to each other what they would wear but agreed that their costumes must display a cherished fantasy. And for the first time Stanley and Van would join them in a double date.

As she was climbing into her Annie Oakley costume, Quinn wondered how Will would get along with her friends. She was impatient with her nervousness; how could three such terrific people not like one another? It was the argument from two weeks ago that had done this to her, she decided. Will's sudden explosion had left her with the uneasy sensation that he was not altogether predictable.

She appraised herself in the long mirror on the closet door. Her fringed skirt was exactly right. The dime-store material appeared worn and discolored, like real suede. In that skirt Quinn might have spent the past twenty days chasing cattle rustlers across the plains. She wore a plaid work shirt, and over it a vest with fringe to match her skirt.

She had bought skeins of corn-yellow yarn, which she had braided into a wig with pigtails. Her plastic ivory-handled six-guns were somewhat small but could be tucked neatly into her belt. She had drawn patterns on her old leather boots in white chalk to simulate elaborate cowboy stitching. Feet apart, she snatched the guns out of her belt, twirled them around her fingers, and shot her image right in the heart.

"Gotcha," she said. Then she flung on her raincoat and headed off for the union. It was a damp January night. Every now and then a snowflake dropped heavily out of the sky and turned to slush the moment it hit the ground. She glanced at her watch. The others would be there already, maybe sitting and staring at one another in silence.

Stanley intercepted her by the door. "I am taking Marvin his beer," he said. "Who's this, Calamity Jane?"

"Aren't you cute, Stan!" Quinn exclaimed, scrutinizing his long velveteen robe with the rat-fur trim. He poked a leg through the folds to exhibit purple tights. "Oh, my," Quinn said. "This has to be Henry the Eighth."

"Your obedient servant," Stanley said. He forged a path through the crowd with his foaming pitcher.

"I should have known. Who's Marvin?"

"Who's Marvin!" Stanley echoed in mock horror. "Your Marvin. Marvin the Magnificent."

Quinn giggled. "Oh. That one. He is, isn't he?"

Stanley had to shout back at her over the din. "If first impressions don't deceive, he's better looking than Quasimodo and smarter than Ed the Talking Horse. More than that I dasn't say."

Quinn poked him in the back. "You dasn't, dasn't you?"

Will and Van sat at a table in the corner behind a solid wall of costumed students. They were talking with heads close together in order to hear over the cacophony.

"I think they like each other," Quinn observed.

"Not too much or heads will roll," said Henry the Eighth.

Will and Van looked up as Quinn reached for her six-shooters. "Pow!" she said.

"Annie Oakley," Van and Will pronounced simultaneously.

"You got it," Quinn said, using her hip to edge her way to the seat next to Will. She examined her friend. "I don't suppose you're Anne Boleyn."

"You won't get it," Van said. She waved arms that were draped in gauzy white cloth. "Isadora Duncan."

"A fine match for King of the Brits, think ye not?" Stanley asked, pouring beer into their paper cups. "We raided the drama department, but there wasn't much left."

"Henry the Eighth was Stanley's finest role. Wasn't it, Quinn?" Van asked.

"*And 'tis a kind of good deed to say well: / And yet words are no deeds,*" Stanley proclaimed.

"I saw you in that production," Will said. "I'm impressed. You were very good. Why are you going to medical school when you're such a good actor?"

"Doctors are the ultimate in royalty back in Brooklyn," Stanley replied.

"Anyhow, I think the impulse to be Henry the Eighth goes beyond remembering the play," Van said.

"Here we go, Freud time," Quinn remarked.

"The impulse, my dear Isadora," said Stanley with a Viennese accent, "is the sublimated urgency to dispose of my wenches when they become too much a pain in the ass. I like especially to chop them off at the head. I find the castration symbolism so gratifying, don't you agree?"

They all laughed.

"But Will," Quinn protested, "you didn't dress up."

He held out his hands to display an old flannel shirt and patched jeans. "I did."

"You won't get him, either," Van said. "He's Henry Thoreau."

"Oh," Quinn said. "Well, at least we're both outdoor types."

"Come on, Isadora," Stanley said. He pulled Van to her feet. "Let's show 'em how to trip the light fantastic. Don't look when she does a pirouette. You can see right through that stuff." They got up and squeezed through the crowd to the dance floor.

"So do you like them?" Quinn asked.

"They seem nice."

"Seem, seem. They are nice. What were you talking to Van about?"

"I don't remember. Beacon Hill, I think."

"Stanley's a dear, don't you think?"

"He's definitely a dear. You want to dance, Annie?"

"No. My feet are killing me in these awful old boots. They've got nails coming through."

"Take 'em off. I want to see if you've got freckles on the bottoms of your feet."

"You're weird, Hank. Did I tell you that I hate your costume?"

"What?"

"Forget I said that."

"Talk about weird."

She moved her shoulders in time with the music. Will tugged on a braid. "Anyway, I like you in pigtails," he said.

"I used to have real ones until I was eleven, but Jake cut them off."

"Oh, is he the family beautician?"

"It was purely a disciplinary event," Quinn said.

"What'd you do to provoke that?"

"I don't remember exactly. My mother wouldn't let me do something I thought I should do, and I got mad and told her I hated her guts. Jake just happened to come into the kitchen and gave me this look like I'd thrown a rotten egg at the Pope. He grabbed a pair of scissors and chopped my braids right off my head and threw them on the table." She paused a moment, then went on thoughtfully, "I had this wicked temper . . ."

"I'm so glad you grew out of *that*," Will said.

"You turkey."

Isadora and Henry the Eighth flung themselves into their chairs. They were breathing hard.

"I don't know how she moved in these clothes," Van gasped. "You can break your neck." She exhibited the well-trod hem of her dress.

"As it happens . . ." Will began slowly.

"Don't tell her!" Quinn said.

"What?" Van asked.

Stanley explained the manner of Isadora's demise.

"Oh, dear," Van said. "I think I should have been Eleanor Roosevelt instead."

The music stopped pounding and Will sighed with happiness. Suddenly Quinn became aware of being watched. The bleary eyes that stared at her from the table directly behind Stanley and Van belonged to Chris Hartley. He wore a tinfoil crown that was too small for his head and a T-shirt with a bright-red heart painted on it.

Chris saw that she had become aware of his gaze. He turned and whispered to his table companions. They laughed uproariously and glanced at Quinn. She felt herself blushing.

"I'm going to slip some Scarlatti into that jukebox one of these days," Will said.

Quinn reached for her six-shooters and pointed them at Will's chest. "You jis' try it, ya' no-good sidewinder. What's a sidewinder, anyway?"

Out of the corner of her eye she saw Chris rise awkwardly and lurch toward their table. He stopped when he reached Quinn, and put a hand on the back of her chair to steady himself.

"Well," he slurred. "The beeyoo-ful Miss Mallory, z' I live 'n breathe."

Quinn kept her voice friendly and neutral. "Hi. King of Hearts, right?"

"Nice costume, Chris," Stanley said. "You're pretty blasted."

"Drunk!" he shouted. "Intoxicated by the beauty of this fair maid. Mallory the Untouch . . . able." He leaned down to put his face close to hers. He was sweaty and smelled of cigarettes. "Am I *so* repulsive to you, mademoiselle?"

Quinn shook her head "no" as she breathed through her mouth to shut out the stench of nicotine. She imagined the rough hand of the garage intruder digging into her mouth.

"You could use a cup of coffee," Will said.

Chris seemed to notice Will's presence for the first time. "Ah!" he said with a clumsy flourish. "The charming Misser Ingraham." He mimed a gesture of tearing open an envelope. "And the winner is . . . William the Conqueror! Virgin Vanquisher!"

"Somebody do something with him," Van said.

Quinn held her hand out imploringly. "Hey, listen, Chris—"

Chris struck it away and tried to focus on Will. "How

was it? As a finalist, I got a right to know. What I lost out of . . . on. She got a nice tight . . . ?"

Will was on his feet, but Chris backed away from the table. His face had collapsed, as if he were about to cry. He waved at them in a kind of apology, but the small movement upset his balance. He slipped on a discarded paper cup and went down with a crash. Will reached to help him up, but Chris was fierce.

"No! Do it myself. Sorry. Not the life of my party." He stood, and with careful dignity, walked across the room and out the door.

The others turned to Quinn, who was pale, almost gray. "Poor thing," she whispered. A dozen onlookers averted their eyes and resumed disrupted conversations. The entertainment was over.

"You okay?" Will asked.

"He smelled like cigarettes," Quinn murmured. "Excuse me." She got up and hurried across the dance floor. The yellow pigtails bounced, more grotesque now than gay. She made it to the ladies' room just in time.

After that the tumultuous atmosphere of the union seemed oppressive. Van suggested Lou's, and since none of them was dressed for the cold, they ran, howling when they intercepted the brutal wind that swept across the Pilgrim River bridge. They arrived out of breath, laughing and delighted with the stares from the conventionally attired patrons. They found a booth toward the back.

"You sure you're up to this?" Will asked Quinn.

"The cold helped. I'm fine."

"You can content yourself with the fact that Chris is no doubt following suit—as behooves the King of Hearts—in the men's room," Stanley said.

Quinn was still ashen. "He was . . . his face was . . ." She looked at Van. "You told me. You were right. I never thought anybody would get hurt."

"Old Chris'll be okay," Stanley said. "He'll drown his grief with Henrietta Foster."

Quinn looked unconvinced. "I wish I could say something to him, do something to make up for it."

"I think the kindest thing would be to just leave him alone," Will said.

Van cleared her throat and said brightly, "Will was telling me about the old loggers he knew when he was growing up."

"That's the Huntington 'change the subject' tone of voice," Quinn told Will.

"I've known a few old lawyers in my day," Stanley said.

"Loggers, loggers, you quahog," Quinn said.

"Like Paul Bunyan and John Wayne and Maureen O'Sullivan?" Stanley asked Will, and whispered to Van, "What's a quahog?"

"More like Pierre Lechat and John Tallfeather and Dooley Donovan," Will said.

Stanley forgot about quahogs and began interrogating. Will narrated the whole story, starting with his grandfather's exodus west from Chicago with the railroad. Quinn sat sipping her ginger ale. The cold air had cleared away most of the choking odor of Chris Hartley's cigarettes, but a faint reminder still clung to her hair. She had thought she had put the garage assault behind her. She would have to learn to live with the smell of nicotine and not be running off to vomit every time somebody lit up a cigarette. The man was still at large, but it wasn't constructive to think about that. She tried to tune in to Will's narration. Stanley and Van were obviously fascinated. They also seemed to like him. It was what she had wanted out of the evening. But why had Will worn that outfit? It wasn't even a costume. And why was it that she only heard that degree of enthusiasm in his voice when he was talking about the Great American West?

The wind had died down by the time they started back to campus. Their pace was a brisk walk, with Quinn and Will ahead of the other two.

"They're okay, your friends," Will said.

"I don't know how you could tell. They couldn't get a word in edgewise."

Will stared at her.

"I'm sorry." She took his arm. "I was desperate for you to like them, and I'm really glad you do."

"What's the matter?"

"Nothing."

"You've been too Goddamn quiet. Is it Chris?"

"Probably."

"Look, this is the first time you've ever accused me of talking too much."

"Was I accusing?"

"Yes," he said.

"You're going to be a great teacher. I've already heard all that stuff and I wasn't even bored."

"Could have fooled me."

They continued walking in silence. Stanley and Van now trailed far behind. Suddenly Quinn stopped short and released his arm. "How come you're Thoreau? I really wish you weren't."

"Excuse me?" He couldn't help smiling, even though her face was deadly earnest under the light of the streetlamp.

"Is that really your absolutely fondest fantasy, to be off in the woods all by yourself?"

Standing still was making them cold, and besides, Stanley and Van were catching up. Will put his arm around her and started moving again. "Not all by myself."

"I never hear much about Mrs. Thoreau." When Will didn't respond, she pressed, "Well, was there one?"

"I don't know."

"I bet she brought the groceries over to Walden twice a week and shuffled off home again to tend the babies."

"If there were babies, he must have been around sometimes."

Quinn didn't smile. "I thought you'd get a big charge out of Annie Oakley. She's so western. I could have come as Fiorello LaGuardia, you know."

"I'm sorry. I didn't think about how you'd see it."

"Will, what is there for me out in the boondocks?" She stared up at him, but he had no answer for her. "If you ever leave me," she said, "I'll hate your guts forever."

He could sense her decision to back off. Relieved, he picked up one of her pigtails, made his fingers into scissors, and pretended to cut.

She jerked her head away. "Oh, hell, we're too nuts about each other not to work it out. We'll do it." She began to run back toward Stanley and Van. "Come on, Hank, let's go get those two snails."

In the distance the streetlight glowed on Stanley's purple tights.

"Hey, Your Majesty!" Quinn called. "You've got regal stems!" Will strode along beside her with his eyes staring off into the darkness.

Chapter 17

The following Monday afternoon Quinn made the forty-minute bus ride to Springfield. She hadn't mentioned to anyone her appointment with Dr. Huntington's colleague at the Western New England Medical Research Center.

She shook hands with Dr. George Loomis and sat down. He seemed barely within shouting distance, on the opposite side of a vast expanse of rosewood desk. It had been polished to such a high gloss that even the ornate pattern on the physician's Liberty of London tie was clearly reflected. There were exquisite glass sculptures on the bookcase behind him. Quinn's eyes searched in vain for the amiable clutter that she associated with her family doctor back home. In fact, the sole personal touch was a collage of children's finger paintings that were handsomely framed but obscured by the array of diplomas and citations. What kind of doctor's office smelled more like furniture polish than rubbing alcohol? At seventy-five dollars a crack, Quinn thought, the guy'd better be a diagnostic brain trust.

"Russell Huntington tells me you'd like an opinion regarding your mother," Dr. Loomis said.

"Yes." Quinn found herself whispering in response to the doctor's hushed tone. Loomis began sifting through the leaves of Ann Mallory's medical history. Quinn watched the top of his head and wished that the skull gleaming beneath the thinning hair were transparent, that she could read the thoughts hidden there before they got translated into that soft, careful voice.

"Ym," Dr. Loomis said.

Ym, what's ym? Quinn wondered. Her heart had begun to thump. Hey, that pile of statistics you're looking at is my mother.

Her eyes wandered to the finger paintings. Upon closer scrutiny she began to suspect that they had been selected by an interior decorator to enhance the colors in the Oriental rug.

Dr. Loomis looked up. His face was bland, eyes a pale, noncommital blue. "I presume you've read this. The prognosis and so on?"

Quinn nodded. The thumping intensified with each movement of her head.

"Without actually examining Mrs. Mallory," the doctor continued, "I find nothing to dispute the diagnosis in Dr. Gunther's letter."

Quinn put her hand on the glass surface of the desk and felt it stick there. "I want to know what her chances are. Whether there'll be pain. Whether she's better off in the hospital than at home. Where there's an experimental program . . ."

"Miss Mallory . . ." The doctor held up his hands to stop the torrent. "I wish I had more to offer you, but I'm afraid—"

"How come nobody wants to answer my questions?" Quinn blurted.

"Because there aren't any answers."

Quinn thought for a moment. There were always answers. It was finding them that was tricky. But she could see that Loomis was trying to be straight with her. "Are you a better doctor than Gunther?" she asked.

There was a flicker behind the pallid eyes. "He has an excellent reputation."

"What would you do if she were your mother?"

"I'd stick with Gunther, and if he asked me to feed her raw dandelion leaves, I'd do it. I'm sorry, but you're up against a disease we just don't know enough about." He looked tired.

Quinn stood up. "I like your art," she said.

The doctor rose too, glanced at the finger paintings, and smiled. "I'm convinced they belong in a museum, of course." He extended his hand. "I wish you luck, Miss Mallory. Lupus sometimes has long periods of remission. It won't be easy, but it's possible that she's got many years."

Quinn clung to his soft fingers, as if by prolonging the handshake she could somehow prolong her mother's life. The doctor held out the file for her, and she was forced to let go.

"Next time you see Russ Huntington," he said, "you tell him for me he's a son of a bitch."

Quinn never did get a bill.

"Will, I want you to come home with me," Quinn said, slapping down *The Evolution of American Foreign Policy*.

Will looked up from *The Golden Bough*. Beside his chair the window framed a swirling blizzard. "Funny you should say that," he remarked.

"Ho-ho?"

He set his book on the windowsill and motioned to

her. She sat on his lap and wrapped her arms around his neck. "I've been thinking," he began.

"I told you never to do that."

"We've got an eight-day break after exams. How about we go to Idaho?"

Quinn stared at him.

"It's not expensive if we fly standby. There's a really cheap Saturday flight."

"How cheap is really cheap?"

"I don't remember exactly."

She rolled her eyes. Sitting bolt upright now, she held her hands folded in her lap. "I've never been west of the Hudson River."

"*Carpe diem.*"

She thought for a moment, then looked at him and said, "You bet your ass, honeybunch. And what's more, on our way back we can fly to Boston and stop over at my house. That way we'll kill four birds with one stone. And I'll have a party so you can meet all the old crowd. They can stare at you and envy me. Will, this is gonna be fun. Idaho. Holy shit. Have you got a map? I want to see where I'm going. Oh, my God, I almost forgot."

"What?"

"The second thing I was going to say, after 'come home with me.' It's going to put a damper on everything."

"Let's get it over with then."

"It's my letter to Ted Manning, the one about a job?"

"I know the one you mean."

"We won't talk about what's going to happen. I am absolutely convinced we'll reach a compromise. Just please take a look at it for me and tell me how to fix it?"

"All right."

She lifted herself partway off him and withdrew a crumpled page from the back pocket of her jeans. Will slipped his hand under her as she settled onto his lap again.

"Nice," he said.

"Here, read." She handed him the letter.

He scowled at it. "I hope you're going to type it. Nobody can read this mess."

She snatched it back. "Of course I'm going to type it. Here." She read aloud. "*Mr. Ted Manning, On the Line, 4141 Avenue of the Americas—*"

"Spare me the zip code, will you?" he interjected.

She went on in a firm voice. "*New York, New York 10019. Dear Mr. Manning: This is partly a fan letter. I watch your program almost every night and you are the most insightful, persuasive, thorough, and exhilarating interviewer in the media.* That's Part One," she explained to Will, then continued. "*That was the fan letter section, and now I want to ask you for a job with* On the Line. *I have terrific grades, my bookcase is full of awards, I've got enormous stamina, and besides, I can type. I am also insightful, persuasive, thorough, and exhilarating. I will be in New York the end of the month and would appreciate an interview with your company. Perhaps you would also be interested in hearing my suggestions for making your show an even greater success—humble suggestions, of course. I hope to hear from you soon. Very truly yours, Quinn C. Mallory.*" She looked at Will expectantly.

"You're hired," he said without enthusiasm.

"Think I overdid the charming impertinence?"

"No." He looked at her carefully. "Quinn . . ."

"*Oh*, no. We're not getting into that, remember?"

"We're going to have to one of these days."

She nestled against his shoulder. "I want you to meet my parents. And Margery, and Jim, and everybody, even Darlene Finney."

"Who's Darlene Finney? Have I ever heard of her?"

"I think I dreamt about her last night. I do occasionally, when I'm paranoid. You ready for the sad tale of my criminal youth?"

"If we can't discuss the future, I guess we might as well discuss the past. But squinch over. That's better."

"Once upon a time, little boy, there was this convent school called St. Theresa's that had a really prigass student government modeled after the Gestapo. Darlene Finney was head of the Hitler Youth." She pulled away from him for a moment to check his face. "You listening?" She could see he was, and she kissed him lightly on the mouth as a reward. "Now, Darlene Finney wore frosted lipstick that made her look like a ghoul, and she lurked around corners waiting to pounce on you with her little demerit notebook."

"Boyohboy, I can hardly wait to meet her."

"In eleventh grade we had all these rules, like wearing gray socks with black shoes and carrying our books in special plastic bags they sold at school for a dollar fifty. Well, I wasn't about to spend all that money when I could use a dry-cleaner bag, which is what I did. But old eagle-eyes Finney popped out from behind my locker one day and grabbed me by the arm and started snarling at me about demerits for my dry-cleaner bag. So . . ." She paused.

"What?"

She smiled, pleased at the intensity of his curiosity. "So I whacked her."

"Unconscionable!"

"But she was hurting me. She had her pointy frosted

fingernails stuck in my arm. Anyway, all injured dignity, she said, 'You can't hit me. I'm on Student Council.' And I said 'You can't hit *me*. I'm a temple of the Holy Ghost.' "

They both laughed. He pulled her face close for a kiss, but she sat back after a modest peck on the cheek, too full of memories.

"I guess I held the record for demerits. Too many you went to school Saturdays, so I spent tenth grade with a six-day week, doing Word Wealth. Aversion: repugnance, repulsion, antipathy, allergy, don't-stop-me-or-I'll-forget, abomination, abhorrence, disgust, loathing."

She took a deep breath.

"Finished?" he asked.

"Are you bored?" she asked accusingly.

"No."

"Then, of course, there was cheerleading. I tried out every year, and every year I was always the first person chosen by the coaches—they posted our names on the bulletin board. And I was always the first person to be crossed off the list by the nuns. I was such a good kid. Why'd they give me a hard time?"

"I can't imagine."

She put her face half an inch from his. "I want you to come home with me."

"I can pass meeting Darlene Finney."

"St. Theresa's was not administered with an even hand. We just won't send our kids to parochial school."

He lifted her off his lap and carried her to the bed.

"Let's hear about Red Falls High," she said.

He kissed her just under the left ear. "I had an affair with the principal's wife."

Quinn sat up abruptly. "You didn't."

"Tell you about it sometime." He wrapped an arm

around her chest and pulled her down again. His hand slipped under her sweater. "Not now."

She felt his fingers move up her rib cage toward her breasts, and decided to let the subject drop for the moment. She didn't believe him anyway.

Chapter 18

They boarded their plane at noon on Saturday. Quinn had never flown before, and was so intrigued with each element of the procedure, from baggage check to boarding, that she forgot to talk. Unaccustomed to such long periods of silence, Will kept studying her face to make sure she was all right.

She raised and lowered the shade, pressed the light button, twisted the air regulator, experimented with her seat position and the food tray. She listened with total concentration to the flight attendant's speech about oxygen masks and emergency exits. Finally, when they were airborne, with a thick layer of clouds beneath them, she turned to Will and smiled.

"Hi there," he said.

"How much you figure it costs to take flying lessons?"

He laughed and glanced at his watch. "Not one word for over fifteen minutes. I was afraid you ate a rusty nail for breakfast and got lockjaw."

"I had my tetanus shot. God, I wish we could have brought Harvey with us. Wouldn't he go nuts? I don't understand why takeoff is so noisy outside when it's not bad at all in here. What kind of insulation do they use?

Or maybe it has something to do with pressurization. I always had this yen to be a stewardess."

"I think you've found your voice again."

"Idaho could be a great big ugly pit, and it'd still be worth the trip just for this."

At Boise they transferred to a sixteen-seater for the flight to Lewiston. The sky had cleared, and there was still a pale shimmer of light when they caught their first glimpse of the Salmon River. From two miles up it seemed like a long curl of silver Christmas ribbon draped across the forests, shiny and, Will knew, deceptively smooth. Sam was to meet them at the airport. Will felt the rush of affection that always engulfed him at the thought of his lumbering younger brother.

"There he is," Will said. "Over by the luggage pickup."

"God, he's big," Quinn remarked. "He's like a bear." Sam stood a full three inches taller than Will and had a bulky, meaty body.

Sam had seen them now. Grinning, he walked over and wrapped a huge paw around Will's palm. "Not even an hour late." His voice was a slow, deep rumble.

Quinn found it hard to believe that this hulking young man was only a high school senior. Though Sam was as dark as Will was fair, she was startled by the resemblance between them. Susan Ingraham said her two boys had inherited the same face, it was just that Sam looked as though he had the shades drawn.

Sam was reaching for Quinn's hand. "Oh, sorry," she said, grasping it. "I'm glad to meet you. It's the bump on your nose. It's just like Will's."

"Dad says that's a dead giveaway of McCaffrey blood," Will explained. He slung their suitcases off the ramp, handed one to Sam, and began walking toward the exit. "Comes from generations of brawling in bars on Saturday nights."

Quinn squeezed into the front seat of the jeep between Sam and Will. There was a fine dusting of new snow on the road, but Sam handled the vehicle expertly. Quinn gazed out the window and enjoyed the sensation of muscular male thighs on either side of hers.

Meanwhile, Will was experiencing the swelling in his chest that occurred whenever he was deeply moved, by a poem, perhaps, or by a particular piece of music. The response always forced him to take deep breaths, as if by expanding he could accommodate the volume of his feelings. Provoking it now was the sight of the pine trees by the side of the road, with their dark trunks rising out of the snow.

He had come home from far-off places many times before, but never had he felt such a profound sense of reunion. Perhaps Quinn's presence somehow made a difference. He put his arm around her and wished, as so often before, that he had been a pioneer like his grandfather when the territory was still practically uninhabited.

William Ingraham, two generations back, had come west from Chicago with the railroad in the 1870s, built himself a cabin in the Clearwater Mountains, and set up the first lumber yard in the region. Soon afterward he'd married Johanna Moore, extracting her from her father, the local missionary, who spent his lifetime converting the Nez Percé Indians. Will still remembered his grandfather, white beard against bright plaid shirt, striding through the mill like a young man, always the handful of sawdust in his left fist. He would hold it out for Will to smell. "White pine dust," he said. "Like gold, only better."

The Ingrahams sold out after Will's father had been injured in the big fire ten years ago. A piece of the roof had collapsed, pinning Matthew Ingraham inside the inferno. The old Canadian foreman, LeChat, had pulled him out, but Matthew never used his legs again.

Will's father now sat in his wheelchair in the shop they'd built for him at home, handcarving cabinets and furniture and fine statues of animals. He claimed the statues never came out quite right. "Wasn't what I had in mind," he would say. One time Susan had put her favorite, the hawk, on display in the living room. When Matthew saw it perched there on the table, he wheeled over and silently removed it. The sculptures remained undisturbed thereafter, and they were not discussed unless Matthew chose to speak of them.

"You'll be flying east too, Will tells me," Quinn was saying to Sam.

"Yup."

Another big talker, Quinn decided. "You guys go a long way for college. Isn't there a veterinary school closer to home?"

"Not like Cornell. Besides, I'll get to live somewhere else for a few years."

"You'll have the rest of your life to explore the world."

"I'll be coming back after I graduate, to set up my practice."

"Tell me, Sam, does anybody from Idaho ever leave the state permanently?"

"Yup. A kid in my class, the whole family just up and moved to Minneapolis." His voice, *basso profundo*, resonated with pity.

Will watched the spooky light flickering against the lower branches of the forest. The woods never looked exactly the same, and yet always enchanted him. He took a breath of mountain air, fragrant with pine. Anywhere east of the Montana line was too far away.

The Ingraham house sat back fifty yards off the Mountain Road. The original structure, Grandfather's cabin, stood at the center and was used as the living room area. Additions rambled off in three directions, reminding Will of the cardhouses he and Sam used to build as boys. Tacking on rooms each time the family expanded had eventually resulted in a dining room that was practically inaccessible to the kitchen. Over the years, helping hands had dribbled soup, fruit juice, and spaghetti sauce in an ineradicable dotted line from the stove through the living room and onto the long maple dining room table. "The Gravy Trail," Matthew Ingraham called it. But there was never any question of tearing down the ramshackle arrangement to begin again. Tampering with Grandfather's living room would be like disrupting the ghosts of pioneer America. Nor would the Ingrahams ever move, not with the exuberant cascades of Red Falls keeping up their end of the conversation a hundred feet beyond the back door.

They had driven nearly an hour before beginning a steep ascent up a road narrowed by towering drifts.

"I've never seen so much snow in my life," Quinn said. "We're like Moses parting the Red Sea." She stared out the window, looking for houses in the darkness. Suddenly Sam turned off into a driveway on the right.

"We're home," Will said.

"Where are all your neighbors?" Quinn asked.

"We passed the Bateses about two miles back."

Quinn thought two miles was a long way to walk to borrow sugar or chat over a cup of tea.

A chorus of deep-throated barking began the moment

Sam, Will, and Quinn started up the front steps. Quinn grabbed Will's arm.

"What's that?"

"Sam's wolves."

"You're kidding me," Quinn said with a quaver.

"Gentle as lambs," Sam assured her.

The door burst open and two large furry bodies flung themselves out onto the porch. A golden retriever and a Labrador, yelping wildly, leapt up on Sam, licked his face, and only then calmed enough to sniff at Will and Quinn.

Susan Ingraham stood in the doorway. "Fred! Flower! I'm sorry. What a welcome. Sam, do something with those two."

Sam squeezed inside, and without being called, the dogs followed, weaving in and out of his legs.

Quinn watched Will bend his head to kiss his mother's cheek. It was a formal gesture. Matthew Ingraham approached them next, braked his wheelchair, and stretched out a hand to Will. While Quinn was being introduced, she examined them: Matthew Ingraham with the blond hair faded and lank over a creased forehead, the wide gentle face that seemed younger than it should on a man who had apparently suffered such pain; Will's mother standing beside the wheelchair, hand resting lightly on her husband's shoulder. Her hair was dark and thick, and though she pulled it back into a knot at the nape of her neck, it sprang loose from the hairpins and softened the severe lines of her face with tendrils like tiny corkscrews.

Will took Quinn's bag and led her to a pine-paneled cubbyhole at the rear of the house.

"I bet Abe Lincoln slept here," Quinn said. She

twisted the knob on a kerosene lamp above the bed. "Do these work?"

"They did when we were kids, but after we set fire to Sam's room, we stuck with electricity."

After he left, Quinn sat on the bed next to her suitcase and took a deep breath. American pioneer homes must have smelled like this room—rough wooden walls and plank floorboards. Raw wood had a cozy, welcoming scent.

Susan Ingraham knocked, waited for Quinn's permission, and poked her head through the door.

"Dinner's ready whenever you are. Would you like more time to get settled, or are you starving?"

Quinn hopped off the bed. "Starving, thanks. I'll be right there."

She was seated next to Will. Sam and Susan sat across from her, with Matthew at the head of the table. There was roast leg of lamb, crisp browned potatoes, a platter of mixed vegetables, and homemade dinner rolls. Matthew watched with satisfaction while Quinn heaped her plate.

"See you brought us a good eater," he said to Will. "Can't abide these skinny glamour girls that swallow one lettuce leaf and half a tomato."

"Oh, you'll go broke trying to feed Quinn just for the weekend," Will said amiably.

"Thanks," Quinn responded.

"Jed Ryan's building a mile up," Sam said to Will. "Bought five acres near the mill."

"Yup," Matthew said. "Getting to be a regular housing development around here."

"Oh, for heaven's sake, Matthew," Susan protested. "I don't know why you bother living in civilization at all."

"Will's just as bad," Sam remarked.

"We had an awful time keeping track of him when he was little," Susan told Quinn. "Always disappearing into the woods where he could be by himself."

So it had started early, Quinn thought.

"Will's birthday one year," Sam explained to Quinn, "they had a dozen ten-year-old kids here and no birthday boy. By the time we found him up by Flat Rock, there wasn't any birthday cake left."

"I didn't mind," Will said.

"Rude antisocial bastard, my brother," Sam commented.

"Maybe I should be a social butterfly like you and spend my entire life with animals. Anyway, I do all right." Will rested his arm on Quinn's shoulder for a moment.

"Not bad at all," Matthew agreed, and reached for Quinn's plate. "Here, have another slice."

There followed a prolonged silence. Quinn made a furtive check, but none of the others appeared to be at all uncomfortable. The click of knives and forks echoed in Quinn's ears until she could bear it no longer.

"I never saw such enormous pine trees. On the drive from the airport," she blurted.

"That so?" Matthew said. "Well, I hear fir trees don't get much more'n knee-high back east. It's the air."

It took a moment for Quinn to realize that she was being teased. Now she understood the origin of Will's deadpan expression.

"We stretch them for Christmas," Quinn replied. "That tree in Rockefeller Plaza's been on the rack for days."

"Hm," Matthew said appreciatively.

Meanwhile Will's eyes kept flickering back and forth from Quinn to his family. There had been no important girl in his life since Marianne, and she had always been so much a part of the Ingraham clan that the interplay was long established by the time Will began to think of her with sexual interest. But even back at college Will found Quinn a member of an alien species. The feeling was exaggerated in the familiar atmosphere of his home. He was surprised that everyone wasn't studying her as they might a rare acquisition on display in the zoo. On the contrary, they were reacting as if she were a legitimate member of the human race. He felt gratified, and yet vaguely disappointed.

Soon after dinner Will and Quinn were left alone by the fire in the living room.

"So?" Will prompted.

"I like them. God, it's weird. I must have been thinking you existed in a vacuum, as if you didn't get born and raised in a regular family like everybody else."

"Sprang fully grown from the forehead of a god, no doubt."

"Your father is so much like you, your expressions, your speech. It's peculiar."

"Well, you and I've been living in a pretty rarified atmosphere. It must be a jolt coming here—new family, new place. Culture shock."

"I could eat you up, starting with your toes."

"I'm surprised you've got any room in your stomach after what you put away."

"That was just to impress your father."

Will laughed. "Do you want to go out, or are you tired?"

"I couldn't sleep if you hit me over the head with a mallet. Is there any place to go out to?"

"We can visit Edward."

"Edward French, the famous literary light of Red Falls High?"

"That's the one."

"Let's go."

Will drove them up the Hot Springs Road toward Edward's house. When they slowed at an intersection, Will felt Quinn smiling at him.

"What?" he asked.

"I've never been in a car with you driving before."

Will cranked the jeep into third gear. "Is there some significance I'm missing?"

"You're a good driver. It's sexy."

"I'll keep that in mind."

Will had been making this trip since he and Marianne were freshmen in high school. Edward, with his L.L. Bean safari jacket and climbing boots, had appeared that year to teach the ninth grade American Literature course. For Will, French's class was like flinging open a great many windows simultaneously. The light was dazzling, the rush of air made him dizzy. The second week of class, in the midst of a lecture on Melville's *Billy Budd*, Will found himself holding on to the sides of his chair to keep from being blown over.

Soon afterward Marianne and Will began their regular Saturday evening trips to Edward's house. The three of them took turns reading aloud: Marianne from Emily Dickinson; Will from John Donne and William Blake and the Lyrical Ballads; Edward from Chaucer, in the original Middle English. It was all food for Will, and he would stumble out of the little house in the early morning hours, exhausted and stuffed like a man well fed.

Will felt a certain trepidation about bringing Quinn to see Edward. Even after Marianne was killed in the car accident, her presence had always hung in the air of Edward's living room like the smoke from his fireplace. Quinn's visit was bound to disturb that familiar haze, and yet her meeting Edward was as important as her knowing his family.

Will pulled into the driveway in front of a shoebox house perched on cinder blocks. Before he could raise his hand to knock, Edward opened the door and stood aside.

"Come in, come in. You must be half frozen."

Automatically, Will ducked to avoid hitting his head on the low frame.

"Quinn, this is Edward French. Edward, Quinn Mallory."

They shook hands. "I'm delighted to meet you," Edward said.

Quinn was trying not to show her surprise. She had imagined Edward as approaching the stature of Paul Bunyan, but the man was hardly bigger than she was. His hands were tiny. He had a square face with deep lines around the mouth, large, rather prominent blue eyes, and thinning hair. Quinn liked the fact that he made no attempt to camouflage the baldness by sporting one of those corny hairpieces or combing the longer strands up from the sides. That kind of futile vanity always irritated her.

"Come sit by the fire," Edward said. "What can I get you?"

While their host went to fetch drinks, Quinn looked around the room. Three out of four walls were obscured by bookcases. Every now and then there was a gap in what seemed an endless array of titles for the display of small, exquisite Japanese wood-block prints. The twin wicker sofas before the fire were upholstered in a bamboo pattern.

Edward set down a tray, poured their beer into glasses, and settled opposite them with his Scotch and water.

Will had purposely occupied the cushion farthest from the fire that had been Marianne's spot. He didn't think Edward would want to see Quinn sitting there.

"Are you an English major too?" Edward asked her.

"No, poli sci. I didn't even like English until this year. We have a great teacher. A little on the affected side, but he knows how to get people excited about books. At least he did it for me." She looked at Will. "And Will helped."

"We had some pretty nasty debates about the Brontës. Quinn has a philosophical preference for Charlotte."

"That was in November."

"Don't tell me you've changed your mind about Cathy Earnshaw?"

"I'll admit she's been growing on me," Quinn said.

"What do you plan to do with your political science?"

Quinn kept her eyes on Edward so she wouldn't have to see Will's face. "I'm applying for a job with a television network in New York. The current affairs department."

"Ah," Edward said. It was a carefully noncommittal "ah." Will stared into the fire.

"Tell me, how's our friend Harvey Jackson?" Edward asked.

"You know Harvey?" Quinn asked incredulously, then realized that no, of course he didn't.

"I feel that I do," Edward said.

"I always pick Edward's brain about how to handle the little bastard," Will explained.

"I could use some help in that department," Quinn said.

"There's some resentment about Quinn," Will said.

"Just a bit," she agreed wryly.

"But he's really getting into the Tolkien. It's just what he's hungry for. Total fantasy, but challenging for a kid his age."

"Just think what he'd have been capable of if he'd had the luck to be born in Shaker Heights."

"You sound as if you're writing him off," Quinn said.

"It'll be a miracle if his intellect can survive, much less flourish, with the road he's got ahead of him," Edward said.

Will drained his glass. "That's all I ask. A small miracle."

"But he's so smart," Quinn protested.

"Maybe he'll make it," Edward said. "I have something to show you, Will." He got up and went to his desk.

Quinn was thoughtful and quiet. She was visualizing Harvey as a grown man nodding on a Roxbury street corner like so many other black men she had seen in Boston. It had never occurred to her that those wasted people could have started out with gifted minds.

Edward returned with a folder. Will took it while Edward explained to them, "She's rather special, I think. Half-Indian, half-Canadian. I'm very excited about this particular story."

Will was already on the second page. Edward watched him read, and when Quinn glanced at the older man, she suddenly saw something that chilled her. Edward's eyes, as they moved from the typed page to Will's face, were full of adoration and pain. The moment lasted for the barest fraction of a second, but Quinn was stunned. Then she began to flush. Edward looked up at her, smiled pleasantly, and rose. He held out his hand and ushered her to his bookcases, where she could get a closer look at the prints.

"You seem a little warm there by the fire," he whispered. "This is a Yoshida. It's my particular favorite."

"It's not a wood block, is it?"

"Yes, amazingly. I don't think anybody in the western hemisphere has mastered the technique."

"What's that light?" Quinn asked. She was staring out the window above Edward's desk.

Edward followed the direction of her gaze and laughed. "Stars."

"That's incredible." She turned to look at Will, who was still absorbed in the manuscript. "Do you think we could go out?"

"Certainly." Edward helped her on with her coat and slipped into a down jacket. "We'll be right back," he called to the oblivious Will.

They leaned back against the jeep and lifted their heads upward.

"I'm grateful to you, Quinn," Edward said in a hushed voice. "It's been a long time since I bothered to look at that."

"It's not the same sky. Is Idaho that much closer to heaven?"

"There's no light to distract the eye. No cities. The nearest town is Red Falls, and everybody's probably turned off the lights and gone to bed by now."

"It's a little scary. I'm not very big to start off with, but this is ridiculous."

"I know just what you mean."

They smiled at each other in the starlight. Soon there was a beam of light from the house and Will's figure appeared in the doorway. They blinked at him like blind creatures.

"Finished. Are you coming in, or should I come out?"

"Let's go in," Edward said, taking Quinn's elbow. "It's cold."

Standing by the fireplace, Edward explained, "We were being reminded of our insignificance."

"I feel like your basic dust mote," Quinn said. "An awed dust mote. How was the story?"

"It's good. It's better than good."

Edward nodded. "She's a lovely girl, too, but I think her classmates neglect her. What a plague to be extraordinary at that age. Quinn, would you like to read it?"

They had sat down again. Quinn took the pages and began to skim through them. It was a story about an Indian child's odyssey to New Mexico, written in a vivid, straightforward style, but Quinn couldn't concentrate. She kept her head down and flipped pages while she listened to Will and Edward.

"If I could have one student like this in a lifetime of teaching, I think I'd be satisfied," Will said.

"Yes. I hadn't had such a thrill since . . ." Edward glanced at Quinn, whose face was invisible under a curtain of hair. She filled in the blank: *Marianne*. "Her first assignment was very rough," Edward continued, "but the purity was there, the power."

"I can hardly wait to start."

"You'd be very fortunate to run into a student like this right away."

"If I can just excite someone the way you did me, that's enough."

Even if Quinn had been involved with the words on the page, her attention would have been caught by the depth of feeling in Will's words. His voice, normally so measured, resonated with eagerness. He drummed his fingers on the arm of the sofa. Quinn had never seen the gesture from him before. She watched his hand, transfixed.

They drank some more and talked about Thomas Hardy, the poet versus the novelist. Finally Will began to yawn, and soon they got up. At the door Edward gave Quinn a kiss on the cheek. He stared into her eyes for a moment. They smiled at one another and embraced. Then Edward shook hands with Will. He followed them out to the porch with his right hand in his pocket. Quinn wondered if he was trying to preserve the sensation of Will's fingers on his.

"Well?" Will said as they drove off.

"He's a dear man. He's also crazy about you."

Will was silent.

"You know what I mean, don't you?"

"Yes," Will said.

"You didn't tell me that, either."

"It didn't seem fair."

"I can understand that."

"He changed the world for me."

"I know. Funny thing." Quinn shook her head. "He won."

"What?" Will asked.

"Nothing. Let me drive, will you?"

The next day Matthew wanted to replenish his supply of reading material at the Red Falls library. He appeared in the living room with a lapful of adventure books to return. Susan helped him on with his coat, then opened the front door and wheeled him down a side ramp to the jeep, where Sam and Will stood waiting. Sam scooped his father up and set him in the passenger seat while Will collapsed the chair and slid it into the back. Then Sam climbed in and started the engine. It was all accomplished in a matter of seconds.

"That was efficient," Quinn said to Will as Sam drove off.

"We've done it a few thousand times."

"How come you don't attach a lift to the back? Then he could stay in his wheelchair and you wouldn't have to carry him."

"Because he loves sitting in front like anybody else. It gives him a chance to feel normal."

Sam and Matthew were back in an hour, and the same ritual was performed in reverse. It had begun to snow.

"We're in for a real storm today," Matthew told Quinn as he wheeled in the front door. His pale cheeks were ruddy with the cold and the excitement of an excursion. "You're likely to be trapped in here for weeks." This time Quinn smiled at him. His expression never permitted a hint of humor, but there was something about his eyes when he was teasing her that she had begun to recognize.

"Never snows like this in Medham, I figure," he said.

"Oh, no. New England flakes are entirely different. Mostly they're square, but sometimes they're the same shape as faces of the Founding Fathers. I especially like the Ben Franklins, but they melt too fast."

Matthew shot Will a look as he wheeled off toward his workroom. "You better watch out for this one," he said, and raised his eyebrows just a fraction at Quinn. "You interested in taking a look at my studio?"

Quinn nodded eagerly. She followed the wheelchair to a room, at the far end of the house, that had its own small fireplace. Across one entire wall hung an array of tools: jigsaws, awls, screwdrivers, picks, each in a variety of sizes. There was a smell of fresh sawdust. Quinn wandered over to a cabinet off in the darkest corner of the room and stared at Matthew's collection of exquisite wood sculptures. He picked out a field mouse and handed it to her for inspection.

"This is lovely. It must have taken hours."

"Days, more like. That one over there was weeks' worth of trouble." He pointed to an eagle that was poised on a rock as if about to take flight. "It's Will's Christmas present. Kept thinking of him while I worked on it. The bird reminds me of him somehow."

Quinn nodded. Yes, she thought. Sharp-sighted, beautiful, and strong. "It's perfect," she said.

"I still have some work to do. Damn thing fell on its beak the first dozen times I tried it."

"I don't know if we have eagles in New England."

"Probably not enough space, not enough sky."

Not for Will either, Quinn added silently. "Would you let me watch you work sometime?"

"Sure, when you come to stay more'n a couple minutes. Here. You keep this."

He handed her a doe that was curled up so that it fit perfectly into the palm of her hand. Quinn stared at him in surprise. She started to murmur her thanks, but he had already turned his chair away and wheeled out into the hall.

As Matthew had predicted, it continued to snow. Quinn stared out the window at the swirling white storm and tried to discern the branches of the elm tree just outside. Will sank into a corner of the sofa with his book. After a few minutes Quinn picked up a copy of *National Geographic* and settled on the opposite end of the couch. Every now and then the wind blasted a cloud of snow against the house, but otherwise all was tranquil.

Quinn leafed absently through the magazine and set it down with a sigh. Pointing a toe at *Middlemarch*, she said, "Planning on finishing that today?" Will was about halfway through the six hundred pages.

"If the storm keeps up, there won't be much else to do. Maybe I'll get through it."

Quinn felt the stirrings of panic. She got off the couch and began to pace back and forth. "If it clears up a little, do you think we could go somewhere? Maybe there's somebody you'd like to visit?"

"Nobody's around now. It's not a regular vacation time."

"What about your old buddy Henry Watson?"

"He's in Boise."

"Oh."

She peered out the window again. "I think it's letting up," she said hopefully. There was a break in the whiteness; she could make out the shape of the tree.

"Come here," Will said.

Obediently she went to sit beside him.

"Let's neck."

"We can't. Not . . ."

He kissed her. "You need something to do. I can tell."

Quinn glanced nervously toward the kitchen door. Will had slipped his hand up inside her sweater. "Oh, God," she said. "You're doing this to torture me."

"You've got blizzard fever. I recognize the symptoms."

"And you've got the cure, huh, doc?"

"That's right." His fingers brushed her nipples. A great throbbing had begun between her legs.

"Will?"

Susan Ingraham appeared in the doorway. Quinn sat

up, blushing furiously. Susan was merciful, allowing a tiny smile but no comment.

"It's clearing."

Quinn stood to look outside and saw that indeed the snowfall had nearly stopped. Occasionally the wind tossed a billow back into the air, but that was all. Will had already picked up his book again. Cool customer, Quinn thought. Or maybe he was used to getting caught messing with girls on his parents' sofa.

"I need some things at the A&P," Susan said. Will raised his eyes above the page. "Oh, heavens, you've got that Do Not Disturb look."

Quinn was startled to hear her familiar accusation come out of Susan Ingraham's mouth.

"I'll go!" Quinn's offer was almost a shout. "Please. I'd like to."

"You'll get lost," Will said, starting to get up.

"I don't like to have you drive a strange car in a new place," Susan said.

"I've been past the A&P. Sit down, Will. Besides, I can drive anything, really. Just give me a list. I'd be happy to go."

Will and Susan looked at one another, then Will shrugged. "Okay, if you're sure."

"Positive."

Quinn knew that Susan was watching out the window and was relieved when the jeep started right up. It felt wonderful to drive. As soon as she rounded the bend out of sight, she roared into fourth gear and began to sing. *Hit the road, Jack, and doncha come back no more no more no more no more no more.* Tomorrow maybe she'd get to the store again. There'd be people in the supermarket, and noise. It was lovely out west; but she was beginning to long for a little tumult, a crowd. Even a traffic jam would help. The novelty of rustic quietude was beginning to wear off.

When she got back, Will helped her unload the groceries. After the last bag had been deposited on the kitchen counter, Quinn followed Will back outside again. He walked ahead of her toward the trees beside the house, his figure disappearing now and then in swirls of snow kicked up by a gusty wind. There was an immense drift against a fence that marked the end of the Ingraham property, and Quinn watched him flop backward into it like a small boy pretending to be shot by the bad guys. When she reached him, he was completely buried except for his face and the protruding toes of his boots. "I'd just as soon lie here forever," he said. "Come on down." He yanked a leg out from under her, and she fell down next to him with a whoosh. He grabbed her in a hug and rolled them both over and over in the snow. Quinn laughed, enjoying the new experience of a playful Will. Finally, breathless, they let go of one another and lay side by side in their soft white cocoon.

"Is it true that you get really sleepy before freezing to death?" Quinn asked drowsily.

"Urm," Will said.

"Then I think I'm dying." She hopped to her feet and hauled him, protesting, back into the house.

After dinner Susan let Quinn help with the dishes. Quinn was pleased to feel less like a guest, and shooed Will out of the kitchen.

Susan had been to Boston once when she was a teenager. They talked about the city for a few minutes, and then Susan said, "Quinn, I wanted to tell you." She hesitated. Quinn stopped drying the gravy boat and looked at her. "I wanted to thank you. We knew over Christmas that something had happened with Will, and when you called that day I put it together. He'd been terribly unhappy about . . . I'm sure you know . . . about this girl who was killed. . . ."

"Yes."

"It was an awful shock for him. But it's been almost two years and he was still, well, subdued." She smiled. "Not that he isn't always on the low-key side." Quinn returned her smile. "You've been good for him. We hope to see a lot more of you." Susan had reddened, and a soapy dish slipped out of her hands into the sink. They both lunged for it and, laughing, rescued it before it crashed.

Their last night in Idaho, Will took Quinn to the movies in Red Falls. Quinn's expectation of a tiny mountain village wasn't far off the mark: Main Street, and a dozen smaller roads that led off it for a few hundred yards and then died. There was a coffee shop, a five-and-ten, a drugstore, and the Red Falls Municipal Building, which housed one lawyer, a dentist, the town clerk, and two empty offices. The Bijou theater showed films two nights a week. Will said it was miraculous that *The Sound of Music* had made it to Red Falls within a year of its being released, the usual offerings being recycled Jerry Lewis movies.

The theater was more than half empty, and its heating system wasn't functioning at full efficiency. But Quinn enjoyed the movie anyway and told Will he just didn't want to admit loving it.

They stood outside and looked up and down the darkened street for a place to get something to eat. The luncheonette two stores down was just closing, but Will convinced the proprietor to serve them a quick snack. There was one other patron at the far end of the counter, a man in work clothes who was chain-smoking cigarettes.

Quinn sipped her coffee. She thought about her suitcase lying open on the bed, ready to be packed. The Boston flights were full, so they had reserved seats on an early plane to Kennedy Airport. From New York they would catch the train to Boston. Quinn could hardly wait.

Chapter 19

Quinn was quiet on the eastbound flight, but this time Will felt her silence emerged from uneasiness rather than absorption in the experience of flying. Each time he had asked how she felt about Idaho, Quinn responded with enthusiasm, but her praise never occurred unsolicited. Will did not like to think what this meant.

They barely made their connection with the Boston train in Grand Central Station. Breathless, they flung themselves into their seats just as the doors slid closed.

Will liked trains. There was more room for his long legs, he was free to walk around, and there was the absorbing panorama that whizzed past the window. Trains held the capacity to thrill. But there was no romance in a Greyhound bus, just endless gray highways with the intermittent littered service area.

Train windows were like skimming a book Will wished he had the time to read. Looking out, there was a general overview of the landscape, but certain impressions registered with greater intensity than others. The frustrating element was that oftentimes a provocative image was snatched past the window too quickly.

Once there had been the house on the line somewhere between Spokane and the Bitterroots. It was a cold January day like today, Will remembered, but every window in the place was raised and the front door was flung wide. More astonishingly, all apertures in the gleaming white structure were filled with people: there were three upstairs windows, each with a head poking through; a window on either side of the front door, again each framing a person, one of whom hung partway out to converse with an upstairs occupant. The other waved at the train as it hurtled along half a mile across the snow-covered field. At the front door a portly woman swept the steps.

The image stunned Will. It was maddening to careen past and know he would never see the house again exactly as it appeared in that particular crystal moment.

Another time on the Springfield to Boston route, Will was tantalized again. Despite the fact that it had been a dazzling spring day, the scene was a grim contrast to the eccentric gaiety of the house in Idaho. There were wild flowers strewn along the roadbed, and the trees were fuzzy with new leaves. Will had been gazing at the blur of foliage and wondering how far spring had progressed back home when, about an hour outside of Boston, a figure appeared beside the tracks. Because of a long curve up ahead, Will spotted the woman several moments before his window reached her. The train slowed on its way up an incline. He watched her stumble toward the speeding cars, then recoil. She straightened, and as Will passed she stared through the window. For a fraction of a second he caught her expression head on. What he saw there froze him. The strong face was a collage of disciplined planes that gave nothing away, that seemed only to endure. But the hazel eyes were circles of terror. They screamed at him as they met his own curious ones, and their image remained with him still. Will had thought of the last pages of *Anna Karenina*, and from then on always pictured Tolstoy's heroine as the handsome, tormented woman beside the train to Boston.

Will had always been afflicted with what he came to call "urgent visual imagery." Now and then his eyes seemed to sustain experiences apart from the rest of his mind and body, in vivid moments that cried out to him years later—to be painted, photographed, expressed in some fashion and thereby released. He had tried sketching, but the primitive scratches that emerged seemed pitifully inept. He tried verbal description, but somehow language was too clumsy for the fragility of the pictures in his mind. He wondered if photography could encapsulate them. Perhaps one day he would experiment with a camera, though he could never be sure of having his equipment on hand when assaulted with one of those moments that demanded recording.

The train struggled over the crest of a small mountain and began its relieved descent. "I wish I were Lorenzo de Medici," he murmured.

Quinn looked up from her newspaper. "Who?"

"I would commission people to paint things for me, things I see. Like that red barn out there. Beautiful, with the color half scraped off in whorls, as if somebody did it on purpose."

"The hand of God."

"I don't suppose Leonardo would have been interested in a red barn, and even if he were, it wouldn't come out the way I see it."

"Maybe a milkmaid with a face like the Mona Lisa."

"Yes."

"Then you'd just behead him," she said. "You know what I see when I look out the window?" Will watched her eyes as they flickered back and forth, back and forth. "Cars. On the turnpike over there. '57 Chevy, '59 Dodge Fury. Another Chevy. '54. I always liked that one."

"You ought to go on one of those quiz shows and do Cars and the Top Ten. You'd be rich."

"Yeah, but I wish I knew everything. Especially about books and music and art, like you. I want you to teach me all of it. Tell me about Bach. He was the one with all those kids, right? Will, where are you?" His face had gone blank on her. She tapped his temple lightly. "Hello?"

He blinked and looked sheepish. "You'll laugh."

"I won't. Maybe."

"I'm getting nervous."

"About my parents? They'd be so flattered. Really, they're nice. Just nice plain old everyday people. You'll love them. They'll love you. Don't worry."

"Uh huh."

Quinn snuggled next to him. "I can't wait to see you all in the same room together. The Big Three, you and Ann and Jake."

"Well, you just keep your hands to yourself while we're there. They'll think I'm responsible for your descent into lust."

"You are. Hey, look at that, an Edsel. Jesus, how'd you like to have that tank named after you?"

She distracted him with her automotive litany, and by the time the train pulled into South Station, he had remembered that basically he was very curious to meet the Mallorys. He tried to keep that curiosity uppermost in his thoughts throughout the twenty-minute trolley ride to Medham.

After a hug for Quinn and a handshake for Will, John drew them into the living room, where Ann was lying on the sofa. Quinn hurried to her mother.

"Mom, you're not feeling well. Why didn't somebody tell me?" She glanced at John accusingly.

"I'm all right," Ann protested. "Just tired."

"This party was a dumb idea. Dumb. I knew it was dumb."

"She's been fine," John said. "It was the tests this morning."

Ann looked up at Will and held out her hand. "I'm sorry I can't get up to greet you properly, Will. Did you have a good trip?"

He had been scrutinizing Ann, searching for evidence of Quinn's features. "It was fine, thanks." Although he failed to find her daughter there, he thought Ann's face was very lovely.

Meanwhile, Quinn was attempting to adjust to the fact that her familiar living room had shrunk, now that it was occupied by the lanky limbs of Will Ingraham. He dwarfed her father's armchair, and his head towered to the top of the china cabinet. She had never been aware of how short her father was. In fact, John and Ann seemed like diminished versions of themselves, about two-thirds of their former size. They studied Will through their smiles. While Ann's face was kind, John's held a hint of challenge. Quinn saw it and decided that her father looked like a miniature deity—stern, dark eyebrows over blue eyes that emitted laser beams into the core of Will's morality. Perhaps this wasn't going to be as simple as Quinn had assumed. She and Will sat down on the piano bench, side by side. She wondered if their potent physical bond rose from her head and Will's like the shimmer of heat off the radiator by the window. Were they fragrant with the musky scent of sexual intimacy? She felt her face grow hot.

"You two smell wonderful. All fresh air," Ann said.

Quinn laughed and the others looked a little startled.

"Tell me about the tests, Mom."

"Oh, let's not get into that nonsense now," Ann said. "We haven't heard a thing about your trip. How was Idaho?"

She'll say "magnificent," Will thought.

"Magnificent," Quinn said. "The mountains are spectacular, just like something out of *Heidi.* The Ingrahams were wonderful to me. It's all very pioneer-ish. Will is, too. Pioneer-ish."

Will forced a smile. "We do have things like running water and television."

"Too bad," John remarked. "Especially the television."

"Listen, what's happening with the party?" Quinn asked. "Who's coming and who's not?"

"Everybody's coming and nobody's not," John said. "Who wants a drink? Beer? Tea?"

"I'd like a beer," Will said. John nodded as if approving.

"Me too," said Quinn.

After John had left the room, Quinn said, "You're really getting him trained."

"Hush," Ann protested, glancing toward the doorway. "I never asked him to. He's just starts doing everything before I can get myself moving. Last night he even made dinner. Stew. Just like his mother used to make."

"How was it?" Will asked.

Ann hesitated, then wrinkled her nose in a ladylike grimace.

"Did you eat it?" Quinn asked.

"No. Actually . . ." Ann smiled. "Well, I put it in my napkin and flushed it down the toilet."

Quinn hooted. "That's my trick!"

"I know, dear, and I'm so grateful." Ann's face was

terribly earnest. When John returned with a trayful of drinks, they were all laughing.

Soon Ann started questioning Will about Red Falls. Well, that's that, Quinn thought, he's off and running now. Her eyes began to drift around the room. On the windowsill a Japanese doll made her graceful pirouette under a bell jar. John had brought her back as a souvenir from the Korean War. The bright-red silk kimono had faded from incessant exposure to sunlight, but Quinn still thought it beautiful. During the scraped-knee and black-eye period of her development, Quinn had spent many an hour with chin resting on grubby fist, gazing wistfully at the doll's creamy porcelain face, envying the mysterious femininity that would surely never be hers.

From the gallery on the far wall Quinn's own face stared out at her—many faces reflecting moments of glory long past, her life like a film reeling off the way she supposed it did when you were about to drown: the gap-toothed but grinning second grade picture, the junior high school majorette, baton held high, bony legs bare under a short white satin skirt (remembering that icy November day, Quinn wondered if the photographer had airbrushed the goosebumps away); the gilt-framed portrait of Quinn and Tommy Flanagan, queen and king of the Junior Prom. Quinn had worked on that pale blue dress every night for a month but never managed to get the bodice just right. It was a little too full for her breasts. In the photo she held her corsage close to the chest. That night, in the front seat of his father's car, Tommy had slipped his hand down the gap and touched her nipples. The delirium of the evening with its romantic music and dreamy decorations, and Tommy's warm fingers on her breasts, had all but overwhelmed her.

Graduation paraded across the living room wall. There was the formal portrait—eyes glistening with confidence, hair a soft halo. There was the collage of snapshots John had taken during the ceremony, dashing from one end of the auditorium to the other in a shiny blue suit, mortifying Quinn with the unremitting explosion of flashbulbs. Despite, or perhaps because of, Quinn's regular attendance at extra disciplinary study halls on Saturday mornings, her grade average for the four years of high school had averaged 3.91. Quinn had admitted to a base-minded and gratifying thrill that she had beat out Darlene Finney by nine-tenths of a point. Quinn was valedictorian, and John's camera had flickered throughout her speech like summer heat lightning. Her favorite picture captured for eternity the oration's stirring close. Eyebrows were knit with earnest zeal and both fists were clenched on the podium. It must have been that bit about committing oneself to action, leaping into the volcano of life, et cetera, et cetera. A dynamite finale. Professor Buxby would have tossed his cookies.

Her gaze shifted from the portrait gallery and settled on her father as he leaned forward, listening, arms resting on knees. She noticed with a pang that his favorite chair's antimacassar seemed soiled and wrinkled. Certainly the pictures hung exactly as they had for years. Certainly the rug was deeply grooved where the furniture nested in the customary niches. But there had been a subtle change. The antimacassar was dirty and a medicinal odor was in the air.

Quinn turned toward Ann and heard her say, "I hadn't done any reading in years. Except for recipes in magazines, things like that. I'm enjoying it so much. I can't imagine that I once thought it was a dreadful chore."

Will picked up Ann's copy of *Hawaii*. She had dog-eared a page about halfway through. "Do you like his books?"

"Oh, this is wonderful. It's the only way I'll ever see the world, and he makes it all come to life."

"Why not?" Quinn asked in a piercing voice.

"Excuse me, dear?" Ann asked.

"I only meant why won't you see the world? You've always wanted to go back to Ireland."

Ann smiled and shook her head. "Oh, I'm too much of an old lady for the grand tour."

"Old lady!" cried Quinn.

"Reading a book isn't anywhere near as exhausting as traveling," Ann said.

"Not to mention cheaper," John remarked.

"Money isn't everything," Quinn said.

"It is if you haven't got it."

"If Mom wants to go to Ireland, she should damn well go to Ireland."

Will saw Ann's discomfort. He slapped *Hawaii* down so hard that a spoon jumped half an inch off the coffee table. Quinn was so surprised that she stopped glaring at her father and instead gaped round-eyed at Will.

"Have you read *Travels with Charley*?" Will asked Ann tranquilly.

"That's Steinbeck, isn't it?"

Will nodded. "You'd like him, I think. Particularly that one."

"I enjoyed listening to you talk about Idaho, Will," Ann continued. "I think you'll be a fine teacher. Quinn says that's what you plan to do."

Quinn watched them smile at each other and wondered what could possibly have drawn them together so quickly. John, on the other hand, was solemn. He was watching Ann, and when Quinn glanced at him, he stood.

"Why don't you two go to the grocery store and pick up something for dinner? All we've got around here is that party stuff."

"Hey, I've got an idea!" Quinn exclaimed. "I'll get some stew meat and maybe Jake'll whip up—" Will's elbow made a dent in her side. Ann's face pleaded for silence. ". . . uh . . . something delicious," she trailed off lamely.

But John was only interested in getting rid of the young people so that Ann could rest. He fished in his pocket for the car keys and told them to be back by six.

"Sure. Gotta see Ted Manning!" Quinn called. She was already halfway out the front door.

"Spare us!" John shouted after them as the door slammed, shuddering on its hinges. He made room for himself on the sofa next to Ann's knees and put his hand against her forehead.

"I don't have a fever, John."

"Oh, I know," he said. She covered his fingers with her own. "What do you think of him?" he asked.

"I think he's lovely."

"Lovely, eh? I hope you never thought that about me."

"I most certainly did, but I knew enough not to tell you so," Ann replied. She closed her eyes and leaned back against the pillows. "I don't understand what he's doing with our Quinn."

"What does that mean?"

"Well, she's an odd choice for a boy like Will."

"She probably chose *him.*"

"I don't think she'll be able to push him around," Ann whispered.

"I wouldn't bet on that," John said, not without pride. "Go to sleep."

"Stay with me," she murmured.

"Always, girl."

Soon her breathing slowed and she was asleep.

Quinn struggled out of bed in the dark at 6:00 A.M. Saturday morning, splashed cold water on her face, and tiptoed downstairs to the kitchen. She had wanted to beat her mother to the stove, in hopes that with a restful day Ann might feel strong enough to enjoy the party.

It pleased Quinn to creep past the living room and catch sight of Will sleeping on the sofa. His legs were tangled in the blankets and his feet protruded ten inches over the arm of the couch. Despite the cramped makeshift bed he seemed absolutely relaxed, so abandoned to sleep that he looked as if he might lie there dreaming forever. He would make a decorative conversation piece at the party, Quinn thought. The guests could hang their hats on those toes.

At the kitchen table over a cup of thick black coffee, Quinn relished the early morning solitude of the house. She imagined that the quiet whir of the refrigerator was the sound of the house sleeping, like a giant purring cat. She set down her cup and said out loud, "Okay." She was fully awake now and ready to begin.

In the refrigerator she found the dozen rolls of cheddar-cheese mixture that Ann had prepared earlier in the week. She sliced them into wedges, arranged them on baking sheets in neat rows, and slipped them into the oven. Next she began combining ingredients for

NEWTON PUBLIC LIBRARY

chocolate-chip cookies. While she worked, the pale winter light intensified outside the steamy windows and the smells of hot coffee and baked goods browning evoked memories of other times. She remembered sitting on the stool beside the sink on sub-zero February mornings to watch Ann concoct the fuel that would carry her family through the day. Sometimes it was oatmeal with brown sugar, sometimes pancakes with maple syrup, but always something hot and sweet to chase away the winter chill and send them out the front door with stomachs as warm and round as potbellied stoves. John would tease Ann sometimes, assuring her that a bowl of cornflakes for breakfast would not necessarily promote immediate pneumonia. He would wink at Quinn and say that when the Mallory family left the house, they exuded enough heat to melt the ice off the Charles River, and that if Quinn and he were to roll down the middle of Gardner Street, Medham taxpayers would be saved the expense of snowplows. Ann would laugh, but she always shut the cupboard door with the cornflakes behind it.

Quinn remembered coming home from school in the afternoons to find her mother exactly where she had left her in the morning, in that core of the house where the best and worst of their lives transpired. Sometimes she was standing at the stove and sometimes she was reading the *Globe* with a cup of coffee, but she was nonetheless there. Of course, there had been the rare occasion when Quinn had clattered through the front door, tossed her books on the table, and heard her sounds die into hollow stillness. On those days there was always a note: Ann had gone to the dentist or to the doctor or to visit an ailing friend. Quinn would grab a handful of cookies, gulp down a glass of milk, and flee.

Out came the last batch of crackers, and in went the first batch of cookies. Quinn dusted the hot cheesy disks with salt and popped one into her mouth. The hot salt and remnants of sweet cookie batter mixing on her tongue were so delicious that she closed her eyes with pleasure. This kitchen. In this kitchen she had confided to her mother that her period had finally, finally arrived; in this kitchen she had sobbed an afternoon away, unconsoled even by hot chocolate and marshmallows, when Margery O'Malley's puppy died of distemper; in this kitchen she had lost her braids to her father's scissors of vengeance.

But this morning it was Quinn herself overseeing the kitchen while her mother lay sleeping to an unprecedented 9:00 A.M. Suddenly she longed to return to a smaller size, when she was proud that her nose had finally reached the level of the refrigerator door handle.

"Damn it," she murmured softly, and for comfort swirled her finger around the edge of the mixing bowl to collect another mouthful of cookie batter. Then she swiped at her misty eyes with the sleeve of her shirt, dumped the dirty dishes into the sink to wash later, and began filling the white wicker breakfast tray for her mother. She glanced at the wall clock once more and shook her head. Nine-oh-six and still not a sound from upstairs. At that moment she heard her father's quick steps moving toward the bathroom. Hurriedly she made her preparations: toast and jam; coffee for two; flowered china creamer and sugar bowl; linen napkins, hand-embroidered with strawberries; fresh orange juice. But still not quite right. In February there would be no flowers cowering under the crust of snow behind the back door, so she rummaged through drawers until she found a long scrap of red ribbon. She cut it in half and tied a bow on each handle of the tray. Satisfied, she crept upstairs and slipped into Ann's room while her father was humming in the shower.

Quinn set the tray down noiselessly on the lace-covered dresser. Ann was asleep, covered with a rough woven blanket sent by an Old Country relative long since dead. With the shower still on they were assured a quarter of an hour's privacy. She knelt beside the bed. *If you make her well, God, I'll quit swearing. I'll give up sex. I'll be so virtuous, it'll make You sick.* But there was no conviction in the prayer. If God could permit Ann's illness in the first place, then there was no point in appealing to *Him.* Obviously, He had no heart. It was a radical thought for a graduate of St. Theresa's, and she wondered when she had begun to lose her confidence in the Almighty. It was one of those topics that required several hours of uninterrupted thought. She resolved to set the time aside to figure it all out, perhaps back in the garage at school. In the meantime she squeezed her eyes shut and willed the positive energy of her young spirit to heal the fragile woman who was once so vigorous, whose features now appeared to have been drawn with the delicate strokes of an Oriental etching, and whose skin was made of the finest rice paper, translucent and too easily bruised.

Ann stirred, awakened, and smiled at Quinn. Through the obstruction in her throat Quinn whispered, "Morning," and pressed her face into the stubbled weave of the blanket, hoping to avoid the scrutiny of those clear eyes. "I've got your breakfast." Surely the muffled sound of her voice could be justified as a mouthful of blanket.

"Wonderful." Ann's hand stroked Quinn's hair. "I'm hungry as a bear."

Quinn looked up. "Are you really?"

"Yes."

Quinn watched with delight as everything gradually disappeared. John arrived, wrapped in a towel and exuding aftershave. She held out her cup to him. "Want some?" she asked.

"Nope." He had combed his wet hair straight back so that the thick springy waves were flattened into a dark helmet. He saw Quinn eyeing it. "I know, I know. My slick weasel look."

Quinn and Ann laughed, both thinking that actually he looked especially handsome, with his muscular arms and naked chest exposed. He gathered his clothes into a bundle under his arm.

"I'll use your room as my boudoir, if you don't mind." He tugged briefly on Quinn's hair and left them alone.

Quinn called after him. "Wake up that hayseed on the couch!"

"If he's got any sense, he'll sleep straight through the party. . . ." John's voice disappeared down the hall.

"Why should he want to do that?" Quinn asked a bit testily. "It's going to be a wonderful party, and he's never met any of my friends."

"Will doesn't strike me as the partying type," Ann said.

Quinn stared at her. "That's what he says." She set her coffee cup on her knee. "I want it to be terrific. Do you think it will be?"

"It'll be fine."

"You haven't said, Mother."

"Said what, dear?"

Quinn crossed her legs on the end of the bed and balanced her saucer on her ankle. "What you think of him."

"What do you think I think?"

"Come on, don't tease me."

"I'm sorry. I guess I've forgotten what it's like, all that." She seemed to drift away for a moment, but Quinn's anxious face nudged her. "I think he's quite wonderful."

"Do you really? Honestly? I mean, *I* think so, but I wanted you to see how special he is. Sometimes he's so damn weird it's hard to tell. He's so quiet, too."

"I didn't notice that."

"Yeah, well, *that's* weird too. I couldn't believe how he was spouting off to you, right away like that. Sometimes we go a whole evening without him saying more than three words."

"As long as they're the right ones," Ann said.

Quinn smiled. "And what about Daddy?"

"Why don't you ask him?"

"Because he won't give me a straight answer. He thinks everybody's Tommy Flanagan."

"I think he thinks he'll do."

"You want to try that one more time?" Over the rim of their coffee cups, coincidentally raised in unison, their eyes laughed at one another.

"I'm going to marry him," Quinn said.

Ann set her cup down. She tried to keep her voice level. "Oh? Have you discussed it, then?"

"No."

They both began to giggle. Quinn's cup tipped, spilling coffee on her sock and soaking into the white cotton fabric. "Oh, damn," she said, only laughing harder. She pulled off her dry sock and mopped at the damp one.

"Don't you think you'd better tell him?" Ann gasped.

"What for?" Quinn replied, and that set them off again.

Finally Ann said, "Dear me," and wiped her eyes with the embroidered linen napkin. "What do you think he'll do when you finally get around to telling him?"

"He'd better say yes."

"Don't push him, darling."

The sudden serious tone of voice sobered Quinn up. "I'll break it to him gently."

"I don't know if it's terribly old-fashioned to ask, but do you . . . are you in love with him?"

For the second time that morning Quinn's eyes grew damp. "Terribly," she said softly. Ann reached out to touch Quinn's soggy toes, the only part of her daughter's anatomy that was within range.

Chapter 20

Quinn was in a flurry, shuffling furniture around in a hopeless attempt to make room for everyone while maintaining some sense of decor.

Will loomed over the china cabinet and watched her with amusement. "You look very pretty," he said. She was wearing his favorite pale blue sweater and a tweed skirt.

Setting the coffee table down in its sixth allocation, she glanced up at him ruefully. "You're not bad yourself, but look at your legs. There's no room for anybody else in here."

"Sorry. I'll stick 'em out the window when it gets crowded. Or maybe I'll just take a long walk."

"Don't you dare." She menaced him with an ashtray.

"Cocktail parties are not my métier. You sure you don't want some help?"

"It's not a cocktail party, and you can't help unless you can add an extension to the living room."

"Reunions are not my métier."

"*People* are not your métier." The doorbell rang and she dropped the cocktail table in a corner by the piano. "Stay there, see if I care," she said to it. "Coming!"

It was Roseann Smith reporting that everyone had apparently arrived at once and there was a jumble of cars at the bottom of Gardner Street. Quinn ran to the kitchen to enlist John as traffic cop, leaving Will and Roseann to look at each other with fixed smiles. They didn't suffer for long, however, because within seconds the mob appeared. Will gathered coats, and Quinn kept up an incessant barrage of introductions.

"Hi Jim. Jim, this is Will. Oh, Noreen! Noreen, this is Will Ingraham. Noreen used to eat erasers off pencils in third grade. What a gorgeous coat. Is it cashmere? Hi, Kathy, where's Norm? This is Will." Finally, laughing, they conceded defeat and Will set off up the stairs with an armload of coats. He dumped them on the Mallorys' bed. Ann was sitting quietly by the window in her rocking chair.

"Are you all right?" Will asked her.

Ann nodded. "Tired, but fine. I'm enjoying watching everybody arrive. It's like going through a photograph album. All Quinn's old chums from kindergarten, grown up now."

Will was silent for a moment, standing beside her, sharing the view. "Are you coming downstairs?" he asked finally.

"Later on. You go ahead and show yourself off for Quinn."

"I'd rather stay here."

"Yes."

She smiled at him, and, reluctantly, he left the quiet room.

Even from the top of the stairs the noise from below was an assault. He remembered watching a television rerun of *To Kill a Mockingbird* when a sensitive scene between Atticus and Scout was suddenly interrupted with a detergent commercial, strident voices shrieking *Ring around the collar! Ring around the collar!* He sighed and started down the stairs, descending into the volcano.

Will held out his hands for more coats.

"Oh, no, you don't," Quinn said. "I'm not sending you upstairs again. Tommy and Margery Almost Flanagan, Will Ingraham." Margery somehow managed to hug Quinn and assess Will simultaneously. As Tommy and Will shook hands Margery mouthed at Quinn silently: *Cute.*

Quinn slammed the front door and fell against it in mock exhaustion. "That's everybody. Thank God."

"You're loving it," Will said.

"You're right. Come on, let's mingle with my past."

"How's your mom?" Margery asked.

"Oh, much better," Quinn said. "She'll be down in a few minutes."

"That's terrific." Margery lowered her voice into an incredulous whisper. Her wild curls quivered with suppressed excitement. "Do you *believe* Mary Frances DeFalco?"

Quinn glanced around, checking out the proximity of Mary Frances. Safe, she explained to Will, "She was the class . . . well, the nuns used to tell us not to kiss boys or we'd"—she lowered her voice—"go the way of Mary Frances DeFalco."

"We thought she was wonderful," Margery said.

"So did we," said Tommy. He winked at Will, who regarded him thoughtfully.

"She's the tweedy one with the horn-rimmed glasses and beehive hairdo," Quinn said.

"She was carrying signs around outside the State House," Margery confided. "First it was abortion. Well,

I guess she had good reason. And now she's all fired up over some Godforsaken place in Asia. You'll see. She's got buttons all over her sweater."

"It wouldn't be so funny if she hadn't been such a, well, nonpolitical person," Quinn explained to Will.

"I can imagine," he murmured.

Noreen and Jim stood beside the piano.

"I was reminding Jim," Noreen explained to Quinn and Will, "about the time Quinn made us take all the knobs off the classroom doors so nobody could get in."

"I didn't *make* you," Quinn said.

Jim took over. "And then this one"—he laid his hand on Quinn's head—"dumped them all in Father Monaghan's confessional so they'd think the guys from St. Andrew's did it."

Noreen rolled her eyes at Will. "My Lord, the things she thought up."

Quinn's Aunt Dorothy beckoned from the doorway, and Quinn excused herself. There was an awkward silence while Will tried to remember what Quinn had told him about Noreen in her preparty briefing. The class beauty, he thought. She had shimmering blond hair, green eyes, and lovely skin. But there was a tense catch at the edges of her mouth, almost a tic that punctuated her speech. It made her look brittle. Jim was tall and gangly in the manner of a loose-limbed star member of the adolescent basketball team. Will thought he seemed so relaxed he might crumple to the floor at any moment.

"I guess she's always getting into trouble up at college," Jim said loudly. Will suspected Jim had had to repeat himself to get Will's attention.

"Not that I know of," Will said. "She works pretty hard."

"The books never stood in her way before, that's for

sure. I hope you college Joes aren't messing up her sense of humor. Noreen, remember the time just before St. Patrick's day when she put green food-coloring in the macaroni and cheese?"

Noreen giggled. "My Lord, it was a classic."

Jim touched Will's paper cup with his own in a toast. "You've got yourself a real kook there, Bill."

"Mm," Will said. He worked up his warmest smile. "Excuse me a minute, will you?"

Quinn squeezed past Tommy Flanagan, who was talking to her father. Tommy was nodding and smiling, nodding and smiling. Come to think of it, Tommy always seemed to be nodding and smiling, and the smile wasn't very convincing. Quinn gave it a ten for oral hygiene and a two for sincerity. She turned her face from the splendor of Tommy's pearly whites. Planting him in the same house as Will Ingraham fixed her perspective, she decided. Tommy expended a lot of energy trying to charm, and Will was charming despite himself—assuming he bothered to open his mouth.

"Left where?" Quinn asked.

"I don't know." Jim craned his neck over the crush.

"Damn it," Quinn muttered.

"Doesn't say much, does he?" Jim asked.

Noreen gave him a warning jab. "I wanted to say hello to your mother. Where's she hiding? Probably in the kitchen as usual, huh?"

"Yeah, probably. Here." Quinn handed them each a cup of beer and moved off toward the doorway again.

Jim called after her, "Hey, when are you two going to make it legal?"

"Jim!" Noreen hooted.

"Well, misery loves company," he said, watching Quinn disappear in the crowd.

"My Lord, you're such a card," Noreen said. She snagged Margery as she passed within range of the piano bench. "Isn't Jim a card, Margery?"

"You coming down, Mom?" Quinn asked.

"Not just now, dear."

"Everybody's asking for you."

"Tell them I'll be down later."

It suddenly occurred to Quinn that her mother was only offering to make an appearance to please her. "It was too much for you, wasn't it, this whole thing?"

"Don't be silly, dear. I loved planning it with you."

"Let me bring you something."

Ann started to decline, but Quinn's face pleaded with her to ask for something, anything.

"I'd be glad of a cup of tea, thank you."

Quinn found Will with Stanley and Van, the three of them rooted to the floor beside the stairs.

"God damn it, Will," she said. "You can talk with these two when we get back to school. Go talk to Mary Frances, will you? Find out how she got to be a Bolshevik."

"I'd rather have another beer," Will said.

Quinn glared at him. "Come on, Van, Stanley." She grabbed each of them by the arm and ushered them into the kitchen.

"Give the guy a break, will you?" Stanley said. "There must be three dozen ex-nuns in there checking him out."

"I went to a whole lot of trouble to throw this party," Quinn retorted. "He can extend himself a little too."

"Yeah, but did he want a party?"

"That's neither here nor there," Quinn said. "Jake, this is Van. And Stanley."

"Hello, Mr. Mallory," Stanley said, holding out his hand.

John took it and smiled. "That's the first decent handshake I've had tonight."

"I think I'll just say hello, then," Van said. "I can't compete with that."

"Ah, Vanessa. Quinn tells me you're the proud proprietor of the Silver Ghost we saw on Gardner Street this evening," John said.

"Well, not proud, exactly," Van said with an embarrassed smile.

"Not proprietor, exactly," Stanley said. "Her daddy is both."

"Such a precise machine," John mused. "Hums and ticks, quiet, like a fine watch, it does."

"If you want to set your eyes on a beautiful specimen of a vehicle, you should see my bus," Stanley said.

John laughed. "I have. And heard it, too, lad. Thanksgiving you brought our Quinn home from school, and it's God's truth I heard you start the engine a hundred and fifty miles off."

"Everybody maligns my bus," Stanley protested.

"Why don't you drown your humiliation with a beer?" Quinn asked.

"What's your pleasure?" John said, an arm draped around both of Quinn's friends.

Aunt Dorothy told Quinn outside the kitchen door that her brother-in-law's brogue became more pronounced under the influence of a pint or two. Quinn was of the opinion that John faith-and-begorra'd in direct proportion to the social status of his companions.

Quinn decided that in short order Vanessa Huntington of the Beacon Hill Huntingtons would render John Mallory completely unintelligible.

Will shut the door behind him. The room, so suddenly still after the hubbub downstairs, was a sanctuary. Ann had leaned back in her chair by the window and fallen into a doze. He crossed the room quietly so as not to awaken her. From his vantage point sitting on the floor beside her, he could watch the light from the streetlamp outside shine on her face. Again, he searched there for Quinn's features but couldn't find them. Eyes open, Ann reminded Will of her daughter, but not like this. Quinn's face was never in repose. It was always mobile, always the barometer of whatever business was going on inside her restless brain.

Will experienced what had already become a familiar sensation of disorientation: what on earth did he think he was doing, hanging around with Quinn Mallory? Wasn't the serenity that radiated from Ann much more akin to his own temperament? He thought of the game he used to play when he was little: Paper, Scissors, Rock. Will imagined himself as Rock and Quinn as Scissors, him silent and inert, her in flashing motion, clicking and clacking, and snipping her world into its proper shape.

One late September five years ago he had sat motionless in his canoe on a mountain lake in the Bitterroots, watching an elk drink at the shore. Suddenly an otter surfaced beside the majestic antlered head. The playful creature, whiskers aquiver, twisted, dove, leapt, rippling the smooth water with eddies and bubbles. Its bright eyes darted to the elk repeatedly in search of appreciation, but the elk, with a single glance of bored irritation, resumed its rhythmical dipping. The furry acrobat kept up the performance until finally, discouraged, it swam off, presumably in pursuit of a more responsive audience.

For a moment Will had thought of drawing his paddle along the water, offering the otter an invitation to play beside the canoe. He had enjoyed the drama of primitive personality conflict being played out across the lake. But finally, like the elk perhaps, Will felt the otter's meddlesome intrusion into the perfect quiet of the evening and was relieved when it gave up and swam away.

It was true that Quinn's perpetual motion tired him. It was also true that he was dazzled by it. But sometimes he longed to clasp her with both arms and make her hold still. Maybe that impulse helped explain the intensity of his sexual attraction for her. While he made love to her, she was, at least temporarily, overpowered. He could contain her beneath his body. After she had reached orgasm, she would lie quiet, sometimes for twenty minutes, before her recharged central nervous system propelled her into action again. He glanced at Ann, so peaceful in her rocking chair, and imagined tying Quinn into his battered recliner back at school. By forcing her to remain immobilized, all that unexpended energy would probably cause her to glow, a pulsating incandescence in the corner, lighting up his room.

All at once Will was aware of being observed. He looked up to see Ann smiling at him.

"What in the world have you been thinking about?" she asked him.

"Your daughter."

"From your expression I would have said politics or religion."

"She's more like her father," Will said.

Ann heard the wistful quality of the comment and was flattered. "And who are you like, your mother or your father?"

"My grandfather, I think. His genes must have skipped a generation."

"Is he still alive?"

"No. I was fourteen when he died."

Ann listened to the distant commotion from downstairs and wondered how long Will had been sitting beside her. He ought to go back to the party. She ought to urge him. Instead she said, "Tell me about him, your grandfather."

Will began to talk, the old man coming to life until Will could almost smell white-pine sawdust in the darkened room. Then Ann told him about her family, with stories of life in Kilkenny before coming to America when she was five years old.

It was nearly ten o'clock when Quinn burst into the room. "Thanks a lot," she said in a voice that trembled with fury. Will and Ann looked guilty. "It's time for people to leave and Will hasn't met half of them."

Will started to get up off the floor. "I'm sorry—" he began.

She cried out, "Oh, what's the point? Just stay up here and rot, for all I care!" She wheeled around and marched out the door, giving it a mighty slam behind her.

Will looked at Ann. Her face was solemn, but her eyes were dancing suspiciously. Will's mouth began to twitch around the edges and suddenly they were both laughing, ashamed of themselves but unable to stop.

"Oh, dear," Ann said, trying to catch her breath.

"I'm in for it tonight," Will said.

"I don't suppose she'll speak to either of us ever again." Ann took a deep, shuddering breath to sober herself up. "I should have sent you downstairs. I had no right monopolizing you."

Will rose now, stretching his legs to get the kinks out. "Most of the time I was here you were asleep. Are you coming down?"

She shook her head. "I don't think so. It would only . . . well, it's hard for other people, my being ill. They don't know what to say, and it makes them uncomfortable."

"It's hard for her, too."

"I know."

Will bent to give her a kiss on the cheek and walked to the door like a soldier going off to battle.

Quinn was already ushering people out the door. Will stood beside her and tried to redeem himself by saying a few words to each person who left. He had a good memory for names and was able to produce a personal good-bye for nearly everyone.

"Good night, Roseann. Glad you could come," he said, then glanced at Quinn in hopes of an appreciative smile. What he got was a cool glare. He observed the stiff set of her head and felt chill icy mountain air swirling around him. Will had never seen this cold anger in her before. He preferred the explosions, the hot exhibitions of temper that quickly fizzled out.

By the time the last guest had left, it was eleven o'clock. It took them two hours to clean up. While John was with them in the kitchen, Quinn was carefully polite to Will, but in their moments alone she spoke monosyllabically or not at all.

John was exuberant. He piled dirty plates next to the

sink for Quinn and grabbed a dish towel. "Fancy staying so late with no dinner. That's the sign of a great party. Oh, and I got such a fine look at the Huntington limo," he said. "There's an Irish driver, fellow by the name of O'Hara. His cousin's at the plant." He winked at Will. "Nice of 'em to hire a Mick."

"Van's not like that," Quinn bristled.

"I know, I know, just funnin' with you, girl," John said with mock offense. "I liked them both, Vanessa and her hairy boyfriend. They're glad about the two of you going over there tomorrow."

Quinn and Will responded to this with silence. John regarded them carefully, then hung up his dishtowel and said, "Think I'll take a glass of milk to your mother." He collected the milk, a clean plate, and two cookies, and wished them a hasty good night. Only Will answered. Quinn continued washing ashtrays with silent efficiency.

"All right," he said, once John was safely out of range. "Let's talk."

"There's nothing to say."

"I told you I was sorry. I am. I let you down."

A serving dish slipped out of Quinn's grasp and shattered in the sink. She wailed.

Will reached for her, but she struck his arm away. The misery in her tear-streaked face dismayed him.

"Did you cut yourself?" he asked her.

She shook her head.

"Quinn, I'm sorry—"

"You hated them, didn't you? I should have known. It's not fair. I wanted, I wanted . . ."

He held her now, and she stood rigid, spilling out words and tears. "God, I had such a crazy idea about how it would be. Crazy, I must be crazy. You and Mom and all my friends, everybody loving the b'Jesus out of each other. And the worst of it is, I don't even know them anymore. I grew up with those people and I feel as though they're off in a different world. They're practically family, and I was bored and lonely. I'm so disgusted with myself, Will. I'm turning into a snob, just like you."

"People grow in different directions. That doesn't make them better or worse, and it doesn't make you a snob."

"But are they growing or standing still?"

Will was silent.

"I didn't like what I was seeing tonight, and I took it out on you. I'm sorry. I guess this was supposed to be one night when everything was all better."

"You mean your mother."

His intuitive grasp of her meaning started her crying again. There was no anger now, only sadness.

"Oh, screw it," she said. "You're not God Almighty. I want you to be, I guess. Will," she sounded tired, "what's going to become of us? I don't even understand why we're together."

He shook his head. "It's one of the great galactic mysteries."

She dried her eyes with the dish towel. "See what I found under the piano bench?" She reached into her skirt pocket and handed him an unopened packet of condoms.

"Whose?"

"I'm truly shocked. The mind boggles." She sniffed noisily. "Maybe it was Father Riley. Pity to just toss them out." She had begun to look more thoughtful than unhappy.

Will reached for her again, but she shook her head.

"No. I'll just start all over with the melodrama. Let's finish cleaning up this mess."

Will was finding it tough to fall asleep. Quinn insisted that for the remainder of their visit Will use her bed while she slept on the sofa. But the bed also seemed doll's-house proportion under his sprawling limbs. Quinn had made him try it out this morning, and when she saw him draped across her mattress with his boots hanging over the edge, she burst into laughter. The bedspread with its frills and flowers only added to the incongruity. She had pounced on him with delight. Now he felt as if he were precariously afloat on a child's rubber raft. Besides, after the emotional intensity of the past hour in the kitchen, his mind was buzzing.

His thoughts leapt to Idaho for comfort, but that topic had recently assumed a menace of its own. Quinn had been like a caged bird out there. She had tried hard, but there was no denying the relief in her face when the plane took off and headed east. He would think of Ann instead, beautiful Ann with the alabaster skin. She had endowed Quinn with her generosity of spirit and blue eyes, but everything else had come from John. Tonight, during that moment by the kitchen sink, Will had caught another glimpse of Quinn's anguish at losing her mother. It was easy to understand. With the image of Ann's face in his mind, he began to float off into sleep.

Suddenly there was a change in the air inside the room, a breeze against Will's exposed arm. A warm body crawled into bed beside him.

"Jesus, what are you doing?" he whispered.

"I got lonely," Quinn said.

"Your father'll be in here with a shotgun."

"They're asleep."

"Uh huh," Will said dubiously.

Quinn pulled her T-shirt over her head, slipped off her bikini pants, and stretched out on top of him, curling her legs around his, and tucking her feet underneath him. She felt his erection grow against her bare stomach.

"This is the bed of your childhood. We can't do this," he protested.

"I'm not a child now. I'll redecorate." She kissed him. "It was so spooky and dark downstairs. I was scared."

"No, you weren't." He ran his hand down her spine; her vertebrae made a delicate ripple against his fingers.

"Promise me you'll never leave me," she whispered. He wanted to cry, but instead smothered the urge against her shoulder, enfolded her, kissed her almost ferociously, on her mouth, her cheeks, her neck. They made love, tumbling about the bed with no regard for John and Ann, who lay awake in the bedroom down the hall.

"In our own house. Mother of Jesus."

Ann snuggled next to him. "Shh," she said.

"How could he, the snake in the grass. And her, too. I blame her as well. They won't get away with it. . . ." He started to get out of bed.

"No." Ann's voice was clear and sharp. John was so startled that he sat back down on the edge of the bed and peered through the darkness at her.

"You let them be, John. It's not our concern."

"In my house it is," he retorted.

"If they want to make love, well, that's wonderful."

"And this from my sweet Old Country convent lass."

"A lot of things don't seem as important as they did once."

He was silent for a moment. The tension from his

body had set the bedsprings quivering, but now it escaped from him like a sigh and he slumped against the pillow. Ann's hair brushed his arm and she curled against him like a child.

"Annie . . ."

"Mm."

"I don't want you to leave me."

"I know."

"If you did, I'd want to go with you."

"You can't think that way."

"I know I couldn't leave her alone. But there's nothing for me without you." His voice sounded thick, and she reached up to touch his mouth.

"*That* would be a sin," she whispered.

They lay quietly together, listening to the rustling noises from down the hall.

"She looked fine tonight, didn't she?" Ann said.

"Same as always."

"She's so full of fire."

"Is that what it is? I thought it was piss and—"

"John, she's almost a woman. She's not your tomboy kid anymore." John thought that over. Now Ann sounded wistful. "It's hard to remember being that young. I was once, wasn't I?"

John bent his head to kiss her. "You've never been more beautiful than you are right now," he said. "And I want you." The last was added in a voice that held many questions. Her illness had made them hesitant.

She responded with deep kisses. After a while she said, "It won't be the last time, John, I promise."

Chapter 21

Van's voice over the phone quavered and buzzed like the upper-register strings inside a piano. "We'll send the car for you. About five, okay?"

"How's it going?" Quinn asked, responding to the strangled hum in her friend's tone.

"I'll be awfully glad to see you. Stan, too."

They hung up. Quinn whooped to Will, "Hey, slip on your spats! They're coming to fetch us in the Silver Ghost!"

At five o'clock sharp, as faces pressed against windows up and down Gardner Street, the Huntingtons' Rolls-Royce glided to a stop outside the Mallory house. Quinn and Will dashed to the car. Neither of them owned dress coats, and preferred to brave the cold rather than drape their army-surplus-style jackets over their best clothes. O'Hara, the chauffeur, ushered them into the backseat. Quinn settled back with a sigh. There was a subtle breath of warm air as O'Hara adjusted the thermostat to their coatless condition.

"Oh, my God, is this heaven?" Quinn whispered. Then she giggled. "Why am I whispering?"

"Damned if I know, honeypot," Will bellowed.

"Shh!" Quinn protested.

As the car pulled away from the curb she leaned forward to wave at the neighbors' animated parlor-window curtains, attempting the familiar stiff gesture of Queen Elizabeth the Second. She turned to grin at Will.

He wore a white turtleneck sweater, a navy blazer, and gray slacks. His hair, freshly washed, had dried in a soft wave across his forehead. The sunstreaks made him look as if he had just dropped into town from Acapulco.

"*You* don't look out of your element in this heap," Quinn said. "You're a natural profligate."

He yanked on a lock of her hair. "Some of the greatest English monarchs were redheads, you know."

"If you value your life, don't mention it to Jake." She hooked a strand behind her ear and listened hard for the engine's purr. "I wish *I'd* had the chance to take a look under that hood. Maybe I can sneak down to the garage after dinner."

"Oh, no, you don't. You're not abandoning me to the Yankee Establishment."

"You're nervous."

"Aren't you?"

"No. What for?"

"Well, I'm just a hick from Idaho. I don't know about this Boston Brahmin stuff."

"Neither do I. But that makes me curious, not nervous. Besides, Ingraham, you're so loaded with class you'll dazzle 'em. Mark my words."

He leaned over to kiss her on the mouth. "They're marked. And I don't care to dazzle. I just don't want to screw things up for Van and Stanley."

The Rolls turned up a cobblestone street that was lined with town houses, mostly brick with white trim. Decorative lanterns shone on graceful wrought-iron railings. Cars were parked along the curb where there should have been horse-drawn carriages; otherwise the street was a portrait of another time. There was a feeling of safety here, of the preservation of valuable things, not just possessions but orderliness, a respect for history, and a kind of stolid optimism.

"There ain't nothin' like it in Red Falls," Will said.

"Not in Medham either."

A butler met them at the front door and reached for their nonexistent coats. Without missing a beat he smoothly withdrew his hands, as if the gesture had been an adjustment of his cuffs. He led Quinn and Will to a high-ceilinged, paneled room that managed to be elegant and cozy simultaneously. Stanley and Van were sitting on an exquisite Louis the Fifteenth sofa. Dr. and Mrs. Huntington faced them on its mate. A glass cocktail table between the two couples held a silver tray of decanters and crystal tumblers, wineglasses, and goblets. Stanley and Vanessa leapt up as if the springs had suddenly burst through the brocade upholstery to hurl them toward the ceiling.

"So glad you're here," they said, bumping noses to kiss Quinn. The butler did not depart exactly; he seemed to fade and become gradually invisible.

Stanley wrung Will's hand until his fingers were white from the compression of blood vessels. Dr. and Mrs. Huntington had risen as well, but stood by the fireplace, waiting and smiling remotely. Quinn regarded them with curiosity over Vanessa's cashmere shoulder. They had beautiful teeth.

"We're so pleased you could come," Mrs. Huntington said. She had Van's long-boned face, but more chiseled so that she was handsome rather than pretty. Dr. Huntington's was fleshy. Quinn decided that he must have been handsome in a standard kind of way when he was young but his small features had not aged well. If it weren't for his height and grace, the man would be quite undistinguished. Van was fortunate to have inherited her mother's looks.

Quinn addressed her attention to Dr. Huntington. "I want to thank you for sending me to Dr. Loomis," she said. "He was very kind to me."

"How was the old man?" the doctor asked.

"He said to tell you for him that you're a son of a bitch," Quinn said.

Mrs. Huntington looked startled, but her husband laughed and propelled Quinn over to the sofa. While they drank cocktails, Dr. Huntington regaled them with reminiscences of macabre pranks from medical-school days. Meanwhile, Stanley practiced drinking martinis, and by nine o'clock his eyes had a certain unfocused glaze. Quinn's stomach had begun to growl loudly enough for Will to raise his eyebrows at her. The butler became visible again beside a paneled section of the wall and ushered them into the dining room.

The seating arrangements were accomplished in an atmosphere as formal and hushed as the room. Quinn made note of the wallpaper above the mahogany wainscoting. It was a reproduction of a pattern she had seen in an exhibit at the Gardner Museum. Will would be interested. No doubt he would also ask her in that deadpan hick voice of his if the Huntingtons were reproductions as well. She caught sight of Van's panicked expression. While Quinn was absorbing the decor, a vast silence had settled over the dinner table. "What lovely silver, Mrs. Huntington. It's antique, isn't it?" Quinn asked.

"Thank you, dear," said Mrs. Huntington. "Yes, it belonged to my great-grandmother, who was a friend of Abigail Adams."

"Isn't that thrilling?" Quinn said to Will. She held

up a teaspoon. "Maybe Abigail drank untaxed tea from this very spoon."

"Actually," Dr. Huntington interjected, "Myra's father swiped the entire set from the Copley Plaza in 1946."

The general laughter was more uproarious than was warranted. Quinn noticed that Dr. Huntington's face had lost the relaxed aura of geniality she had seen in the other room. The eyes were bloodshot, and there was something fraudulent about the smile. Hadn't Van once told her something about her father's being terribly impressed with his wife's social prominence? Apparently he resented it, too; that was a nasty crack about the silverware. Mrs. Huntington had laughed a stiff decorous death rattle, but was patently wounded. She didn't look at her husband. And neither of them ever seemed to look at Stanley. Quinn wondered if they knew that Stanley once had an audience with the queen in Buckingham Palace. It was the sort of thing that would impress them. Her mind began to whir. She saw that Will had already started on Mrs. Huntington. Lord, he could charm the peel off a banana if he only set his mind to it.

"For a westerner, the history of New England is maybe even more precious," Will was saying. "A place like this, Beacon Hill, for example. It hurts to see even one old town house cut up into apartments. It must be like the death of a friend."

Go get 'em, Uriah Heep, Quinn thought. But Mrs. Huntington was leaning toward him with a flushed face.

"Isn't that amazing?" she gushed. "I was just feeling that very same way recently when the Stanfords next door sold their house. Apparently some real estate person bought it for speculation, and heaven knows what will become of it in the end. Probably it'll be razed and made into a parking lot. Imagine, it was built in 1791. I don't know if I can bear to look Amanda Stanford in the eye again."

That end of the table accounted for, Quinn concentrated on prodding Dr. Huntington into a conversation with Stanley. The doctor sat at the head of the table with Quinn on his right and Stanley on his left, a perfect configuration for her purposes. The challenge plus four ounces of expensive wine brought an attractive blush to her cheeks.

"Van tells me you've been doing volunteer work with the clinic," Quinn said.

"A couple of hours a week, yes," Dr. Huntington answered.

"I never think of doctors as rating very high in the altruism department. Aren't you pretty exceptional?" Quinn's face was all admiration. She kept glancing at Stanley to include him. She didn't want him sidetracked into another conversation.

Apparently the subject put a hairline fracture in Dr. Huntington's crust of bemused detachment. He went so far as to shake his forefinger at Quinn for emphasis. "I keep trying to persuade my colleagues that it's not only a humanitarian gesture. If every physician would only donate a few hours a week, we wouldn't be facing the specter of socialized medicine."

Ah, bless you, she thought. Unwittingly he had precipitated the arrival of Quinn's conversational destination.

"Do you think socialized medical care would be so disastrous?" she asked.

"Unquestionably. You'd see such a decline in quality, patients would be dropping like flies. Thank you, Evelyn." He helped himself to a slab of roast beef from a heavy silver platter. Evelyn had well-developed biceps, Quinn noticed.

"I wonder how it's working out in England," Quinn said. Dr. Huntington began to reply, but Quinn quickly rushed on. "Stan? What was your feeling about socialized medicine when you were in London? You know, if it's working out." Almost home.

Stanley swallowed an enormous lump of beef unchewed. "As a matter of fact, I had an opportunity to sample the system firsthand. The emergency room was slow and inefficient, but once they finally got around to fixing me up, they did a good job of it."

"What was the problem?" Dr. Huntington asked him.

"Food poisoning."

"Must have been the crumpets from your visit with the queen." Quinn dropped it ever so casually. Stanley smiled at her, and she read his eyes: *You devious little thing*, they said.

Myra Huntington's face snapped around from the foot of the table, bringing to an abrupt halt her lamentations regarding historical preservation in Newport, Rhode Island.

"You're kidding," Will said, fully aware that she was not.

"Stanley had tea at Buckingham Palace," Quinn reiterated firmly.

"How interesting, Stanley," Myra Huntington said. She kept her voice mild, but her curiosity showed in the eager arch of her torso. She was eight feet away from Stanley, but somehow seemed to be leaning close enough to touch noses with him.

"It's not all that interesting," Stanley said with just the right touch of modesty. But by Myra Huntington's standards there was plenty to tell, not so much his being chosen to participate in a summer drama apprenticeship at the Royal Academy, but rather the list of notables present at the palace reception. Stanley recalled the names of nearly every lord and lady, embellishing the list with only one imaginary luminary named Randolph Higgenbotham-Ramsey.

"You never told us Stanley was so active in the drama," Mrs. Huntington accused Van.

"No," Van said. She restrained herself from adding *Would it have helped?*

The conversation had loosened now. When Stanley spoke, he was granted the courtesy of full attention from the Huntingtons rather than the cool gaze usually reserved for other people's ill-mannered children.

After dinner Dr. and Mrs. Huntington said good night and left the young people by the fireside to evaluate the evening.

"An abundance of snow in the area tonight," Stanley remarked.

"A blizzard was just what we needed," Van said. "Thank you, both of you."

"If we could only install you here permanently," Stanley continued.

Quinn adopted a heavy brogue. "In the words of my aged father, the queen sits on the pot just like everybody else."

There was a burst of laughter. "It would have been comforting if you'd mentioned that while we were on the subject of Buckingham Palace," Stanley said.

"I was too busy imagining Vanessa's father on the toilet."

"Very crass," Will said. He draped an arm around Quinn's shoulder and pulled her next to him. "Look at the way that decanter shatters the light from the fire. Prisms all over the ceiling."

Van snuggled against Stanley. "Will," she said,

"how'd you know Mother was such a Henry James fanatic?"

"Intuition," he answered. "And the bookcase."

"If she could have eaten her chocolate soufflé out of your hand, she would have."

"The good doctor is taking us to his club for dinner tomorrow night," Stanley said. "The membership's all turning out to see what a Jew looks like."

"Just be yourself and try to look biblical," Van suggested.

"They've all got kids with names like Hilary and Darcy and Muffin," Stanley said. "I like John Mallory's advice better. In my mind's eye every Queen Anne chair shall become a commode."

They sat drinking wine and talking until there was nothing left in the fireplace except soft red coals. In the car on the way home Quinn asked Will if he had noticed the exquisite wallpaper reproductions.

"No," he answered. "Are the Huntingtons reproductions too?" Quinn's delight baffled him, but he endured her enthusiastic kiss without complaint.

Chapter 22

Will and Quinn heaved their luggage onto the trolley and climbed gratefully out of the piercing cold of Commonwealth Avenue. The car clicked and rocked, slowing as the traffic became more congested near Boston University.

"Place looks more like a factory than a college," Will said.

"That tower's the law school," Quinn told him. "So how come you never told me what you thought of Tommy Flanagan?"

"Will you explain to me someday how your synapses transport you from one subject to the next?"

"If you tell me what you thought of Tommy Flanagan."

"He has nice teeth."

"I wish you'd try to be a little jealous."

"Find me a worthy opponent and I will be."

"I always said you were an arrogant bastard," Quinn remarked. "You know, it's amazing," she continued slowly. "I have this sort of mild curiosity about him now. I wish him well, but there's no . . . passion."

"Glad to hear it."

She leaned against his shoulder. "It's kind of scary."

"Why?"

"I don't want to get too *too* involved with you."

Will laughed.

"Don't laugh. I think I'm getting clutched."

He wished she hadn't said it. He depended on Quinn for optimism. From the very beginning she had always insisted that everything would work out, she'd make it work out. Now, as the trolley dove into the tunnel below Kenmore Square, Will's stomach took a plunge as well. When Quinn admitted fear, a chasm opened up under him.

"I'm scared about Ann, too. I keep willing her to go into remission and she's not cooperating."

"How realistic is that?"

"It's possible. Lupus isn't cancer." She laced her arm through his and held on tight. "Jesus, it's dark in here." Will leaned his cheek against the top of her head. Her hair was smooth and warm.

She drew away and stared up at him, her face an ashen moon in the sepulchral light of the underground. "If you ever take off on me, I'll kill you. I swear, I'll come after you with a pickax and stab you through the heart."

Will put his hand behind her neck and pulled her against him again. They sat in silence until they reached their stop and boarded the bus for Springfield.

Back at school a strain began to develop between them. The jokes about life in New York City versus the wilds of Idaho grew forced and were soon eliminated from their conversations altogether. An accidental mention of the future precipitated long silences. Quinn received a letter from Mr. Ted Manning himself, granting her an interview. She didn't tell Will about it for two days.

They survived by avoidance. Quinn was inundated with work in the garage, and Will was struggling with Harvey, trying to find a way to ease the separation that would come with graduation. February arrived, and with it a thaw that produced record mild temperatures and the inability for anyone to tend to business. Will and Quinn decided to take Harvey fishing.

That Thursday was particularly mild. The ground was covered with a soft mist, and everything smelled fresh and damp. Quinn was nervous. She hadn't seen Harvey since that initial trip to the bowling alley, and did not look forward to his expression when she showed up with Will at school. Will had prepared him, but Quinn suspected that he had prayed all week for her to contract the flu or break her foot.

"H'lo," Harvey said dutifully, eyes downcast. Will handed Quinn the fishing rods, wrapped an arm around each of them, and headed for the bus stop.

The seats in the front half of the Forestport bus were built to hold two people each. Harvey slipped quickly into a window seat. Will reached for a small brown hand and hauled Harvey to the long row of empty seats at the back of the bus. They waited until Harvey chose a spot so that he and Quinn could sit on either side of him. Harvey kept his face turned rigidly toward Will.

"It's hot back here, man."

"Yup," Will agreed.

"Gotta put the niggers in the back of the bus."

"Oh, shut up, Harve," Will said.

Quinn was staring at Harvey's sneaker. It had come untied. "Better fix that shoelace or you'll trip," she commented.

Harvey glanced down at his right foot. "Can't," he said.

"I'll tie it, then," Quinn said quickly and reached down.

"No!" Harvey jerked his legs out of her reach. "I like it that way, man."

Suddenly she understood. Harvey had outgrown his sneakers, and kept the laces undone to allow maximum space for his cramped toes.

"Oh." Her voice was stricken.

"One of these days we'll have to get you a new pair," Will said.

"I don't need anything from you," Harvey murmured.

"It would give me pleasure to buy you a present, you little creep," Will said. "You'll just have to put up with it."

Harvey's eyelashes were spiky with unshed tears. Quinn was nearly overcome with the urge to grab the little body and hold on tight, but she sat on her hands and looked out the window. The bus had carried them past the ghetto streets and out into farm country. Finally it stopped with a hiss and let them off by the Forestport post office. There was a short walk past half a dozen shoebox-style houses, and then they turned down a dirt road that wound through the woods. The ground was squishy beneath their feet from patches of melting snow and ice. They inhaled the clean, sharp smell of wet earth. Quinn began jumping over intermittent puddles in a kind of hopscotch game. Harvey watched her curiously.

"Spring fever," Will commented to him. He didn't answer, but every now and then his feet would skip over a watery spot in unconscious imitation. Then he would quickly slow up again.

At the end of the road was the pond, fronted by a small clearing. A ramshackle boathouse slouched at the water's edge. In an ancient chair by the doorway sat a very old man. When he saw them, he rose with surprising agility and approached on legs that appeared to have spent half a century wrapped around a horse. His face was withered and brown like a dried-apple doll's.

"Early this year," he remarked to Will.

"Yeah. Good day for perch."

"Should be."

The presence of the auburn-haired girl and the small black boy seemed to cause the old man not a moment's puzzlement. Will reached into his pocket, but the man waved his hand. "Pay me later." He gave them a coffee can full of dirt and worms and gestured toward a battered blue rowboat.

"Come on, troops," Will said. He and Quinn held the boat while Harvey hopped in. It bobbed gently under the boy's weight. Quinn got in next, then Will planted one foot in the stern and shoved off from the dock with the other. Harvey looked impressed.

"Took me a few times of landing in the drink before I could pull that off," Will said. For the first time that day Harvey offered him a quick grin.

"Just out of curiosity," Quinn said, "are we legal? Don't we need a license or something?"

"The old gentleman isn't much of a stickler when it comes to state regulations. He's very independent."

Quinn gazed across the water. Birch trees lined the shore, their white bark dazzling against the dense woods behind. As Will pulled on the oars the boat slid rhythmically toward the center of the pond.

Quinn sighed. "All I need is a parasol." She let her hand trail overboard. "Shit, that's cold!" she yelped when her fingers hit the water.

Harvey looked at her, measuring, and Will said, "What're you trying to do, scare away our fish?"

"I *beg* your pardon," she said in a stage whisper. "What I meant was, *shit, that's cold.*"

This elicited a wan smile from Harvey. Ah hah, thought Quinn. Perhaps entry to this kid's heart is via profanity.

Will showed them how to thread worms on the hook.

"Don't that hurt 'em?" Harvey asked.

"Supposedly not, and I'd just as soon believe it," Will answered.

"Yeah," Harvey echoed fervently. He draped his rod over the edge of the boat and stared into the water. "Come on, you fish."

"It might take a few minutes, Harve," Will cautioned.

"I got the whole entire afternoon. Fish, I'm gonna get you."

Quinn tossed her line in and Will settled back against the stern and closed his eyes.

"Hey, don't go to sleep, guide. What do we do if we get a bite?" Quinn asked.

"You just let me know," Will murmured. Quinn glanced at Harvey, and they exchanged their first look of mutual exasperation. Encouraged, Quinn averted her eyes before the moment could cool.

Then they sat. They sat for twenty minutes without moving, lines trailing in the water. Harvey and Quinn stared into the shiny depths. Nothing happened.

"Hey, man," Harvey said. "How long we gotta wait here?"

"Peaceful, isn't it?" Will said sleepily.

"You gettin' a suntan and we just sittin' here like a cork in a bathtub. Maybe all the fish went south."

"Mm," Will said.

"Let's do something, Harvey," Quinn suggested. "Uh . . . maybe a word game?"

"Ah, shee-yit," Harvey said.

"You got a better idea?"

He thought this over. "What kind of word game?" he asked.

"Botticelli."

"Never heard of it."

Quinn explained the rules. She was pleased at Harvey's interest, however grudging.

"Let me go first," he said when she was finished. "*C*."

"Is this somebody who wears a bright red suit in December?"

"It's not Santa Claus," Harvey answered instantly.

"Okay. Is this another December big wheel? A long time ago."

Harvey thought for a moment. "Jesus Christ!" he answered triumphantly. Quinn shook her head, hunting for a person she was sure he would know. Harvey tried not to look pleased.

"All right, I've got you now," she said. "Is this an American scientist who figured out what to do with peanuts?"

"Not George Washington Carver!"

They both laughed.

"You're a true pain in the ass, you know that?" Quinn said. "I'm *never* gonna get a free question." The only names she could think of were Czerny and Clementi, from her early piano-lesson days. Harvey would never know them. "There's not a single *C* left in my head. Sure you don't want to switch to *M*?"

Harvey shook his head, grinning, and Quinn turned to Will for assistance. She prodded his foot where it dangled over the gunwale. "Help me, Will. This kid's too smart."

Will replied with an incoherent grunt.

"I don't think I'm very impressed with fishing," Quinn said.

"Hey!" Harvey exclaimed suddenly. His line had dipped, tugging the end of the fishing rod down into the water. "I've got somethin'!"

Will opened his eyes. "Reel him in, Harvey."

"Come on, you mother," Harvey said.

"Look at that, look at that! It's a big one!" Quinn yelled.

The fish slapped its tail along the surface, splashing wildly. In his excitement Harvey stood up too abruptly, setting the boat rocking. He arched his body in a sudden violent motion, trying to right himself without giving up his death grip on the rod.

"Sit down!" Will commanded. He leaned toward Harvey, but the boy teetered out of reach. Just as he was about to plunge over the edge, Quinn stood up and hooked him by the belt. She yanked him back onto his seat, but the force of the movement sent her off-balance and the boat began to tip even more wildly. At this point Will stood up too. Quinn grabbed his arm, and both of them plunged tailfirst into the pond.

When they surfaced, gasping with the cold, Harvey was beaming down at them from the boat. He held tightly to the gunwale with one hand, and with the other he displayed a fourteen-inch rainbow trout.

Quinn shouted, "Look at it! He got it!"

"Terrific," Will sputtered. "If you're so damn smart, Harve, how about fishing us out of this ice water?"

Will maneuvered their reentry into the rowboat. It was difficult with their soaked clothes weighing them down, and Quinn was rendered helpless by laughter. Finally, firmly ensconced, they examined Harvey's catch respectfully.

"Some fish," Quinn said.

"How's it gonna die?" Harvey wanted to know. "We don't kill it, do we?"

"Not unless you're so inclined," Will said, starting to row.

"I didn't get your *C*," Quinn said.

"Want me to tell you?"

"Oh, damn it. No. Yes. Tell me."

"Cassius Clay," Harvey said with a grin.

"Beautiful," Quinn said. "You wait. I'll get you."

Back at the boathouse the old man observed them expressionlessly as Quinn and Will dripped puddles all over the dock. "Good-looking fish," he remarked. Quinn decided his comment referred to the soaked, half-frozen bipeds rather than Harvey's trout.

"Coulda caught more, prob'ly, if they didn't fall in," Harvey said.

The old man disappeared into his shack and emerged a few moments later with two wool jackets that smelled of mildew. Quinn was reluctant to borrow the jeans that were offered, suspecting that they were the boatman's only extras. But the old man took her by the hand, nudged her inside the boathouse, and waited outside until she had finished changing. The one large room was surprisingly neat. There was a faded poster of the Eiffel Tower above the fireplace. Quinn wished she knew everything about the old geezer. She hauled on her soggy pantlegs until they finally unpeeled with a cold, sucking sound. Truth to tell, she wished she knew everything about everybody.

When they boarded the bus, Quinn and Harvey broke into giggles at the loud squishing noises from

Quinn's and Will's shoes as they walked to the back. But the seats were warm, and by the time they reached the North End, Will's backside at least was dry. They delivered Harvey to his building and stood in the doorway downstairs.

Harvey eyed Will's sodden pantlegs. "I don't know if . . . well, maybe Leroy's got something," he said tentatively.

Will knew that the man who shared Harvey's mother's bed was vain about his clothing and would never allow anyone to touch his things, certainly not soggy white folks.

"We'll take a cab from here, Harve," Will said. "Be back on campus in a few minutes. But thanks."

"You caught your family some fine dinner," Quinn said. She held out a near-frozen hand. "I'm proud to know ya'."

Harvey took it, and the two grinned at one another. Then the boy gave Will an affectionate rap on the arm and went clattering up the stairs with his fish carefully cradled in its newspaper blanket.

"Well, then, it was worth it," Quinn said with a shiver. "You poor guy, you must be a block of ice."

Will dug into his clammy jeans to check the money supply. "I have to tell you that my enthusiasm for fishing's somewhat dampened."

"Glad to hear it," Quinn said.

Between the two of them they scraped together enough for the long ride back to campus, then took long, hot showers to get their frozen blood circulating again, and recovered without even so much as a runny nose.

Chapter 23

Will had reluctantly agreed to accompany Quinn to New York. Heading south on the bus, he asked himself how it had happened. Maybe it was the sad desperation in the way she had asked him, with none of her usual cracks about how she'd written ahead to make sure all the thieves had left town for the annual Muggers' Convention in New Jersey. When he said all right, her eyes had welled up and she buried her face in his sweater.

As they left the Berkshires behind, the snow outside the window seemed to melt away, as if they were watching a series of time exposures. Neither of them had spoken for nearly an hour.

"What about your mother?" Will asked.

"What?" She had been trying to anticipate the questions Ted Manning might ask her tomorrow.

"If you get the job, what about Ann?"

"She's doing so much better. I think it's happening for her, Will. I talked to Jake this morning and they're even going to a party at the O'Malleys' tomorrow night. And I can commute home every weekend."

He was silent.

"I know you don't want me to get it."

"That's not fair."

"It's something I've wanted for, well, forever. I'd be right in the middle of everything, I'd be involved with people who make things *move*, Will."

"Where the action is." The words were uncharacteristically sarcastic.

She winced, and he took her hand in apology.

"I hope you snow the hell out of him. Who knows, maybe I'll love it so much you won't be able to force me back to school."

Quinn lifted his hand to her mouth and held it there. "I'd be your devoted slave forever," she murmured against his fingers.

The Port Authority terminal was teeming with rush-hour bustle. A stampede of commuters heading for the New Jersey buses hurried past. People jammed against stairways marked "Subway," pressing impatiently against one another. In the center of the station bewildered tourists turned around and around like windup toys, hoping for a shove in the right direction.

Quinn set down her bag. "Isn't it wonderful?" she exclaimed.

"Let's try this way," Will said. He steered her toward the nearest exit.

As they emerged onto Eighth Avenue, panhandlers sidled over to them with their grimy hands extended. Quinn looked at them curiously, but Will prodded her past and began walking uptown toward Forty-second Street.

"Manning did a thing on those guys a few weeks ago," she gasped. "You know, some of them make over a hundred a week, tax-free. Jesus, you can move when you want to. This is the wrong direction, you know. The hotel's downtown."

At the curbside an elderly man stood beside them

with his hand clutching the door handle of a taxi. The door was stiff and the old man was feeble, but finally he pried it open. As he let go to pick up his suitcase, a man in a trench coat, henna toupee askew, hurtled into the backseat and slammed the door behind him. The taxi sped away, and the old man's fingers, still outstretched for the door, trembled.

"We'll get you a taxi," Quinn said. Then she stepped out onto Eighth Avenue, flagged down a Checker cab, and ushered the old man into the backseat with his suitcase.

Will gaped at her.

"I wish I'd had the presence of mind to snatch the wig off that bastard's head when he flew by," she said. She spun around on the pavement. Lights flashed, advertising peepshows and pizza. "I love it, I love it, I love it!" she yelled. Pedestrians, unfazed, merely adjusted their paths to accommodate her swirling arms and moved on down the sidewalk. Will shook his head.

The lobby of the Hotel McAlpin on Thirty-fourth Street was humming. Groups of students, knapsacks drooping from overload, stood jabbering in Italian, French, and something liltingly Scandinavian. Perfectly coiffed airline stewardesses threaded their way through the tumult with their automatic smiles.

"I hate to go upstairs," Quinn said.

Will signed the register. "I hope you gave us a quiet room," he remarked to the clerk.

While they waited for the bellboy, Quinn's head swiveled from one point of interest to the next, as if she were watching a crazy tennis match. Will leaned against the reservations counter and stared at an empty corner of the lobby near the Thirty-third Street exit. It was good to look at something that didn't move.

In the elevator two young women with heavy

makeup kept up a dialogue punctuated with the snap of chewing gum.

"So I walked troo duh door and it's rainin' like a pump," said the tall girl with the maroon lips. "Like a *pump*."

"Ya shoulda went right home," answered the round girl, who exuded a cloud of Ambush with every ripple of her jaw muscles.

"Yeah, but I din't."

The elevator stopped on Nine. Will and Quinn followed the impassive bellhop out into the hallway.

"Was that English, or were they with the foreigners?" Quinn whispered.

"That's what happens after a couple of months in this town. Renders you completely unintelligible."

Their room was small and dark. Will tipped the bellhop while Quinn plunked her overnight case down on one of the twin beds.

"Let's go over to the Empire State Building," she said. "It's just down the block, in person."

Will flopped onto the other bed and kicked off his boots. "Go ahead. The view suits me fine right here."

"Ugh," Quinn said, staring up at the water-stained ceiling. "I don't want to go without you."

"Aren't you worn out?"

"No. This place gives me energy."

"As if you needed extra."

Will's voice had begun to fade, and Quinn knew he was already drifting into sleep. "Take a nap and then maybe you'll feel like going. We've got to eat anyway." She bent to give him a kiss. He draped his arm around her shoulders, pinning her down, but she extricated herself. "Oh, no, you don't. We mess around now and we won't get out of this cave until tomorrow."

"Yrm," Will said.

When he woke up, Quinn was sitting at the window staring down at Thirty-fourth Street. Even her back looked eager.

"Don't jump," he said.

"They're making a movie or something out there, right in front of Macy's. Nobody even pays attention." She sat down on the edge of his bed and opened her mouth to speak, but before the words could come out, her stomach interrupted with a long, delicate arpeggio. They both listened in fascination.

"Care to repeat that for the nice folks in Staten Island?" Will said, poking her navel.

Her stomach retorted with a short, erratic *harrumph*. They laughed.

"All right already. I'm coming," Will said, and reached for his boots with a groan.

The desk clerk glanced at their faded denims and recommended a health food store around the corner on Thirty-third Street. It was packed with foreign students who puzzled over their menus, trying to decipher the Swedish or Thai equivalent of "ambrosia deluxe." Will and Quinn waited a quarter of an hour for two seats together at the counter.

Finally a wheezing waitress plodded toward them carrying menus and a soggy towel that had met misfortune in the carrot juicer. She swiped at the Formica, catapulting crumbs onto Will's lap. Then she coughed on Quinn's menu and retreated to the assorted salads.

"I think I'll have the tuberculosis special," Quinn whispered. "Look at that chef."

At the far end of the counter the cook alternated between stuffing pita bread with bean sprouts and blowing his nose. His neck was scaled with a mean-looking skin affliction.

"Let's get out of here before we catch something

fatal," Will said. As they were on their way out the door a janitor struggled to sweep the rubble from under the seats. He was missing half an arm, the left one severed at the elbow. Quinn and Will spotted him at the same moment and flung themselves out onto the street before they burst into laughter.

"It's not funny," she gasped. " Poor man."

Will grabbed her hand. "I don't think health food has much of a future. For Christ's sake, let's go find a Howard Johnson's."

They set the telephone on the floor, removed the table, and slid the beds together. Lying crossways they could avoid sinking into the crack.

She traced the outline of his ear. "It was fun tonight, wasn't it?" she said.

"Yes."

"It's not so bad, then."

He didn't respond. Instead he kissed her low on the neck, knowing her nipples would stiffen. His fingers slipped under her blouse to confirm it.

Quinn squirmed against him. "I feel like doing something really sinful."

"I'm never averse to debauchery in any form," Will murmured. There was a sprinkling of freckles under her right ear that formed the rough shape of a star. He traced it with his tongue and felt her shiver. Then she rolled away from him and stood up on the bed.

"Whistle me a tune and I'll be Gypsy Rose Lee."

Will propped himself up on an elbow and began to whistle *The Battle Hymn of the Republic*.

"No, you jerk, something sexy." She began to hum a slow, madeup tune and pulled her sweater off, an inch at a time. The blouse underneath hitched up for a moment as she arched her back, revealing a patch of bare stomach. Her face was hidden by tousled hair, but Will caught a glimpse of mischievous eyes glinting at him. He decided to humor her.

To his whistled rendition of David Rose's *Stripper*, she turned her back and watched him over her shoulder. He knew she was unbuttoning her blouse. To keep her balance on the mattress, she had spread her legs wide apart. The blouse unbuttoned, she let it creep down her back, then gathered it into a ball and turned, half covering her breasts. Her face was flushed and she was not smiling anymore. She tossed the blouse onto the floor, closed her eyes, and clasped her arms behind her head. Her nipples had shrunk into hard little knots, and Will could whistle no longer. He lowered the zipper on her pants, and slid them off her hips. When his hands touched her skin, he could feel her shudder. He held her from behind and buried his face in the pale hair between her legs. She sighed and dropped slowly to her knees. Lying back on the bed, she grasped her thighs with her hands and pulled them farther apart, opening herself wide for him. He stayed with her, moving his tongue against the swollen curls of flesh. He pressed his mouth against her in a deep kiss. She cried out, and he felt her muscles contract in spasms against his lips. Before she was finished, she was urging him up. He pulled off his clothes and lifted himself on top of her. He was so engorged he was afraid of hurting her, and penetrated her slowly. But she wrapped her arms and legs around him and pressed him close to her. Her face was wild and full of pleasure. When she felt him all the way inside, tears spilled down her cheeks, and she said in a choked voice, "I love you. Oh, Will, how I love you."

Chapter 24

Friday morning Quinn dressed for her interview with Ted Manning. Will was lounging in bed watching the weather report on the *Today* show.

"Why is Frank Blair crying?" he wanted to know. "Listen, the man is sobbing on every word."

Quinn checked her stockings for runs. "The weather report's giving him a frog in his throat. It'd do the same for you."

"Maybe something tragic happened in his life."

"Will, you're not going to lie there in bed all day, are you?" She stood at the edge of the bed in her tweed suit and trench coat. He hooked his finger in her belt and pulled her down next to him.

"The young professional woman on the make in the big city," he commented.

She was pleased. "Is that what I look like?"

"Yup."

"Really, you're not going to stay here all morning."

"There's a classic Errol Flynn movie on."

She pulled away from him and stood up. "You're supposed to be out there on the streets learning to love it."

"Good luck this morning. Nervous?"

"Yes. Are you going to get off your ass?"

"I'll go, I'll go. You can trust me." She looked dubious. "A man has to eat breakfast."

"You'll poke your nose out as far as the health food store and come right back to the room and vegetate by the boob tube."

"I wouldn't risk my life entering that pit of disease. The only healthy creatures in there are the cockroaches."

Quinn studied him carefully for a moment, then leaned down for a kiss. He watched her walk to the door. She moved comfortably in high heels. If she would teeter a little, maybe he wouldn't feel so uneasy. He preferred the faded jeans and sneakers.

"I'll see you at the Museum of Modern Art. Twelve thirty." She waved and disappeared into the dark hallway. Will felt a shock as the door clicked, a sense of loss, as if she had just boarded a ship bound for the other side of the world. Then he got angry. Who did she think she was, dancing out the door like that, Goddamn Loretta Young? A college kid had no right to look so poised and confident. For sure they'd give her the fucking job. They'd eat her up.

He lunged for the television, snapping off Hugh Downs' observations on *Zorba the Greek*. Then he went to the window and peered out at Thirty-fourth Street, hoping to catch a glimpse of Quinn. She emerged onto the sidewalk, nine floors down, newspaper folded under left arm, handbag strap over right shoulder. He watched her standing at the traffic light, then crossing with the crowd. Most everyone was hurrying, probably late for work. She fell easily into the rhythm of the street, effortlessly weaving past the old fat woman with the cane, sidestepping an unruly clutter of schoolchildren, never altering her stride. After a moment she disappeared up Sixth Avenue. He turned away from the window; the bustle on Thirty-fourth Street held no attraction for him once Quinn no longer occupied it. In fact, the idea of subjecting himself to the tumult below dismayed him. He sighed. First a shower, then breakfast. Then he would make his way on foot up Fifth Avenue and give the place his best shot.

Quinn stepped into a self-service coffee shop on Forty-second Street and Sixth Avenue. Behind the counter a Puerto Rican man smeared butter onto slices of toast with the speed and efficiency of a printing press. She imagined the sound of heavy machinery throbbing as the brown fingers churned out stacks of buttered whole wheat, white, and rye. "Next?" he shouted. His eyes remained fixed on his hands' business. No wonder, Quinn thought. A split second's loss of concentration and there'd be dry toast and buttered fingers.

"I'm next," howled a minute old woman with blue hair whose nose barely cleared the cabinet. "Gimme a bagel, down, with cream cheese, a regular coffee, two sugars."

Quinn let her "next" pass in the interest of observation. The ritual was a far cry from the chaotic chatter of the cafeteria line back at school. Finally hunger overcame fascination, and she carried her Danish and coffee to a table in the back of the shop. A man in a tattered gray coat hunched at a nearby table. He was unshaven, and a fragment of dirty, frayed shirt-collar poked above his coat. A low, muttering sound emerged from the toothless hole beneath a swollen red nose. Instinctively Quinn inched toward the wall. She forced her attention back to the counter, where customers marched in and out in a matter of seconds, as if they had been scrupulously choreographed.

Suddenly there was a loud snort from the next table. Repugnance succumbed to curiosity, and she glanced at the derelict. He had leaned back in his chair so that Quinn was now able to see *The New York Times*, open to the editorial page, on the table beside his coffee cup. There was another indignant snort. Quinn was too far away to determine which article was provoking such disgust, but for sure she would inspect her own copy later on and try to figure it out. In the meantime she amused herself speculating about the ragged old fellow's history. Perhaps he had once taught nuclear physics at Harvard, or maybe he had sat at the head of a multimillion-dollar conglomerate. What intrigued Quinn most was the fact that seeing the *Times* under that alcohol-ravaged nose had suddenly turned abhorrence into fascination. New York City promised to be full of tricks. It was thrilling.

She wondered if Ted Manning would surprise her too. Occasionally she admitted the possibility that she might be ignored and wind up as somebody's secretary. But in her fantasies she learned everything Manning could teach her, and then took off in a meteoric rise to produce her own program, which, unlike his, would direct its attention primarily to international political figures. More often than not Quinn's fantasies solidified into fact. She had learned to trust her dreams.

The network offices floated atop a glass tower on Sixth Avenue. Quinn felt her throat constrict as the elevator climbed to the thirtieth floor. For the duration of that brief ride she was uncomfortably aware of her status as a college undergraduate with no television experience and a talent for fixing cars. She noticed a grease mark on her trench-coat pocket. The buckle on her left shoe was loose. It would fall off. Then her shoe would fall off. Then she would fall down, probably at the precise moment Ted Manning extended his hand to shake hers.

The elevator doors slid open, and she stepped out into a quiet reception area. A middle-aged woman in a soft rose sweater smiled pleasantly at her from behind a typewriter. Quinn felt encouraged.

"Quinn Mallory to see Mr. Manning," she announced.

"Please have a seat. I'll let them know you're here."

Quinn sat. She'd gotten this far by pure nerve. The worst she could do was make an ass of herself.

In a few moments a slim woman with the shortest haircut Quinn had ever seen on a female appeared in the doorway at the rear of the reception area.

"Miss Mallory?"

Quinn got to her feet, wishing she'd had her coat dry-cleaned. The woman ushered her down a long hallway.

"You will be meeting with Mrs. Smedley in Personnel. Her office is in Room 3056."

From behind, Quinn had been marveling at the remarkable brush cut that came to a V at the base of the slender white neck. She stopped in her tracks. "But I'm supposed to have an interview with Ted Manning. Mr. Manning." She dug into her handbag to produce the letter that was signed by the great man himself.

The woman gave her a cool smile. "Mr. Manning hasn't time for job interviews. He's about to catch a plane for Los Angeles." She hesitated. "I will say he liked your letter."

"Are you MK?" Quinn asked. "At the bottom of his stationery, the initials after TM."

"Yes. Here we are. Oh!"

Around the corner hurtled a man, briefcase in one hand, suitcase in the other. He braked and tried to dodge Quinn, but in her attempt to avoid a collision, she moved in the same direction. They crashed. Quinn's handbag shot down the hall at sixty miles per hour, and the man's suitcase snapped open. Underwear and shirts tumbled out onto the marble floor.

"Christ!" Ted Manning said. He had grasped Quinn by the arms in a wild dance as they tried to regain their balance. He let go now. Her face was red with excitement and confusion.

"Are you all right?" he asked.

She nodded. "Are you?"

"Yes, but my intimate lingerie is all over the floor." MK had already begun repacking, slim legs folded up like a slide rule under her compact derriere.

Carpe diem, Quinn thought, and took a deep breath. "I'm so glad you ran into me," she said, carefully deadpan. "I'm Quinn Mallory. I wrote you a letter about a job." Manning looked blank. "I have some suggestions about your show . . ."

"Ah, yes, the cheeky Miss Mallory. I can't resist anyone who doesn't think I'm perfect." He appraised her face and body. "You don't look like a co-ed."

"I'm very mature," she said, holding eye contact.

"What do you want to do around here anyway?" he asked.

"I want you to teach me how to be you."

Manning laughed. He bent down, stuffed the last of his underwear into the suitcase, and snapped it shut. MK rose. Quinn noticed that Manning didn't thank her.

"Tell Smedley I'm sending Miss Mallory back when I'm finished with her." He handed Quinn his briefcase, grabbed her arm, and propelled her down the hallway at such speed that she was practically skating across the floor. "We'll do this on the run. I've got to catch a plane."

Manning dashed out onto Sixth Avenue, hailed a cab, and ushered Quinn into the backseat. "Pan Am building. Heliport," he said, and slammed the door. "The limo's on the fritz," he explained to Quinn. "Lousy timing."

Quinn's hair was disheveled and she was perspiring and breathing hard. Ted Manning, on the other hand, looked like an advertisement for Hathaway shirts.

"What?" he asked.

She blinked at him.

"I thought you asked me something."

"Actually, I was wondering how come you don't sweat." Quinn drew her fingers through her hair in an attempt to subdue it.

"Television personalities aren't allowed to. Look what happened to Nixon when his upper lip glistened through the Kennedy debates."

The cab careened across Fifty-seventh Street while Manning talked in his famous honeyed voice. Quinn studied him. An ordinary-looking man, really. Midforties, medium build, medium brown hair. Face attentive but not intrusive. Warm hazel eyes. Only his tan and the devastating smile hinted at celebrity. And there was a peculiar electric tension surrounding him that was compelling.

Perhaps it was confidence, the prestige of his position. She wondered if the extraordinary personal dynamism preceded his fame or if it had developed as a result of his career? The image of John Kennedy's face flickered in Quinn's mind. Whatever the quality, Kennedy had been luminous with it.

Quinn was aware of being thoroughly scrutinized as

well. Manning had asked her the typical questions: family, schools, hobbies, grades. If he followed his typical pattern, she expected him to zero in soon on the things that really counted. The cab began its ascent through a tall archway and up the ramp that curled around 230 Park Avenue to the heliport entrance of the Pan Am building. In just a moment the interview would be over.

"When are you going to start prying into my darkest secrets?" she asked him.

Manning smiled. "Right about now. You sound as if you're looking forward to it."

The cab stopped. Quinn sighed. "Too bad," she said. "Once in a while I can be incredibly interesting."

"Oh, you're coming with me."

"A helicopter!"

"You'll like it. Come on." He got out and paid the driver through the window. Quinn saw him glance at her legs as she climbed out of the backseat.

"How will I get back?"

"Cab."

Inside, the elevator whooshed up the shaft like a rocket ship. Quinn wondered if her dizziness resulted from the rapid climb or from the proximity of Ted Manning. Old clichés clicked through her head like ticker tape: *it takes my breath away*, *it sweeps me off my feet*, the "it" being comfortably impersonal.

The elevator shuddered to a stop, and they rushed through the glass-enclosed waiting room. A blue and white helicopter stood waiting with its huge rotary blade revolving slowly. Inside, there were only four other passengers, businessmen who looked practically identical. Three out of the four held their briefcases on their knees in precisely the same position.

The propeller whirred, and soon they lifted off the

rooftop. For a moment they seemed to hover at the edge of the building like a gigantic hummingbird. Quinn stared down at Park Avenue while her heart lodged under her larynx. She tried to swallow, but the lump stuck there, thumping. Finally, slowly, they began to gain altitude, as if the city had finally relinquished its constraints on them and set them free. The massive buildings were toys constructed with blocks on a living-room floor. Down in the harbor the Statue of Liberty was a tiny friend, waving good-bye. They crossed the East River with its bridges like spider webs stretched across the water.

"What do you read?" Manning asked her.

"Nonfiction, mostly, but I want to change that." The helicopter was loud. She had to lean close to him to make herself heard without shouting. Manning could feel her breath beside his ear.

"Like what?"

"*Games People Play*."

"What did you think of it?"

"Pretty silly."

"No novels?"

"No, except for my English course. Unless you count *In Cold Blood*."

"What did you think of that?"

"Brilliant."

"Did you see the Capote interview a couple of months ago?"

Quinn nodded.

"Well?"

"You were both . . . excessive."

Manning laughed. "That's probably tactful."

"I'd say definitely."

"Excessive, eh? What do you hate?"

"Laziness," she blurted, then seemed startled at her own response.

"What do you love?"

"This machine." She would love to get a close look at the instrument panel. Wait till Jake heard about this crazy ride.

"Got a boyfriend?"

"I hope so."

"You're not sure?"

"No."

"You seem pretty sure of everything else."

"Yup."

"But not the boyfriend."

"No."

Manning waited, but she only smiled blandly at him. "Why not?" he asked.

"He's unusual." The smile turned to a grin. Sunlight beamed through the window and sent a rainbow through her hair and across her cheek. Manning felt professional curiosity lurch one step closer to a compulsion to know everything. He frowned.

"What?" she asked.

"You have a rainbow in your hair," he said absently.

She shifted in her seat so that the light streamed into the cabin unobstructed. The ray, now alive with dust, shimmered its way straight into Manning's crotch. They both stared.

"Oh, dear," Quinn murmured.

The helicopter set down with a gentle bounce at Kennedy Airport. The clichés began ticking in Quinn's head again: *feet on the ground, coming down to earth, head out of the clouds.*

With their arrival, Manning's face became the pleasant television mask she had seen in the cab. Quinn realized that he must have dropped it at some point or she wouldn't have noticed its return. She scrambled along behind him through the terminal. Until today she had never truly understood Van's complaints about trying to keep up with Quinn's mad dash.

Manning ushered her into a cab, gave the driver instructions and a twenty-dollar bill. He leaned his arms on the window. "Smedley'll give you some forms to fill out. You won't make any money, so find a cheap apartment. See you in June." Then he rapped on the roof and the taxi pulled away.

"That was whatsisname, Manning, right?" the driver asked, craning his neck to look at Quinn. "Who're you?"

"Oh, nobody," Quinn answered. "I just work for him." She felt herself expanding with elation. She would inflate into an enormous balloon-version of herself, so that they'd have to pop her with a pin to get her out of the taxi back in Manhattan. She could hardly wait to tell someone.

Will! Jesus Christ, she'd forgotten about Will. She glanced at her watch. There was no way she could make the museum by twelve thirty, and Mrs. Smedley was waiting too. She instructed the driver and in forty minutes emerged at the museum entrance on West Fifty-third Street. She found Will in the sculpture garden. Suddenly her excitement disappeared, just as if someone had indeed punctured her balloon.

Damn Will Ingraham. This was the triumphant moment of her life. A job with Ted Manning! An interview in a helicopter! Damn Will for robbing her of her victory.

He turned around. His face brightened, and her anger disintegrated. She grabbed him around the waist.

"Well?" he asked.

"I'm not finished yet."

"Jesus, what're they doing, a genetic study of the family tree?"

"It's been a wild morning. Let's stay out here for a second and then I have to get back."

They strolled while she told him about the interview, the helicopter, her impressions of Ted Manning, and finally that she seemed to have been hired as of June.

"That's wonderful," Will said. He kissed her on the cheek.

"How come I suddenly don't feel so terrific?"

He looked down at her silently. Her eyes reflected the dark shapes of the sculptures.

"Will, did you have a good time this morning?"

"It was diverting."

She released his arm. "I guess I'd better go."

"Okay."

I don't have to go, Quinn thought. I can just say screw Smedley, and Manning will think I'm some weird little number he made up out of an overactive imagination.

"I'll meet you back at the hotel around four. Go ahead." He put his hands on her shoulders, spun her around, and sent her marching away from him. When she turned to wave, he was studying a brass figure at the far end of the garden.

Ouch, Will thought. His head seemed to be filled with cartoons. While Quinn was describing her introduction to Manning, the crash in the corridor, Will had imagined their bodies colliding, and, the word *OOF*! in a balloon above their heads. Maybe it made the experience easier to bear, encapsulating it, trivializing it. En-Capp-sulating it, he thought, and winced.

He sat down beside a small pool. A scrawny little bush provided a meager hiding place. He wondered how people found privacy in the city, other than withdrawing to lock themselves into the boxes they inhabited. He had been in New York one day, and already his central nervous system was screaming for space.

Listening to Quinn's tale, he had found himself drifting off into the mountains back home. She talked of helicopters and he thought of the great Salmon River that the Indians called the river-of-no-return. He had half heard her. Obviously, Manning had been enchanted. Obviously, for the rest of his life Will would never watch the man's program again.

Will had decided that the only way to survive her departure just now was to become an active participant in it. For a moment, when he'd taken her shoulders in his hands and sent her on her way, he hadn't felt quite so helpless. He tossed a twig into the pond and watched the reflection of his face ripple and twist. There was a soda bottle resting on the bottom under the exhausted lily pads.

Quinn and Will walked up Madison Avenue in search of a restaurant that was cheap and reasonably clean. As Quinn wove her way along the crowded sidewalks, Will lurched, stopping and starting awkwardly and often standing aside to let someone rush past. Because of his unpredictable pace he was elbowed, poked, bumped into, and cursed at.

They finally had dinner at a coffee shop on Madison and Forty-third Street. It was a quiet meal. As soon as Quinn's voice began to vibrate with excitement about her future, she would check herself and drop her eyes. Soon there didn't seem to be much to talk about. Will stretched his hands across the table and held her fingers. It was as if her success was a cross to be borne by them both. He did not accuse her; she felt no guilt. They were miserable and frightened.

Over coffee she said, “Will, I wish I didn’t want it.”

“I wish you didn’t too.”

“It’s like I’m not responsible for it, as if God or Jesus Christ himself said ‘Quinn Cathleen Mallory, you were born to do this thing in the communications media.’ ”

Will laughed.

“It’s not funny.”

“No.”

“I feel this”—she put her hands against her heart—“this welling up, like I’m going to burst if I don’t do something important. I think it’d kill me if I didn’t try. I’d just shrivel up like a dead plant.” She was quiet for a moment. “You feel that way about teaching.”

“Yes.”

Her blueberry pie lay half finished on her plate. “What’re we going to do?” she asked him.

“I don’t know.”

“We’re going to make it somehow.”

He said nothing.

“I know you don’t.”

“I don’t what?” he asked.

“You don’t think we’re going to make it.”

Again he said nothing.

“You hate it here, don’t you?”

“I guess that’s a pretty fair description.”

“But Will, you were nice to try.”

“I’m a nice guy.”

“You’re a fucking wonderful guy.”

“Watch your mouth.”

“I’m watching yours and I wish I could kiss it.”

“Nobody’s stopping you.”

She got up and walked around the table to squeeze onto his lap. She gave him a long kiss. A woman glanced at them from the counter, and with a bored expression returned her gaze to the *Daily News*.

They strolled back to the hotel by way of Rockefeller Plaza. Skaters circled the rink, pirouetting and colliding to the strains of piped Lennon and McCartney. Will wished he'd worn his gloves. There was no wind, but the air was damp and promised snow. Quinn stood in front of him, and he wrapped his arms around her chest. His grandfather had told him that body heat is released through the top of one's head, so he rested his chin where Quinn's warmth would be escaping like steam from a tea kettle. The music switched from the hectic "Can't Buy Me Love" to "Yesterday." They swayed together, watching the skaters glide past below and listening in their heads to the unsung lyrics: "Yesterday, love was such an easy game to play . . ."

Quinn turned in his arms and gave him a fierce hug. Suddenly neither of them could wait to get back to the hotel. They half ran all the way down Sixth Avenue to Thirty-fourth Street, and for the rest of the night they made love—wildly at first, then with silly good humor, and finally, at 4:00 A.M., with great tenderness.

Both of them slept most of the way back to school on the bus.

Chapter 25

Will and Quinn had not spent ten minutes alone together since their return from New York almost a week before. There were class notes to copy, assignments to catch up on. Quinn had spent her last nickel in the city and was putting in extra hours at the garage. When Stanley suggested a double date for Saturday night, they accepted eagerly. Neither of them wanted to discuss the trip. Stanley and Van would distract their attention for the evening.

The four of them sat in the smoky red light of Lou's listening to Nat King Cole on the jukebox.

"So how're things in the asphalt jungle?" Stanley asked Will.

"Primitive."

Van glanced at Quinn uncomfortably.

"Not impressed, huh?" Stanley went on. This time Van squeezed his thigh in a warning, but Stanley misinterpreted the pressure. He drew her close to him and kissed her cheek.

"I liked Rockefeller Center," Will said.

"That place was always off limits for me in the winter," Stanley said. "Too *goyishe* with all those angels and the giant tree. I think my parents figured if I looked at it long enough, I'd turn into a Methodist."

"So naturally you spent every waking hour hanging around the skating rink," Van teased him.

"Naturally."

"See why I'm irresistible?" Van complained. "It has nothing to do with *me*. I'm just another Christmas decoration."

Stanley went on: "I saw myself as this choirboy type, all robed and ethereal, singing *Silent Night* with the Italians down the block. They had fantastic stuff in their windows—Santa Claus and Rudolph with this big fat flashing neon nose. Shit. Finally my parents had no choice but to play Chanukah for all it was worth. I got a present every night for eight nights, and my mother made potato pancakes till they were bursting out of my—"

"Not to worry," Van broke in. "Next year we'll have eight days of *dreydls* and holly." She and Stanley exchanged a look full of secrets.

"You tell them," Stanley said. His brown eyes were glistening.

"We're getting married in August," Van announced.

"What?" Quinn whooped. She leapt up and threw her arms around them both, practically lying across the table to accomplish the embrace. "Wonderful! I can't believe it! Of course I can believe it!"

Will was beaming. He shook hands with Stanley and leaned over to kiss Van. "Come on, let's celebrate." He held up his hand and called imperiously. "Waiter!"

Quinn giggled. "Look at this."

The waiter appeared, and Will said, "Champagne. Your best New York State, but no twist-off top, if you please. We shall have a cork."

Will opened the bottle, which obliged by making a

resounding pop. Then he and Quinn slid out of the booth and stood with glasses held high.

"To the bride and groom," Will said solemnly. "Happiness together always."

They drank, then Stanley half rose from his seat and pronounced, "To Quinn Mallory, the toast of New York, to her success. To chutzpah."

"Thank you," Quinn said with a forced smile.

The silence that followed grew heavy. Quinn quickly began to pepper Van and Stanley with questions about the impending marriage. Every time Quinn glanced at Will, his face looked absent. She imagined that his eyes were filled with reflections of pine trees and white-capped mountains.

It was 1:00 A.M. when they started back toward campus. Stanley and Will walked ahead while the girls strolled along behind, arm in arm.

"I like to think of you ten years from now," Quinn said. "God, you'll probably have a couple of little kids crawling around. Mrs. Vanessa Markowitz and her brood."

Van laughed. "Vanessa Huntington Markowitz."

"I think you ought to hyphenate it."

"What about you and Will?"

"Oh, well—"

"You're going to New York after graduation and he hasn't said anything about changing his plans, and I sort of wondered . . ."

"You might just be a bridesmaid yourself one of these days," Quinn blurted.

Van stopped short and stared at Quinn. Then she hugged her. "That's terrific! Why didn't you tell me?"

"Well, it's not exactly formal," Quinn said.

Van started running, dragging Quinn by the arm. Before Quinn could stop her, Van had caught up to the others and thrown her arms around Will.

"You sneaks. All that time we were babbling on and on about our own plans, and here you two are holding out on us."

Stanley and Will looked equally stunned. Quinn's face was burning.

"They're getting married too," Van explained to Stanley patiently.

"Hey, that's fantastic!" Stanley gathered Quinn into a lung-crushing bear hug. Her eyes, over his shoulder, implored Will.

"This makes everything perfect," Van said.

Quinn took Will's hand and clung to it. His fingers were as stiff as his smile.

Stanley watched them carefully.

"Uh, we'll go on ahead," Van said finally. "See you at the dorm." She pulled Stanley's arm, and they were soon just shadows under the streetlights far ahead.

Will's face appeared to have frozen over. Quinn was afraid that if he opened his mouth or blinked, he would crack right down the middle, forehead to chin, like a glacier cleft by a jagged fissure.

"I don't know how it happened, Will," she said. "It just slipped out before I knew I even thought it. Then she just, well, it was too late and she got to you before I could stop her." Tears had begun to fall down her cheeks.

"Is this your way of making things all right?" The face didn't crack, but she felt a blast of polar air.

She shook her head. "I don't know."

"Well, you sure as hell complicated things. Jesus."

She let go of the rigid fingers. "They were so happy and I guess I just wanted us—"

"How do you think I felt?" he interrupted angrily.

"It was as if you were sticking pins in me. We're not going to get married, Quinn. It's cruel what you did."

"It's cruel to me, too." Her voice broke. "Don't you think it hurts me, too? Ever since we got back from New York, it's been awful. We can't even talk to each other." She was crying in earnest now, choking out her words between sobs. Will's face began to thaw. Out of remorse he touched her arm lightly. They started walking toward the campus gate now visible up ahead. Stanley and Van were just entering. Their shadows made a grotesque shape with four legs.

"Well, then, I guess it's time we talk," he said. "We sure as hell can't keep this up."

Fear had taken Quinn's voice away.

"Tonight was just the beginning," he continued. "We're only going to keep on hurting each other. Let's not drag it out."

"Oh, Will."

"Do you see any way?"

"I'll come with you to Idaho. Maybe—"

He interrupted her. "You going to turn down the Manning job? It's a phenomenal break. You'd hate me in three minutes."

"Can't we stay together until summer?"

"No."

"You sure don't seem very willing to fight for it."

"Not when there's no point."

"How can you just give up like this?" The tears stopped. A tiny splinter of anger floated to the top of her sea of misery. It felt good. She clung to it, using it as a life raft to keep her from drowning in her own helplessness.

"It depends on how you want it to end," he said.

There was challenge in his voice, she thought. Maybe

he needed anger too. Well, God damn him, he was going to have it. "Got any suggestions?" Her voice was as cold as his.

"No."

"Just like that." She looked up at the lights of the women's dormitory just ahead and wondered how they could have gotten to the end so fast.

"I'll walk you to the door," he said.

"Don't bother."

"I said I'll walk you."

Both of them felt finality swallow them up in a great roaring wave, all splinters pitifully useless now. They stopped at the door and averted their faces from the other couples who were kissing good night.

"Oh, God," Quinn said.

Will turned without a word and walked quickly away.

Van went straight to Quinn's room. The door was closed. When she tapped on it, there was no answer.

"Quinn, it's me," she called softly. "Hey."

Still no answer.

"Come on, let me in." She tapped louder. "I'm going to stay here all night unless you let me see you're okay."

There was a muffled noise.

"I guess that means come in," Van said, and stepped inside.

Quinn was huddled on her bed in the dark. "Close the door," she said.

"I can't see you."

"Exactly." The voice was barely recognizable.

Van shut the door and groped her way to the bed. She put her hand on Quinn's back. It felt steamy. "What happened?" she asked, her voice hushed in the presence of tangible misery.

"It's finished."

Van restrained an exclamation of shock.

"I'm such a jerk," Quinn sniffed. "All that stuff about getting married. I don't know. I just got carried away. I want it so much and I can't figure out how, so I just said it, I guess. He was so angry. You wouldn't believe the way he looked at me. Will. You know our Will. He wouldn't swat a spider if it sat on his nose, and for a minute I thought he might even hit me." She started crying again. "Oh, shit. I can't believe this."

"You'll work it out," Van said. "Really you will."

Quinn shook her head. "It's a curse, this job thing. I'd go live with him in Siberia if that's where he wants to go, but he says no. He says I'd hate him."

Van was silent.

"He's right. I would."

"Don't you think he'd get used to the city?"

"Oh, it was pathetic, Van, like watching a wild animal in a cage. He tried. Every time a siren went past, he was in torture." She reached for a tissue, blew her nose, and poked at her pillow in disgust. "It's going to take three weeks for this thing to dry out. Christ Almighty, how did I let myself get mixed up with that guy?"

"He's something special, that's how."

"Listen, Huntington, can't you be a friend and tell me what a shithead he is?" Their eyes had adjusted to the dark and they stared at one another helplessly, two pale moons in the murkiness. Quinn gave Van a wan smile. "Thing is, I can't figure out how I'm going to live without him."

Van thought of Stanley and her eyes filled with tears.

Quinn said, "Oh, for God's sake, don't you start or they'll have to come in here with a pump. Go on. I'm okay now. Thanks. It helped."

Van hugged her, the long dark hair cool and smooth against Quinn's hot cheek.

"Van," Quinn whispered. "I'm so glad about you and Stanley."

"I know."

Van stood in the doorway for a moment. The hall light shone on Quinn's puffy face.

"Don't worry. I'll get over it," Quinn said.

Chapter 26

But she didn't get over it. Each morning Quinn would wake up at 7:00 A.M., eager as always to jump out of bed and plunge into the day. It took about three seconds to remember, and then she wanted to roll over and go back to sleep. Sometimes she woke up crying before she knew why, and slunk through the hours with swollen eyes. She would stare at herself in the mirror and marvel that she didn't look more sickly.

The worst was seeing him. They knew each other's schedules well enough to avoid confrontation when possible, but there were the three English classes. The first Monday, Professor Buxby raised his eyebrows when they took seats on opposite sides of the room. Mercifully, he did not remark on it. Quinn experimented with her view, and by Friday had discovered that if she chose the front left-hand corner of the classroom, only half a dozen students were easily visible. Neither she nor Will spoke up in class. Professor Buxby, making his own guesses, left them alone.

The dormitory on Saturday night was an eerie place. Everyone, even poor Mavis Underwell, had gone out. Quinn decided to take advantage of the silence and get into bed early. Surviving the week had worn her out.

She expected to fall asleep immediately, but instead lay in the dark and wondered what Will was doing. She imagined him out with another girl, perhaps the small dark-haired one she'd once seen him with. Maybe he was kissing her, or worse. She squirmed with jealousy, and flung herself over on her stomach. Time to start naming nuns.

Instead of beginning with kindergarten, tonight she would work her way back from senior year, in imitation of anesthesia. One hundred; ninety-nine, ninety-eight; Sister Mary-Catherine; Sister Edwina; Sister Celestina; Sister Carmine—God, what a horror; Sister Margaret-with-the-Moustache; Sister Philippa. Who else that year? Sister Penelope, the home economics teacher. Quinn amused herself by inserting Will's face into a wimple. Sister Wilhelmina. He would have made a great nun, she thought. Better than her, for certain.

It was useless. The lump formed in her throat. Oh, no, you don't, she vowed. Her pillow could not absorb another drop. She remembered an old shirt of Will's, borrowed weeks ago, that hung in her closet. She crept out of bed, found it with her fingers in the dark, and held it to her face. Then she slipped back under the covers, clutched the flannel ball to her midsection until finally she drifted into sleep.

On Tuesday she telephoned home, alerting John and Ann to expect her on Friday evening. A weekend in Medham would snap her out of it. She would take care of Ann, which would force her to stop feeling sorry for herself.

But what Quinn felt when she set eyes on her mother was shock. No one had prepared her for the drastic change in Ann's appearance. Quinn was still calling home twice a week and had always been assured that her mother was improving. Now it was obvious that her parents had either tried to spare their daughter or that they were unwilling to face the truth themselves.

Quinn set down her suitcase and knelt beside the sofa in the living room. She kissed her mother's pale cheek, but very gently, for fear of bruising the skin.

"Why didn't you tell me?" she pleaded. "I would have come home."

"The doctor says I'm doing very nicely. And besides, I don't want you hopping back and forth to Medham when you should be studying. How's Will?"

"I don't really know."

Her mother was silent.

"We're not together anymore."

"You didn't tell us," Ann said. They both smiled, acknowledging their habit of sparing each other bad news.

"Was it the job?" Ann asked.

"Sort of. Yes. We're just so . . . going off in opposite directions." Ann looked terribly sad, so Quinn added, "I tried to pine away, but I think I put on a couple of pounds instead. Anyway, think of all those other young swains out there ready to fall for my considerable charms."

"I'm sorry," Ann said.

"I'll take a shower and come talk to you later," Quinn said. "Have a nap, okay?" Ann's eyes were closed before Quinn was out of the living room.

Instead of showering, Quinn marched out to the driveway to confront her father, who was half-hidden under the hood of his decrepit Ford. He held a flashlight in one hand and with the other fingered wires, twisted bolts, tinkered, and hammered. Quinn knew his absorption, understood the comfort of working with one's hands. The streetlamps cast erratic illumination. If she squinted, Quinn could transform her father into geometric patches of light and dark.

She envied him in silence and admitted to herself that coexistent with the desire to nurse Ann had been the impulse to come home and lick her wounds. Her parents' house had always offered solace. But tonight, instead of warmth and peace, she had found dread. A shadow that had skulked in an inaccessible corner of her mind for months had suddenly expanded into a black monster.

John straightened up and handed her the flashlight. "Hold this, will you?" he said.

She took it. "Why didn't you tell me about Mom?"

John began manipulating spark plugs. "A little closer. That's it."

"The whole way from the bus station, not a word."

"She's doing okay," he said.

"She's not doing okay."

"You've got to have a little faith."

"She needs healthy kidneys, not prayers."

John glanced up at her. "I don't like that kind of talk. All those ideas you get up at college don't make you smarter than the Pope."

"You can't convince me a bunch of Hail Marys and some holy water are going to keep her out of renal failure."

John snatched the flashlight out of her hand. "You're coming to mass with me Sunday morning, girl, and you'll pray for your mother and for forgiveness."

"Oh, come on," she murmured.

John whirled around, his hand raised as if to strike her. She ducked out of his way.

"Just when did you get to be the big theologian?" she blurted angrily. "How can you go to mass and sit there kowtowing when Ann's in there dying? She never hurt anybody in her whole life and she's only forty-six God-damn years old!"

"It's God's will." He held the flashlight like a weapon.

"Bull*shit* it's God's will! There's no way I'll go to church and thank God for doing this to my mother. You're not going to get me down on my knees to that bastard—"

"You shut your mouth," John said. He strode around the front of the car, but Quinn darted toward the side-walk, keeping her eyes on him every moment. Then he stopped short and suddenly deflated. Seconds ago his face had been fiery and his eyes, defying the darkness, had flashed bright green. But now he was washed as colorless as the portrait on Quinn's desk back at school. She halted her backward escape and gaped at him.

"Do what you want," he said finally. He turned and walked into the house.

Quinn stood on the sidewalk for a moment, swallowing hard against the familiar ugly taste that rose in her mouth. Ivory soap. The first time she could remember challenging her father was when she was six years old. She had sassed him and then refused to apologize. John dragged her to the kitchen sink by the pigtails, stuffed a bar of Ivory soap into her mouth, and held her jaw shut. It was a small piece, very shiny and soft. It melted quickly. The punishment proved effective, and was repeated on several occasions until one time Quinn swallowed a large chunk and suffered three days of diarrhea. The technique was thereafter abandoned, but even now an angry look from her father brought the same bitter taste to Quinn's mouth. If she visited a public rest room that offered only Ivory, she washed her hands with water. The lingering sweet scent on her fingers invariably made her gag.

She glanced across the street at the neighbors' windows where faces quickly disappeared. The argument had drawn an audience. Well, they'd witnessed plenty of battles between Quinn and John Mallory, and they'd probably see more. She slammed down the hood of the car and went inside to take her shower.

Dinner was uneventful, with John and Quinn being carefully civil so as to avoid upsetting Ann. It pained Quinn to watch her mother swallow a few slivers of chicken and set down her fork. Afterward Quinn cleaned up while John helped Ann to bed. By the time he came down again, Quinn was twenty minutes into *Casablanca.* John sat down gingerly on the sofa next to her and watched in silence. When Ingrid Bergman admitted that she still loved Humphrey Bogart, Quinn began to cry. The tears flowed straight through the foggy finale. John made no comment on the surreptitious sniffling, just fetched a box of Kleenex and tossed it into her lap. She said "Thanks" without looking at him.

He went upstairs after that, but Quinn was too restless for bed. Her thoughts hopped back and forth between Will and her mother. She told herself how pointless it was to dwell on either subject. The trouble was, both were *full* of points, jagged, tearing points that pricked and stabbed, making her raw. She twisted the channel knob. The news was over, and the late movie was a grade D Jane Russell melodrama. Johnny Carson was host to Tiny Tim, displaying him like a freak for the amusement of insomniacs across the nation. She snapped the hirsute soprano off in mid-warble and headed for the kitchen where she consumed six Oreos, two glasses of milk, and a Fig Newton. Then she crept upstairs. Tonight, perhaps, she would have to resort to reading.

Ordinarily she relished the moments before sleep. She would lie in bed in the dark thinking about life. In New York, Will had said she was like a small child in a crib who lay like a turtle on its back, counting toes and reliving the day out loud, reluctantly, gradually, giving it up to sleep. *Mommy*, it says—not calling, just remembering. *Daddy . . . baby . . . stroller . . . rain, rain*—a kind of evening news report to round off the day before relinquishing it. Quinn's presleep ruminations often included the future as well, though perhaps a child's do too. Planning, she called it. Plotting, Will said.

As she tiptoed past her parents' bedroom she saw that the door was ajar. Surprisingly, a light was still on inside. There were strange muffled sounds. Quinn peered through the crack and froze. Her mother sat in the rocking chair by the window. John knelt beside her with his head buried in her lap. He was sobbing quietly. Ann stroked his hair, her own tears falling so that the back of her hand was wet and gleaming. Quinn stared at them with a kind of horror. Her throat felt constricted, as if she were strangling, and yet she could not draw her eyes away from the tableau. She watched in silence as her father lifted his head and pulled Ann's face down to his. They kissed, a deeply passionate kiss, not at all the chaste, mechanical parents' kiss she had observed at least a thousand times, good-bye in the morning, welcome home after work. This was a lovers' kiss.

Quinn crept to her room, taking care to avoid the single groaning floorboard. She sat shaking on the edge of her bed. She felt disoriented, almost as if she were dreaming. In her dream she was standing at a threshold. Behind her was a comfortable room, a bit cramped, perhaps, but familiar. In front of her loomed a cavernous shadowed interior. Furniture with sinister carvings were dwarfed by towering stone walls. She felt an invisible hand pressed cold against the small of her back. A voice whispered *Enter. This is where you belong.* She was like a blind person in this dream, groping and feeling her way. If only she were allowed a few exploratory steps ahead, with comforting visits into the old place every now and then. But the door slammed behind her, and she was all alone.

She shivered. Without undressing she curled herself into a ball under the bedspread and tried to pray. The irony of the impulse after her argument with John did not occur to her. She was a child lost in the dark, turning her face toward a light. *Hail Mary, full of grace, the Lord is with thee. Blessed art thou among women. Blessed is the fruit of thy womb, Jesus.* Mary's face, hooded with gentle blue folds, melted into Ann's, and finally Quinn fell asleep.

Saturday she awoke stiff but rested. She peeled off her jeans and wondered if the seam marks on her thighs would ever disappear. Then she looked out the window at a startling deep-blue sky and imagined that if she reached up, her fingers would touch a solid iridescent shell. The bright morning had burned away the fear and loneliness of last night. She was young, tough, smart. Ann would be strengthened by the mere presence of such vitality. It had to be catching.

And as for William Ingraham, well, what was one less intelligent, sensitive, poetic, sexy person to her anyway? A dime a dozen. She'd just shop around, that's all. She tried to think of someone she could call. Not Tommy, of course. Jim was married. There was Dennis Riley, but his too-pretty face repelled her a little. No sober, reflective types, but someone out for a good time, someone lively. She thought of Johnny Sullivan and wondered what he was up to. He had appeared at her party without a date. When she got angry with Will, she had flirted with Johnny. He teased her and said he had always been crazy about her. She would call him.

They decided upon a movie. Quinn was grateful, since she wasn't sure how much she would feel like talking to him. It would be strange, looking into someone else's face, walking beside a body whose proportions weren't the same as Will's.

They saw *The Pink Panther*. She found herself laughing at the slapstick gags, and she was pleased with Johnny's reaction too. Will was not fond of broad humor. He would have chuckled now and then, perhaps, but Quinn couldn't imagine him howling unabashedly, like Johnny. After the film Quinn felt so grateful that she held hands with him during their short walk to the corner pub. He told her about his job at the print shop.

"It's got a future if I take a couple of courses to learn about the new machines. They're starting with the computers now. You gotta look ahead and protect yourself. The unions can only do so much."

"Do you like it?"

"I don't mind it."

"I'm crazy about machines."

"I remember."

"You must be, too. Presses are really interesting."

Johnny shrugged.

"You going to do it the rest of your life?" she asked. Johnny's hand was smaller than Will's, and his grip was a little too tight. She tried to wriggle her fingers.

"Why not?"

"Well, isn't there something you really want to do?"

"Sure. I want to make a bundle and retire at forty-five."

"Yes, but *then* what would you do?"

He gave her a puzzled look and ushered her inside The Dugout without answering. The bar was noisy and crowded, but a booth soon emptied near the door. Quinn studied the handsome face across the table. Johnny had thick jet hair, blue eyes, an easy smile. He had always been surrounded by admiring girl friends.

"How come we never went out?" Quinn asked him.

"You were always too busy with Flanagan."

"Not all the time, I wasn't."

"I asked you out once."

"You did?" She was surprised.

"See? You were so stuck on him you don't even remember. I heard you'd broke up, so I figured I'd make my move."

She shook her head. She believed him, and it bothered her to think she could have forgotten such a thing.

He ordered hamburgers and a pitcher of beer, and as they ate she asked, "Did you ever really want anything? I mean so much that it screwed everything else up?"

He looked thoughtful for a moment. Then he replied, "Well, yeah, I wanted a white Corvette. I guess I still do, but I wouldn't steal to get it."

"I was thinking more about, I don't know, goals."

Johnny looked away, his eyes searching the bar restlessly. "I don't think so, no. Hey, there's Maureen and Jack Conley. Let's get them over here."

Before Quinn could protest, he had beckoned to them. The four sat reminiscing for an hour and a half—about old times, about the destinies of their classmates; who had kids; who was married; who had a good job. The feeling that she had experienced at the party surfaced again. These were lifelong friends, and yet she was a stranger here now. The others' voices seemed far away. Nothing touched her. She was no longer real. Not without Will. Not without Ann and Jake the way they used to be. She could not get rid of the image of her parents kissing, nor the sound of her father's hoarse sobs, nor the scent of Will Ingraham's body.

"Johnny!" They stared at her. She must have interrupted someone in midsentence. Or perhaps she had shouted. "Take me home, okay?"

"You all right?"

"Uh, no. I think I'm sick. Sorry. Virus or something." Johnny bid a reluctant good night to the Conleys and walked Quinn to his car. They did not hold hands. Johnny was proud of his new, bright blue Chevy, proud that it was almost paid for, and annoyed that Quinn hadn't even remarked about it. She'd changed, that was for sure. She used to be such a good sport, funny, always up to something. And some body on her, too. That hadn't changed, at least. Must be college that did it. He thanked his lucky stars he hadn't bothered with it if it could take the piss and vinegar out of a live wire like Quinn Mallory.

She listened to the tires squeal as he drove away, and thought, well, so much for that.

Sunday morning John asked her in a neutral voice if she would be coming to mass with him. She declined politely. After he left, Quinn made up a tray for her mother. Her inclination was to load it until it sagged under the weight of pancakes, cereal, pastries, and fruit, food to pad Ann's too prominent cheekbones. But she resisted and kept it simple, just two slices of toast, juice, and a cup of tea. Otherwise the leftovers would be too discouraging for them both.

Ann was propped up in bed reading the Sunday

Globe, with her glasses perched on the end of her nose. When Quinn appeared, she whipped them off.

"Vanity, vanity," Quinn said, setting down the tray. "You look nice in glasses. How come you're always hiding them?"

"Oh, it's silly. I keep thinking I just got them and have to adjust." She laughed. "It must be ten years now. How lovely, dear. This is really very nice. Come sit."

Quinn sat on the end of the bed, cross-legged as always, sipping her coffee. Ann munched deliberately at her toast.

"How do you feel?" Quinn asked.

"All right. Fine."

"No. I don't want the bullshit. I want to know really."

Ann regarded her daughter over the rim of her teacup.

"I need to get ready," Quinn said. "If I have to. Do I have to?"

"I'm not getting any better."

"Today you're not, or this week? Or ever?"

"Darling—"

"Please, Mom. It's the not knowing I can't take. It's no protection being in the dark. You just trip yourself up."

"Well, Quinn, sometimes I'm not so sure who I'm trying to protect." Ann's eyes filled with tears. "I think you give me too much credit."

"I feel like I can't talk to you anymore about anything. Not with this big question hanging here." She traced a giant question mark in the air above their heads.

"All right." Ann paused, then stretched out her hand to touch Quinn's foot. "I think God's made up His mind about me."

Quinn dropped her eyes. In a moment the tears that

had collected at the tip of her nose splashed onto the bedspread. "How long?" she asked in a choked voice.

"I don't know. It gets a little better, then a lot worse. I've had estimates anywhere from six months to a few years."

"Estimates," Quinn echoed.

"I'm sorry, darling."

Quinn looked up fiercely. "Don't apologize." She swiped at the tears with the back of her hand, the way she had done as a child. "What does Dr. Gunther say?"

"He's not guessing."

Quinn was silent.

"I don't know how to help you live with this," Ann said.

Quinn blew her nose. "You're going to have to put up with a lot of tender loving care, that's for damn sure. I'm not going to leave you alone. You'll throw up at the very sight of me."

Ann touched Quinn's toes one by one, her fingers remembering the old game: *This little pig went to market.* "I can't imagine having a child who could give me more pleasure." The next thing she knew, Quinn was in her arms, sobbing.

"Oh, Mommy, I love you. Please don't leave me. Please."

The cups had spilled onto the bed, coffee and tea soaking all the way through to the mattress. But Ann just held her daughter's trembling body and let her grieve.

Chapter 27

Despite the formal disbanding of the Big Brother program, an earnest sophomore named Steve Sawyer had volunteered to replace Will for Harvey Jackson. At four o'clock in the afternoon on a brilliant early April Thursday, Will and Steve stood in the doorway of Harvey's building. Will was despondent. He stared at the graffiti—a new artist had been hard at work. Primary blue paint to match the primary blue spring sky. *Cops suck.* Someone else had smeared the "Cops" with white paint and substituted "Pigs."

"Pretty grim," Steve said, looking around.

Will nodded. Was graffiti a symptom of the decade, he wondered, or was the impulse for public inscription a timeless one? He thought of the stone walls surrounding medieval English towns. Perhaps in centuries past there had been scribblings on those rough surfaces, too. *Alison doon it up-swa-dune.*

"How long is he going to be?" Steve asked. Reluctantly, Will shook himself into the present. He seemed to be dwelling in past history a lot these days. Steve rapped his knuckles against the doorjamb in a nervous drumbeat.

Finally they heard footsteps descending the stairway inside, not the usual eager clatter but measured, dutiful, soldier steps. Will chastised himself for delaying today's confrontation. *Here, kid. Here's your new surrogate Dad. You like?*

"Harvey Jackson, Steve Sawyer," Will said.

Harvey stuck out his hand, but kept his eyes on the floor. Steve sent Will a look of dismay.

"Come on, let's go shoot some pool," Will said. In trying to figure out how to win Harvey over, he had sat in Steve's room last night, asking questions and delving into Steve's motivations for volunteering. There was something reminiscent of Stanley Markowitz in Steve Sawyer, a clean-cut version. Like Stan he was gentle, dark, rounded at the edges. Steve gave an initial impression of reserve; his room, however, was anything but quiet. Rock 'n' roll pounded throughout Will's visit, and there were posters taped from ceiling to floor: Ike and Tina Turner, Chuck Berry, Little Stevie Wonder, Ray Charles.

It came out that Steve was proficient at billiards. Harvey appreciated competence, so Will's decision was to spend the afternoon beside a green felt table. Unfortunately, the only game close enough to Harvey's apartment was in the bowling alley of the first disastrous outing with Quinn. Will hoped Harvey would associate the place with his present regard for her rather than his initial sullen resistance.

Will was not looking forward to being there himself. He remembered too well Quinn's rueful grin after her ball had crashed to the floor and wobbled into the gutter. He remembered her triumph when she had accomplished a strike. Small body, compact energy, easily mastering the necessary motions. Jesus. He closed his eyes against the memories, but they clung inside his lids, images in merciless rerun.

"How's school?" he heard Steve ask Harvey. The bus

was coming, thank God. How long had they been standing at the curb in silence?

"Okay," Harvey answered in monotone.

Damn her, Will thought. She was not going to screw this up, too. He vowed to concentrate on the matter at hand.

Will did most of the talking. First he spoke to Harvey, then he spoke to Steve, taking it slow. He had thought about the seats, and engineered it so that Harvey sat between them in the back row. There would be Will's familiar body on one side and Steve's on the other. Let Harvey get used to Steve's size and bulk.

Steve showed Harvey how to choose a stick and chalk the tip, while Will talked to the attendant, bribing him with five dollars extra to let them remain uninterrupted past the allotted half hour, just in case it worked.

Steve broke first. The balls careened around the table, and the green solid ticked into a corner pocket. Harvey tried to look bored. Steve showed him how to rest the cue against the fleshy part beside his thumb. He drew the unwieldy stick back and plunged it into the felt. It missed the ball altogether.

"This is stupid," he muttered.

"My turn," Will said. His ball struck two others, neither of which landed in a pocket. Steve chalked his cue as he circled the table, checking out possibilities. Will prayed for a truly impressive shot. He wasn't disappointed. The ball bounced off the side, clicked gently against the solid red, and spun it neatly into the center pocket. Will glanced at Harvey. The boy's black eyes said *I know what you're doing. So he's good. Big deal.* Will sighed.

Finally, Steve missed. There were only three balls left on the table, with the cue ball positioned so that it was in a direct line with the striped blue. What's more, the shot was within easy reach of Harvey's ten-year-old arms. When Harvey bent over the table, Steve winked at Will.

The cue ball struck the blue striped, and it plunked into the pocket, clean and swift.

"Way to go!" Steve said.

Harvey smiled, not exactly at Steve, but in his general direction. Steve put his hand on Harvey's shoulder. Instantly the boy froze and moved away. Steve realized his mistake at once and winced. Will watched the exchange. Steve was a sensitive guy, he decided. It was going to be okay. He felt a sudden bleak loneliness. *Come on, Harve. Put up more of a fight. I'm losing you, too.*

They ate in the coffee shop attached to the bowling alley. Steve sat across from Will in the seat Quinn had occupied. Under the table she had wrapped her stocking feet around his ankles, crawling up his leg with her toes until every piece of erectile tissue in his body stood at attention. When Harvey had wanted another Coke, Will had asked Quinn in a croaking voice if she would fetch it.

"I'll treat you to a hot fudge sundae," Steve said.

Harvey glanced suspiciously at Will. It was his favorite treat. "I'm not hungry," he said.

"Get one for yourself, Steve," Will suggested. "If you don't eat it all, somebody will."

Harvey's eyes narrowed. *I will not.*

Harvey had nearly finished his Coke. Will nursed a cup of coffee, and the only thing melting was Steve's gooey sundae. Nobody was saying anything. Will began to despair. He was exhausted. The jukebox blared: "I wanna hold your hand." Your gland, Quinn always piped. Will had never known a girl who was so comfortable with profanity. Ironic that she was Catholic, though perhaps that was why. He'd give it some thought. No, he would *not* give it some thought.

He slipped out of the booth. "Going to the john," he explained. Steve and Harvey looked at him in mutual panic.

On his way back from the bathroom Will dropped a quarter in the jukebox and pressed K-4 three times: *Fingertips*. Neither Harvey nor Steve saw him do it. When he got back to the table, they were sitting as before, silent and miserable.

As soon as the music started, Will began to fret. "Explain something to me, Harve. What do you see in this stuff?"

"That's Little Stevie *Wonder*, man," Harvey protested.

"I heard he's working on a new album," Steve said. "The best one ever."

Harvey stopped fiddling with his straw.

"Don't tell me you're a fan," Will said to Steve, remembering the posters and the thumping cacophony of Steve's room. The record began again: "Jesus, what are they trying to do to me?"

"I've got every disk he ever cut," Steve said with a touch of reverence.

This was too much for Harvey. "Yeah?" he said, looking directly at Steve for the first time.

Steve nodded. "People keep saying he's finished, but I don't think so."

"Right," Harvey said. "He's a real genius, man, and he's only a kid." Suddenly he caught himself and clamped his mouth shut tight.

Steve waited a moment, then said quietly, "He's coming to Springfield for Memorial Day."

"You're shittin' me," Harvey said, glancing at Will for confirmation. Will shrugged. What did he know about such things?

"I've got tickets."

"Wow," Harvey whispered.

"You want to go?"

Harvey couldn't believe it. Steve smiled at the astonished face, and Will felt his throat tighten. *'Bye, Harve.*

"Yeah, man," Harvey breathed finally. "I wanna go."

"Good." Steve was matter-of-fact. "I was looking for somebody with real appreciation."

Harvey eyed the soupy remains of Steve's hot fudge sundae. "You gonna eat that?"

Steve shook his head and slid it over. The boy dug in.

Fingertips began its cycle on the jukebox again. When Will groaned, Harvey laughed out loud.

Chapter 28

Quinn kept finding excuses to delay her departure. First she decided to take the late bus back Sunday night. Then, as Sunday afternoon wore on, she began to talk about how she could work on her Religion term paper in the Medham library and go back to school later in the week. She waited on Ann constantly, bringing her cup after cup of tea, fetching magazines Ann hadn't asked for, and hovering either at bedside or just outside the door.

While Quinn doted, Ann grew increasingly anxious. No one in the family had ever achieved a college education. And here Quinn was so close. Ann saw her daughter's degree being sabotaged, perhaps forever. On the other hand, every moment spent together felt precious now.

At eight o'clock that evening Ann said to Quinn, "Pack your bag."

"What?" Quinn said. She had just plunked herself down on the end of the bed to read Ann another chapter from *Travels with Charley*.

"Get off my bed and pack. You're going to be on that ten o'clock bus and make no mistake about it."

Quinn stretched out her hand imploringly. But Ann's face did not yield. Quinn dipped her head.

"Go on," Ann urged.

Slowly, wordlessly, Quinn crept off the bed and left the room. When the door clicked shut, Ann clasped John's pillow to her face and wept.

John drove Quinn to the bus station. The atmosphere inside the Ford was relaxed, the steam from their argument having evaporated out of a shared concern for Ann. This morning as Quinn had watched John go off to mass in his best blue suit with his hair slick from the shower, she vowed to restrain herself from further outbursts against God. If religion offered him consolation, she wasn't going to spoil it.

Quinn tossed her suitcase on the bed at 1:00 A.M. and without unpacking sat down to write Ted Manning a letter turning down the job. She felt no conflict, only gratitude that there was something in her life worth sacrificing. *If I lay this lamb at your feet, God, will you give me back my mother?* The pain felt good.

Her reading assignments sat neglected on her desk in piles that looked like the Manhattan skyline. For the past two weeks everything had seemed so pointless. The only thing that mattered now was somehow enduring until graduation, grabbing her diploma, and hurrying home to care for Ann.

Wednesday evening she was on the garage floor under a broken fuel line when Gus appeared to tell her there was a phone call. She stood up and wiped the grease off trembling fingers.

Carefully Gus said, "It's Vanessa."

"Oh." Quinn had never spoken with Gus about not seeing Will anymore, but he knew.

"You've had a call from Springfield General," Van said. "It's Harvey."

Quinn's heart began to thump. She clung to the phone, dreading what she would hear, yet frantic for information.

"There's been some trouble at home and he was hurt. Will's there and wants you to meet him in Pediatrics."

"Do you know the floor?"

"Five. Quinn, he's all right."

"Thanks. I'm on my way."

Quinn stripped off her overalls and borrowed the campus pickup truck. She took the highway rather than the more direct route through the residential streets. Stop signs were intolerable. What she wanted was speed.

She tried to prepare herself. A dismayed expression on her face would frighten Harvey. She wanted to comfort, not inflict more pain.

Simmering beneath her fright was the realization that she would see Will. Soon. Despite her effort to suppress it, there was a stirring of hope.

Just inside the Emergency entrance was a narrow slot marked "Official Vehicles Only." She pulled in. The university insignia on the truck was official enough.

The nurse at the fifth-floor reception desk directed her to Harvey's room with an admonition to keep it short. These were not formal visiting hours.

Three of the four beds were unoccupied, with Harvey a small lump in the other. Will's back was toward Quinn, but she could see that he was holding the boy's hand. She moved to the bedside. Harvey seemed to be asleep. His left eye was bruised purple, and swollen to the size of a fist. The long eyelashes were invisible. An ugly slash down his cheek had required eight stitches, and a plaster cast on his shoulder forced his right arm to jut out at a bizarre angle.

"God," Quinn said. Will turned and she saw his face through a watery blur. "What happened?"

"Leroy." Will's voice was strange. She must have forgotten the sound of it. She stared at him numbly without understanding.

"Leroy did this," he repeated. Quinn realized now that the unrecognizable color in his voice was something she had never heard there before. It was hatred.

"Why?" she asked.

"He was drunk."

"What about that eye?"

"They say it'll be okay. Everything's superficial." Quinn understood the bitter irony. There were internal injuries that would never heal.

"He was so scared," Will said.

Quinn's stomach felt as if it had been kicked hard. She put one hand on her solar plexus and reached out with the other to touch Harvey's soft kinky hair. "Baby," she whispered. He was so small. His feet made little points in the sheets halfway down the bed.

"Where's his mother?"

"At the police station trying to get Leroy off."

Quinn shook her head. "How'd he get here?"

"They brought him in a cab, and the hospital called the cops."

"But how did you find out?"

"The resident in Emergency called the school. Apparently he kept crying for me and wouldn't let anybody near him. They couldn't stitch him up until I got here." He gazed out the window into the dark, remembering. "What a mess. Thank Christ they took the other two away before I got here. I would have murdered them both."

She believed him. The quiet voice did not dilute the ferocity of his rage. Her own anger lifted a little in the presence of his, and she was able to think about what they should do now.

"Can we get him out of that house?"

"I don't think so."

"Then we've got to find a way to keep him safe. Somebody's got to scare the shit out of Leroy."

"He was so blasted I don't think he even knew what he'd done."

"What if we take him away for a little while. Medham . . . somewhere."

Suddenly she stopped herself. There was Quinn and there was Will, but there was no longer a "we."

"We'll think of something," Will said. The tiny particle of hope quivered again. Quinn noticed he was wearing the Christmas sweater she'd knit for him.

A nurse swished into the room. "You'll have to leave. It's past visiting hours, and we only made an exception because the patient was so upset."

Will sat. Quinn knew no one could pry him out of that chair until he was ready to leave.

"I don't want him to wake up and be alone," Will said.

"He won't wake up, sir. He's had a sedative."

"We can take turns sitting with him, just for tonight," Quinn said. "We'd be very unobtrusive, and there's nobody else in here."

The nurse smiled. "I know it's hard to leave him. But listen, I'll look in every fifteen minutes all night long. I promise. I can also promise he won't wake up until it's light."

Reassured, Will got to his feet. He swayed a little.

"You okay?" Instinctively, Quinn touched his arm. With the physical contact she recoiled as if he were electrified.

"I don't want to go," he murmured, mainly to Harvey.

"Please," the nurse urged them. "I won't let you down."

They left the room and walked down the hushed hallway to the elevators.

Will and Quinn were back together again. Neither of them wished to examine the reasons, since what had changed was that Harvey now wore a shoulder cast and a nasty scar on his face. Nothing else.

Quinn had received a personal letter from Ted Manning, offering Quinn his sympathies regarding her mother and a job with an affiliate news program in Boston. He assured her that the door was open whenever she felt ready to come to New York. Quinn waited several days before she mentioned the letter to Will, and when she did, it was without joy.

On Thursday afternoon, two weeks after Harvey's hospitalization, Will and Quinn were drinking coffee in the union. Will was about to head for the bus to the North End.

Quinn grumbled over her newspaper. "Would you look at what Johnson's doing to his dog? Somebody ought to pick *him* up by the ears." Suddenly she cried out. "Hey! Guess who's coming to Ferguson's this weekend."

"Mm." Will was engrossed in his philosophy notes.

"Will, listen, the entire cast of Harvey's favorite TV show, *Infinity*. They're making a promotional tour for the movie. Wouldn't Harve go ape?"

"That's the cartoon thing," Will said absently, outlining a sentence with yellow Magic Marker.

Quinn snatched it from his hand. "It's a regular science fiction program. Harvey'd give up hot fudge for life if he got a chance to see those guys."

Will was paying attention now. "When?"

She folded her paper open to the advertisement and read. "Uh . . . Filene's Friday, Ferguson's Saturday. This Saturday afternoon." She looked up. "Let me take him by myself. I want to do something special for him, and Thursdays are shot now with the cafeteria job."

"I think he'd be ecstatic."

"Tell him I'll pick him up at one, and he should wear his Sunday best. We'll go out to dinner afterward, a fancy date."

"Did you get this worked up to go out with me?"

She forced a smile. "Saturday night without you ain't champagne, believe me."

"Root beer?"

"Flat root beer, with a lousy aftertaste."

"I know the feeling." He regarded her for a moment. Finally he said, "Are we ever going to talk?"

"Not if I can help it."

He shook his head.

"Let's just drift for a while, okay?" She grabbed her stomach. "I'm still trying to stick my guts back inside."

"I suppose the solution is a lobotomy for us both."

"Good," she said. "We could sit on the front porch in our rocking chairs, holding hands and gazing blankly into space. Forever."

"What am I going to do with you?"

"Sure and it's damned if I know, lad."

"Lad?"

"Did I say that?"

"You did indeed."

"I used to do that with Jake sometimes when I wanted something. Colleening around. 'Ah, and it's me, Daddy, your own girl Quinn' and all that."

"What're you after now?" Will stretched his hand across the table, slipped it behind her neck, and drew his fingers up through her hair. Her eyes were deep blue, with the glistening black flecks he had noticed in Ann's. Maybe Quinn was becoming more like her mother.

"Your ass," Quinn said.

Will laughed. Then again, maybe she wasn't.

"What?" she asked.

He shook his head and began gathering his papers together. "Steve's waiting at the bus stop." He gave her a quick kiss on the mouth and strode toward the door. She watched him leave, thinking that when he really wanted to move, he could be plenty fast on his feet.

The clock over the exit told her she had twenty minutes before leaving for the cafeteria. Twenty minutes to think, and nothing safe to think about.

"Hi," Stanley said, plunking down his books.

Quinn flung her arms around his waist. "I love you, Stan," she said.

He laughed. "They all do." Extricating himself, he took a close look at her. Then he set about cheering her up with stories of mayhem in the Markowitz family regarding the Great August Disaster, which was how the wedding had come to be known. How the Markowitzes wanted to hold the ceremony in a kosher hotel in the Catskills and how the Huntingtons insisted it transpire in their living room, where they could serve watercress sandwiches instead of chopped chicken liver.

The twenty minutes flew by.

Chapter 29

On Saturday morning Quinn put on her best sweater—pale lime-green cashmere—and her gray wool skirt. As she slipped into high heels she felt a twinge, hastily quelled, remembering the last time she'd worn them, for the interview with Ted Manning in New York. Well, anyway, the mirror said that today was a particularly good day. Her hair had dried just right, and this morning's phone call to Medham had left her feeling optimistic about Ann.

Van walked in while she was contemplating her reflection. "Well, Vanity, and where are you going, may I ask?"

"I've got a hot date this afternoon. Don't I look smashing?" Quinn reached into the recesses of her closet for the treasured green topcoat, carefully bagged in plastic. "Harvey Jackson and I are going to meet some very important television stars. And then we are going out to supper at a chic spot where they serve wine and Shirley Temples." She planted a kiss by Van's ear and breezed out the door. "Don't wait up," she called.

It was a brilliant cool spring day that even the litter-strewn streets of the North End could not eclipse. She was a little early, but Harvey was already waiting for her in the doorway of his tenement. From a block away she could see him peering through a pane of broken glass. She walked briskly past a group of black teen-agers who were bouncing a ball off the roof of a stripped automobile. Harvey emerged from the doorway and approached her with the dignity befitting his formal attire.

"You look wonderful," she said. He was wearing the shoes Will had bought for him, navy blue and polished to a glassy shine. His slacks, hand-me-downs from someone on the block, were gray, his shirt white with tiny blue stripes, his tie black watch plaid, and his jacket deep green.

"We even match," Quinn said. She pirouetted for him. "What do you think?"

"Nice," Harvey said. The flesh around his left eye was still yellow. The stitches had been removed from the cut on his cheek, but the scar's track was clearly visible.

"I look like Frankenstein, right?" he asked.

"You're too glamorous for Frankenstein." She touched his shoulder carefully. "Where's your cast?"

"They strapped me up in a Ace bandage." The jacket was a size too big and hung loosely.

"You're going to need a coat."

"No!" Harvey said fiercely.

Quinn realized he did not want to spoil the effect of his outfit with a baseball jacket. There was no other coat in his closet. She drew him close to her as they walked down the street.

"I'll keep you warm," she said.

"Did you catch the show this morning?" Harvey asked. "Leroy let me watch and I didn't even do the garbage."

At the mention of the name, Quinn felt her back teeth clamp together. Leroy had been released the morning after Harvey's hospitalization with a warning from the police department. Ever since, Quinn had found herself constructing fantasies of revenge. She imagined Leroy being mugged by a gang of toughs who would torture him before beating him senseless. The final blow, administered with a heavy fist to the left eye, was always accompanied by a howl of angry voices raised in unison. *This one's for Harvey*. Once at night Quinn dreamed that she broke into Leroy's closet and systematically ripped up all the fancy finery that provided his self-respect. Hatred had never been a part of Quinn's nature; she resented Leroy all the more for introducing her to it.

Harvey machine-gunned a trash can. "You shoulda seen Marfax. Oh, man, he was great this mornin'. There's this monster after Golon, y'know, the chick, and he was this real greasy, re-VOLT-in' snaky thing . . ." He wriggled away from her and skipped up ahead, making grotesque faces and clawing the air with his hands. "An' Marfax, he jus' hangs in there cool, bidin' his time with them magic eyeballs, ready to zap anythin' that breathes, and . . . eep, erng, erng, here comes the monster with Golon hangin' out of his big slimy claw, and she's screechin' her brains out, and WHAMMO! Magic eyeballs to the rescue! And the monster, man, he drops Golon like she's electrified, and then he kicks it . . ." Harvey performed his rendition of a monster succumbing. "Ungh, ooo, uhh . . . ahhh." He started to drop to the pavement but caught himself just in time to preserve the Sunday best. Then he flashed Quinn a smile of such gentle complacency that she grabbed his sleeve and captured him in a hug.

Harvey's limit for such demonstrations was three seconds, tops. When she released him, he marched beside her, matching his strides to hers. "You really think Marfax is gonna be there himself?"

"Yup."

On the bus trip downtown Harvey provided her with a historical overview of the *Infinity* adventures, beginning with the very first program two years ago through this morning's show. The gaps due to Leroy's intervention had been filled in by detailed cross-examination of Harvey's friends.

The ground floor of Ferguson's Department Store was crowded with Mother's Day shoppers. As Quinn and Harvey passed the lingerie counter, a saleswoman eyed them curiously. Quinn was trying to imagine the speculations she and Harvey must be engendering, when up the aisle shuffled a robot. Harvey spotted him first.

"Zindar!" he shouted. "Quinn, hey, look, man! It's Zindar!"

The robot stopped, whirred, and projected a stiff hand toward Harvey. A pair of brown eyes glistened behind the aluminum helmet.

"Oh-humanoid-you-come-to-observe-Infinity," the robot intoned.

Harvey was overwhelmed. He gazed up at Zindar, speechless.

"You-shall-encounter-Marfax-on-Eight," Zindar said. "I-will-shake-the-hand-of-the-female-humanoid." He picked up Quinn's hand with his silver gloves. One brown eye winked at her.

"Thanks, Zandor," Quinn said.

"Zindar!" Harvey howled.

"I beg your pardon," Quinn said humbly.

The robot bowed in little rigid lurches and made his way, ticking and humming, toward a group of children half hidden behind the glove counter. Their faces were fascinated and terrified.

"Infinity-on-Eight, Infinity-on-Eight," intoned the receding Zindar.

"Wow!" Harvey breathed. "Come on! Marfax is up there! Shee-*yit*!" He tugged on Quinn's hand. "Man, I hope he brung them magic eyeballs."

On the eighth floor a replica of the *Infinity* spacecraft had been constructed against one entire wall. Above the huge model the word "Infinity" flashed in pulsating red light bulbs. The show's soundtrack boomed and throbbed. A young man in astronaut gear guarded the display. He wore a button on his chest that announced: *I work for Ferguson's. Let me help.*

"Hi," Quinn said. "Where's the crew?"

The astronaut peered inside the rocket. "Don't know. I just came on."

"Zindar said they were on Eight," Quinn said. Harvey slipped his hand into hers.

"Who?"

"Zindar. The robot on the ground floor."

"Just a minute." He headed for the service desk.

Quinn looked at Harvey. The boy's face was heavy with disappointment.

In a moment the guard returned with a sheet of paper. "Says here *Infinity* crew . . . hm, hm . . . yeah." He checked his watch. "Should of been here a half hour ago, and stayed till three. Try Nine. They were scheduled for noon up there in Children's Shoes."

"Okay. Thanks." They hurried to the escalator, but Harvey's excitement had become tentative. Quinn was tugging at him now.

The salesman on Nine said *Infinity* had passed through his department about twelve thirty. It was now one fifty. Weren't they supposed to be on Eight? Quinn explained. The salesman fingered his *Let Me Help* button.

"Well, try the Cafeteria on Five. They were down there earlier. The kids went crazy."

"Let's take the elevator," Quinn said.

Harvey was quiet. His scar formed a rough exclamation point that punctuated the yellow stain beneath his eye. Quinn resisted an impulse to kick the elevator door.

A serpentine lunch line had formed on Five outside the cafeteria, but there was no *Infinity*.

"Stay here," she commanded Harvey. "Excuse me," she said to the cashier, "but do you know if *Infinity* is going to be here?"

"What's that, miss?" The cash register clanged open.

"*Infinity*," Quinn repeated. "From the television show."

"Don't know anything about that. Better try Eight. That's where they have all the kiddie stuff."

Quinn marched back to Harvey. He checked her face for good news, then dropped his eyes as they began to fill with tears. She ushered him toward the escalator, taking care not to jostle the injured shoulder. She stalked up the moving stairs with Harvey scrambling along behind.

Ferguson's astronaut stood where they had left him, his face alternating steadily between pink and white with the flash of the *Infinity* lights above his head. He watched the twosome approach: attractive redhead, real classy and trim, probably from one of those towns like Lincoln or Wellesley. Working in a place like Ferguson's, you got to know the type after a while. What in hell was she doing with the little skinny colored kid? Beat up like he was in an accident or something, and looked like he was crying.

Quinn backed the guard up against the spacecraft

and halted six inches from his face. She narrowed her eyes at him and said, in a low but menacing tone, "Where the fuck is *Infinity*?"

The young man's jaw dropped.

"I said," Quinn repeated, decibels building, "where the *fuck* is *Infinity*?"

His mouth opened and shut silently.

"This little kid has had a miserable couple of weeks, and this is the best thing to happen to him in his whole life. Now I want to know where the *FUCK* is *Infinity*?"

"I'm sorry, madam."

"You bet you are. Now I want to talk to the president of this place and I want to talk to him now. Where's the store phone?"

The astronaut pointed wordlessly.

"Come on, Harvey. We're going to find your Marfax."

Harvey's tears had dried into two chalky streaks. His head jerked back and forth between the equally enthralling spectacles of the dumbfounded Ferguson's employee and the enraged, heroic Quinn. When she walked away, Harvey trotted along behind with eyes full of unspilled tears and awe.

Quinn picked up the phone and waited for the operator.

"Hello," she said pleasantly. "Can you tell me the name of the president of this store, please? . . . Fine. Mr. Murdock. I want you to ring Mr. Murdock's office for me, please, and tell him Miss Mallory has urgent business with him." There was a pause while she listened politely. Then she continued, "It concerns my attorney, whom I intend to telephone this minute if I can't reach Mr. Murdock. And possibly the police. Definitely the police."

Harvey hung on every word. There was no chance of

Infinity's matching this performance, and he knew it.

"Mr. Murdock's office? Fine. I'm Quinn Mallory; who's this? . . . What's your title? . . . I see. All right, you'll do." She related the afternoon's adventure, beginning with Zindar's tantalizing introduction in the lingerie department. At the end of her narrative she said, "And if we're not standing in the presence of Marfax and Golon and the entire crew of the spaceship *Infinity* within five minutes, I will personally launch Ferguson's Department Store into outer space. I mean it. I am very pissed." Then she replaced the receiver. Harvey smiled.

In three minutes and twenty seconds—Quinn monitored her watch—six members of the *Infinity* crew arrived via escalator, all present with the exception of Zindar, who was presumably still circling the bras and girdles. Marfax was a splendid green-scaled tower. He regarded Harvey with neon eyeballs.

"What is the name of this small humanoid?" he demanded in a voice like thunder. Quinn wondered if there was an amplifier hidden in the costume.

"Harvey Jackson," Harvey croaked.

"Marfax wishes private communication with Harvey Jackson," Marfax said, and picked Harvey up in one swift motion. Quinn winced for the wounded shoulder, but Harvey's face peering at her over the chartreuse biceps was at war between delight and terror only. Pain, if in attendance at all, did not signify.

The crew began to chant, "Harvey Jackson, leader of the humanoids," and followed Marfax in a parade up and down the eighth-floor aisles.

Harvey nestled comfortably against the massive chest. "You got your magic eyeballs, Marfax?" he asked.

"You dare to ask such a question of Marfax?" boomed the creature. "Naturally I've got 'em." A buzz sounded from somewhere behind the mountain of a head, and the eyes spun into crimson whirlpools.

"Shee-*yit*," Harvey murmured. Marfax set him down outside the spacecraft.

"The humanoid leader will enter the *Infinity* ship and serve as captain," Marfax announced.

"Captain Jackson!" cheered Golon, resplendent in skintight mauve satin tights. Blond hair spilled down her back in a tangle of polyester curls.

After Harvey had entered the hatchway, Quinn tugged at Marfax's scaly elbow. "Where were you?" she demanded.

"Marfax takes coffee breaks like humanoids," he answered.

"You were supposed to be here at one thirty." She held up her watch and tapped the crystal. "See that? Two thirty."

The monster lowered his voice. "Coffee breaks cause certain physiological changes in Marfax's creature body."

"I don't give a damn about your physiology. You should have been here."

"Marfax!" Harvey called from inside the ship.

"Listen, lady." The neon eyes spun. "Do you have any idea what it's like trying to get out of this thing to take a piss?"

"Oh," Quinn said.

"They don't make zippers on Planet Orbicom."

"Oh," Quinn said again. "Okay. Maybe you could tell somebody next time."

"Right." Marfax began to thunder again as he disappeared under the doorway, bumping his head in the process. "Harvey Jackson, humanoid captain of the primary star force! Marfax desires communication with you!"

Quinn didn't see Harvey again for half an hour. By then a horde of eager *Infinity* fans had accumulated outside the spacecraft. Now and then a crew member emerged to mollify the crowd. Finally Harvey stepped out, his hand invisible in Marfax's giant paw. Golon planted a kiss on his cheek, and Harvey rejoined Quinn. The crew stood at attention and with Marfax conducting shouted together, "Farewell to Harvey Jackson! Farewell to our beloved captain!"

The other children stared at Harvey with faces radiating envy. "I bet they think I'm on the TV show," Harvey whispered to Quinn. He took her hand. "Thanks . . . thanks for . . ."

"A pleasure," she said, stepping onto the escalator. "You know something, Harve? Standing there next to Marfax just now, your eyes were as bright as his. I think maybe yours are magic too."

They were both so hungry that they ate dinner in the first restaurant they could find with tablecloths and candles. There were no hot fudge sundaes on the menu, but Harvey didn't seem to notice.

Chapter 30

In Will's mind he and Quinn were closing in on summer as if they were doing a headlong dash on tiptoe. It wasn't easy to maintain the awkward gait, and both felt the strain.

On a Saturday afternoon two weeks before graduation, they were studying in Will's room. Outside, a gray sky sulked close to the ground, heavy with its burden of rain but unable to release it.

Quinn closed her notebook. "Was that thunder?"

"No." Will was stretched across his bed, trying to absorb Professor Buxby's final lecture on Thomas Hardy.

"I wish it would pour," Quinn said. She tapped her foot restlessly. Will's T-shirt had shrunk, exposing an inch of skin above his jeans. She stared at it. "Can we take a break?"

Will looked up. Her face held a familiar suggestion.

"Sure." He collected his papers and piled them on the floor beside the bed.

Conversation was dangerous, so their lovemaking had become a silent rite. Quinn's body performed a languid dance under his hands as if too full of sensuality for motion. His orgasm was early and explosive, but Quinn made a long, slow climb. He reached into her with his fingers, the mingled liquid of their bodies warm as she strained toward him, then pulled away, then arched again. He felt her flesh swell, then begin to pulsate, and suddenly she was sobbing through her climax. She tried to muffle the deep cries against his shoulder.

"What is it?" he whispered. But he knew.

The tears slid out the edges of her eyes to make dark streaks in her hair.

"I love you," he said.

"Yeah."

"You're the one who's big on action. Tell me what to do."

As she reached for the tissue box, her shoulder pressed against his face. Her skin tasted faintly of salt.

"I've been giving the matter some thought," she said, mopping her face. "Somewhere I read that every seven years or so your body replaces all its cells. Maybe it'll happen to us. We'll be total strangers and it won't matter anymore."

"I don't know if I want that."

She blew her nose. "No. Except sometimes." She allowed herself to look directly into his face. His mouth barely curved in the strange smile that seemed to contain both apology and amusement.

"I'm sure my cells would still lust after your cells," he said.

She choked out a kind of laugh. "Pitiful, isn't it?"

It had finally begun to rain. The sky was as dark as late evening. Quinn's hair looked almost black in the shadows, but her eyes shone up at him like chips of aquamarine. "The way I figure it," she said, "we've got until the wedding. I could kill them for moving it up. I liked the August plan a whole lot better."

"Their families won't be speaking by the end of June."

"They haven't even *met* and they're not speaking." She blew her nose again, tossed the wadded tissue at the wastebasket, and missed. "Oh, well. This way Mrs. Markowitz only has time for one heart attack and the Huntingtons think everybody's so busy with graduation nobody'll notice their daughter is marrying a Jew."

"It's going to be tough to celebrate, honey."

"At least somebody's getting married."

Will sat up on the edge of the bed. She ran her hand down the hard ridge of his backbone. "I should have known you were going to be a stubborn bastard, with your fucking iambic pentameter. God, how I wish I didn't have to do the things I have to do."

Will dipped his head to peer at her over his shoulder. "Ain't it the truth?" Then he got up and began to get dressed.

Quinn listened to the rain, its soft, comforting swish against the window, and snuggled down under the blankets. She never wanted to leave this room with its sweet dusky smell of intimacy. If only it would keep raining forever.

Chapter 31

On Thursday afternoon, while Quinn labored through her last exam, Will set off on the bus to say good-bye to Harvey. He had made repeated attempts to prepare himself, but dread still sat like a sickening mass in his stomach. Once, in the middle of the night, cowardice had overcome him and he composed a letter that began, *Dear Harvey, I'm sorry I couldn't say good-bye in person. My exam schedule is so brutal that* . . . and so on.

Mercifully, the boy was participating in a school concert this evening. Their last afternoon would be brief. Will knew a plan was obligatory, otherwise they would simply drift through the two hours in mutual misery. Once again he opted for the pool table. If nothing else, Will's ineptitude would remind Harvey of how accomplished his successor was.

The day was steamy hot. Harvey waited by the school steps with the heat from the pavement shimmering all around him. He wore jeans and a too-large T-shirt that was the same pale blue shade as Will's. Will watched Harvey note the coincidence and then avert his eyes.

Two games of pool elapsed without conversation, but with each of them sneaking long looks at the other. Will stared at the scar that sat like an ugly worm on Harvey's cheek. If it happened again, would Harvey call for Steve, or would he, in pain and fear, forget and cry Will's name?

Will put down his cue. "Harve."

Harvey took a good look at Will's face and set his stick down too. He stood straight, a fragile soldier child, realizing that the time had come to be brave.

Will shook his head. "You are some kid, you know that?"

"Sure, I know it."

"You make me a promise, tough guy?"

Harvey shot him a look of mock suspicion from under the thick lashes. "That depends."

"You ever need me, you call collect. I expect you to write plenty of letters, but there's the phone, too. Okay?" He cupped the small brown chin briefly.

"Yeah. Okay." Harvey turned toward the table. "Can we play now?"

"You break this time." *Break my heart, you little monster. I'm going to grab you and stuff you in my suitcase.*

Will escorted Harvey to his building without saying any of the things that filled his head. Nor did he deliver his declaration of faith, a speech carefully worked out last night, about Will's confidence in Harvey's future, in his ability to bust free of ghetto futility and make a life for himself. Will had planned to wind up with a stirring grand finale about how people could be together in important ways even if they weren't together physically. *Et cetera, et cetera, et cetera*, as spake the Siamese monarch in *The King and I* who abandoned everybody in the end.

They stood inside the doorway, graffiti encircling

them like old friends whose profanity had finally become endearing.

"Well, Harve," Will said. Harvey stared up at him with a face full of questions. "I'm going to miss you a shitload."

Harvey's chin began to quiver. He stiffened the muscles around his mouth, trying to deceive. Will watched, and wondered if his greatest cruelty had been in befriending this child. The small face gave way and crumpled. Will dropped to his knees on the filthy floor, and Harvey was in his arms. The wiry body heaved against him in three violent sobs. Then Harvey wrenched himself away, shoved inside the door, and clattered upstairs.

Will was left kneeling like a supplicant in prayer. His heart shouted through the broken panes of glass and up after the stumbling footsteps: *But I didn't tell you!*

Like a whipped dog, Will limped to the bus stop. The only thing he wished for now was that the bus would drive him straight to the airport for the first flight west. No more amputations.

Chapter 32

Quinn's last exam was Thursday morning with graduation the following Monday. She had decided that each hour would be so full and rich that time would slow from the sheer weight of condensed experience. Somehow, though, she slipped into Friday before she could absorb the departure of Thursday. Already the morning had been gobbled up with packing. Quinn sat on the stripped bed and stared at her watch, wondering how it could possibly be eleven thirty. Last she'd looked, it was ten-oh-eight. At least one hour misplaced, unaccounted for, as if she had been knocked unconscious or had been anesthetized. She looked around the bare room at the cartons, mostly closed, taped, and neatly labeled with marking pen: *Linens; Religion Notes; Lit. Books; Junk;* and so on. Somebody had packed them; it must have been she. So she'd been here the whole time after all, except for her soul, which had spent the past hour hanging around over at the men's dorm.

Quinn got up stiffly and began to fill the last box. In went four years of letters from Margery. In went four years of newspaper clippings from her mother. Next were the notebooks from Professor Buxby's class. She hesitated, then began to riffle through them. Their margins were copiously decorated with doodles, a living record of the many months of cartoon correspondence with Will. The pages seemed as elaborate as the illuminated pages of antique manuscripts they kept in glass cases at the library.

She taped the box, then shoved it into the hall to join a mound of luggage just outside. From the doorway she gazed back into her empty room. Paradoxically, with her belongings cleared away, it seemed smaller. Sunlight streaked through the window and bounced off the bare white walls, making her blink. The only inhabitants were dancing, swirling dust motes. *I lived here*, Quinn protested with a sudden twinge of sympathy for Kilroy. Remembering her first day, freshman year, unpacking her suitcases in another room in another hall, she felt more than four years older. That girl with the quick smile and easy confidence had gradually been displaced. Just like the room, she had once been sunny and uncomplicated. It seemed appropriate to be relinquishing her cubicle just as she was relinquishing that laughing girl. She turned her back and closed the door behind her.

As a graduation present Gus loaned Quinn and Will a truck to transport Quinn's paraphernalia to Medham. Quinn spent the first half of her trip wailing along with the radio. Will sat in the passenger seat with one foot on the dashboard and one resting on the carton marked *Misc. Memories*.

"*Tonight you're mine completely. You give your love so swee-eet-ly . . .*"

"When do you have time to learn those things?" Will asked.

"Osmosis. It's in the air, can't you hear it? *Tonight*

with words unspo-oh-ken. You said that I'm the only wuh-ha-huh-ha-hun . . ."*

"Hey!"

She stopped singing and looked at him.

"What about Harvey?" he asked.

"What about him?"

"You think he's okay with Steve?"

"Uh huh, but he's going to miss you."

"He'll miss you, too."

"Oh, he's coming to Medham for the weekend once a month, as long as it's okay in terms of Mom. Marylou from the cafeteria says she'll put him on the bus, and I'll pick him up in Boston."

"What if you end up in New York?"

"I'll stay with the Boston job until I'm sure Ann's in a real remission. Anyway, even if I go to New York, I'll be coming home on weekends. Harvey can come too."

"I wonder why he didn't tell me," Will mused. Quinn kept glancing at him to try to decipher his expression. Finally he gave her a wry smile. "I'm jealous."

"Who of?"

"Both of you."

"You've got visitation rights," she said.

"You're pretty blasé."

"You bet your ass. It's the only way to make it through."

"Okay. Sorry. I know you're not blasé."

She took one hand off the steering wheel and pointed her finger at him. "I'm going to ask you one question, and then I want you to promise we won't talk about it ever again."

* Lyrics from "Will You Love Me Tomorrow" by Carole King and Gerry Goffin. Copyright 1960, 1961 by SCREEN GEMS-EMI MUSIC INC. Used by permission. All rights reserved.

"How can I promise if I don't know the question?"

"I won't ask it, then."

"All right. I promise to try."

"That'll do. I want to know, do you think we'll ever see each other again, after Van's wedding?"

He gazed out the front window. His eyes flickered involuntarily as they captured speeding images and then let them go. "I don't know, babe."

"That's not an answer."

"It's the best I can do."

"It's a chicken answer. Come on, be brave. I can take it. What do you really think, in your heart of hearts?"

"I think we won't see each other again."

"Ever?"

He nodded.

"All right. Now let's not talk about it anymore."

She turned up the volume on the radio and began to sing along with Mick Jagger.

That night Quinn lay in her bed and thought about *ever*. The word had an important ring to it. She tried it backward. *Reve. Never* was better and it served the same purpose. *Never, reven, raven.* Quoth the raven, Nevermore. She kicked her legs restlessly under the blanket. The only way to endure the next few months would be to tell herself she would see him again, maybe tomorrow, maybe next week, maybe five years from now. That was how her father had quit smoking, first assuring himself that he'd have a cigarette in ten minutes. The ten minutes would pass, and so would the peak of his craving. Once he could make it through several hours, he began telling himself he'd smoke one tomorrow. Then he extended it to next month, then to next year, until finally he didn't need the pretense anymore.

He said it took about four years to truly kick it. Well, maybe by 1969 she'd have rid her system of the William Ingraham habit.

1969. It seemed so far off. Would Ann be with them then? After so many false hopes the doctors now said she was in a true remission. She was even planning to attend graduation. The atmosphere in the house had changed; it seemed to be sighing with gratitude. John's relief had caused him to relent on the issue of Aunt Millie, who was coming to tea next week. Quinn sent silent thanks in the direction of her ceiling. It was a habit left over from childhood when some aching wish had been fulfilled, like the Christmas ice skates that weren't even hand-me-downs but were all stiff and new with the tag from Filene's stuck to one blade. In those earlier times she had voiced her gratitude to particular names, like St. Theresa or St. Christopher, but they had since become as impotent as figures out of childhood mythology—Rumpelstiltskin or the Tooth Fairy. Only the impulse was left, like knocking on wood.

Downstairs, Will tried to arrange his body on the living room sofa in a position that might permit sleep. Soft light from a streetlamp outside filtered through the curtains, illuminating the picture gallery against the far wall. Will's favorite, Quinn's sixth-grade portrait, beamed at him with braids, freckles, and a grin that displayed teeth too big for the preadolescent mouth. Already evident in that saucy face were the qualities that had attracted him in the first place: curiosity; optimism; adventurousness; generosity. As a young woman, however, she had developed certain extras, among them an astute intelligence and a tantalizing, robust sexuality. Will shook his head. Quinn's twelve-year-old face seemed to shake hers back at him, mocking.

He wondered what she would be like at thirty-five. Quinn's adult personality seemed less predictable to him than his own. Will assumed that he would remain the same. The person he had been at six was mostly what he was today. But Quinn was a changeling. She slipped away, eluding the categories he provided for her in his compulsive effort to possess her somehow, even if only within the cold, echoing chambers of his intellect.

He stretched his feet over the arm of the couch and tried to think about time in its grand perspective. This day, like the day of their good-bye next week, was a mere blink, meaningless in historical terms. Their pain was a tiny twinge compared to the accumulated miseries of humanity, the wars, famines, the systematic cruelties. Will stood perched at the edge of the universe and regarded the two of them. They didn't matter. A wink, a pinprick of light extinguished, that's all.

He shivered, feeling the chill of empty terrestrial darkness whirling about him. He drew his feet up under the blanket and finally, half frozen despite the warm spring night, fell asleep.

Graduation was a bright blur for them both. When many years later Quinn viewed Stanley's home movies of the occasion, she was struck by the identical expressions on their faces, Will and Quinn staring into the camera with the dazed look of tourists who have lost their way.

They walked up the platform on legs unsteady from the impact of four years slamming them into this final moment. They took the dry white scrolls, shook the dry, white hand, and marched down the other side of the ramp, no longer college students.

Chapter 33

The wedding had been deliberately arranged for Tuesday, an inconvenient day that might discourage curious relatives. Both the Markowitzes and the Huntingtons breathed the heavy atmosphere of shame; both prayed in secret for poor attendance. But despite entreaties for heavenly intervention, two dozen people showed up at the rehearsal dinner Monday night. Vanessa had chosen Anthony's Pier 4 down by the docks.

When Quinn and Will arrived, Van greeted them with haunted eyes and the red blotches on the sensitive skin of her neck that served as a stress barometer.

"Help," she croaked.

"Where's Stan?" Quinn asked.

"Placating his mother. She started to cry after her first glass of sherry."

Will draped his arm around her shoulder. "This time tomorrow it'll be all over."

Quinn felt her throat constrict.

"They made him get a haircut. I don't recognize him." Van's blotches were spreading to her cheeks.

"Have you had anything to drink?" Quinn asked. "Come on, honey. Let's get you smashed."

They led Van to her table. The picture windows framed Boston Harbor, which was pink and glistening in the sunset.

"Did you get our present?" Quinn asked.

"We're not going to open it until tomorrow night, when we're alone and married."

Will's eyes flickered to Quinn's for a moment, then retreated to the spectacular light show outside. The clouds were laced with silver now, and the smooth water was gold. *Make new friends, but keep the old; some are silver and the others gold.* He wanted to reach out and touch Quinn's russet hair.

Their present was an antique silver picture frame that held a photo of the four of them leaning against Stanley's bus. Stanley looked fierce, the camera having misinterpreted the stubbly shadows of his face as sinister. His eyes were dark with mystery. Quinn wished he'd worn a golden earring. Van was self-contained, with lowered eyes and half-smile only a trace too haughty for the quintessential madonna. Will, a head taller than the rest, looked foolish and goofy, with the relaxed grin Quinn usually saw only after they had made love. Quinn herself, nestled under Will's shoulder, was a trembling fragile flower, hanging on to the arm of her man for protection. She carried a wallet-size copy with her everywhere.

Van had seated Quinn and Will to either side of Mr. Markowitz's sister. Aunt Sarah was a concrete hulk of a woman with tight little curls that clung to her head like terrified blue caterpillars.

In a voice smaller than expected from a diaphragm of such magnitude, she asked, "What's that?" pointing to a bowl by the centerpiece.

"Bacon bits," Quinn answered, then hurriedly elaborated. "Uh, for salad or baked potato. You don't have to eat it. I don't like it much myself, bacon."

Aunt Sarah regarded her impassively. Quinn wondered at the incongruity of the woman's gaily flowered dress.

"I'm Quinn Mallory," she said, and extended her hand. "That's Will Ingraham on your right. We're friends of Stanley and Van's."

Suddenly Aunt Sarah's face registered her arrival at some private conclusion. She smiled. Quinn felt a rush of pleasure as the grim face surrendered to half a dozen dimples. There was a childish space between her front teeth.

"Stanley is my favorite nephew," Aunt Sarah said. An Eastern European childhood was evident in her pronunciation. "I love him very much."

Quinn was at her mercy. "Me, too," she echoed.

"I see he is happy, thanks God."

"Yes," Quinn said.

Then Aunt Sarah turned to beam at Will, allowing Quinn the opportunity to watch his face fill with astonished delight.

Despite her charms, however, Aunt Sarah was a formidable obstruction between Quinn and Will. They couldn't hold hands; they could barely see each other. When she finally excused herself to visit the ladies' room, Quinn asked, "When do you think we can leave?"

"Empty bed in an empty hotel room, what a waste," Will agreed.

"I have to cross my legs."

At the Arlington Copley Hotel they warmed their tiny room with lovemaking, some of it ferocious enough to leave bruises on Quinn's rib cage. She fell asleep at 4:00 A.M., half waking an hour later to see Will writing at the desk. Wads of paper littered the glass top like giant popcorn balls. She drifted back into a dream about the fir tree in Rockefeller Center.

When she woke, he was lying beside her. Panic snatched her eyes open: today was Van's wedding, today Will would fly away. She watched him sleeping. His eyelashes were dark near the lids, but the tips were pale. It was a detail she had never noticed. How many hundreds of similar discoveries she had yet to make in an adventure that ought to absorb a lifetime.

"Will," she whispered. He slept on, so she began to trace the shape of his ear with her fingertip. His face was ruddy while he slept, as if he'd been in the sun too long. Finally he opened his eyes.

"You bastard," she whispered.

"Ym," he said and slipped an arm around her waist. "M'ere."

At first the bruises and cramped muscles protested, but soon her body softened under his hands and the pain melted away.

Afterward they lay in silence, staring up at the ceiling. There was a crack that formed a rough cross. Bless this bed, Quinn thought. Or maybe, *Requiescat in Pace.*

"Are you really going to do this, Will?" she asked.

"Yes."

"Do you . . . is it . . . well, if you were polite, you'd sound a little more miserable about it."

He rolled over to face her. The pale tips of his eyelashes had darkened with tears. There were shiny hollows under his eyes.

"Oh, Will." She reached for him, trying to drive her body through his skin and be enclosed. He would be forced to carry her with him everywhere, and she would have no choices.

"I dreamed I saw you writing," she said into his shoulder.

"No. I was up."

She pulled back to look at him.

"Needed to set a few things down."

"Let me see."

He shook his head.

"Please."

"Not now. Sometime."

There wasn't much sometime left, she thought, then took a deep breath and plunged out of bed.

The Silver Ghost was waiting when she stepped out of the marble lobby into a hazy summer morning. There would be sailboats on the Charles River today, like brides with their crisp white veils. Sinking back into the seat, she tried to think of Stanley and Van's union without envy. But the irony stung.

"Shit, piss, and corruption," she said.

"Excuse me, miss?" asked the driver.

"Oh," Quinn said, thinking fast. "Sure to be instructions. About the wedding. I'm a little nervous."

The Huntington house was filled with lilacs, and with their sweet fresh scent. A maid led Quinn upstairs to Van's bedroom, where the prospective bride was screwing on the pearl earrings Stanley had given her as a wedding present. She wore a creamy silk dress with an Empire waist and lace trim on the sleeves and bodice. After much indecision she had opted for wearing her hair down, just clean and straight, the way Stanley liked it most. She was beautiful. My friend, Quinn thought, watching from the doorway, and tears welled up.

Sensing someone's presence, Van turned, saw Quinn and the tears, and held out her arms. Blue jeans and T-shirt were enveloped in clouds of silk.

"Does this stuff water-stain?" Quinn asked.

"It better not." Van held her by the shoulders. "You know what I wish for most of all?" she asked. "For you to be as happy as I am."

Quinn's chin trembled. "One of these days it's bound to happen." She broke away and paraded in her jeans. "Think I'll look cute sashaying down the aisle?"

"There's a part of me that would just as soon you wore that."

"There's a part of your mother that would pick me up by the ears and dump me into the chicken liver."

"Please," Van said. "In this house we call it *pâté*."

Quinn giggled. "How does she explain gefilte fish?"

"Quenelles, my dear."

"Well, pretty soon you and Stan can ride off into the sunset and let the Montagues and Capulets fight it out on Beacon Hill."

"Have I told you how much I'm going to miss you?" Van asked.

"Have I told you how much I wish you'd zip it up?"

"Are you going to be all right?"

"Of course I'll be all right. Did you ever know me when I wasn't?"

"I mean about Will."

"I know what you mean. I'll survive."

"Mother has a copy of our itinerary for you."

"Oh, for heaven's sake, I'm not going to bug you on your honeymoon."

"You will if you need us. Won't you?"

"In a dire emergency. Ingrown toenails. Hemorrhoids, something like that."

"We'll see you as soon as we get settled in New York. If your mom's okay, maybe you'll be there too."

"Could be, but don't you be thinking about me on

your wedding day. It's only once. Enjoy it. I'm going to."

"Enjoy it? With that crowd?"

"Nothing to it," Quinn said. "But I'd better get dressed or you'll have a tacky-looking maid of honor."

Quinn watched the living room ceremony through a mist. She could make out that Stanley was almost clean-shaven, and that he, too, was close to tears. Quinn scanned the rows of guests and spotted Will toward the back, with his legs stretched out into the aisle. His hair was dark and slicked down with water from his shower. She liked it this way, a hero from an F. Scott Fitzgerald novel. She also liked it when it dried, full and sun-streaked and wild. He felt her eyes on him and winked.

While Quinn watched the bride and groom, Will watched Quinn. She was wearing a pale lavender dress that matched the lilacs spilling over the mantelpiece. Will tried to memorize her solemn expression. He knew she was trying not to cry.

". . . pronounce you man and wife," intoned the judge. He was an austere-looking man with purple veins in a chalky face. He produced a tiny smile while suggesting to Stanley that he might kiss the bride. Stanley had lapsed into a trance, so Van was obliged to nudge her new husband with an elegant elbow. The kiss lasted a long time. Quinn watched Mrs. Huntington glower as the congregation began to titter. Finally Van's shoulders started shaking with laughter and Stanley had to let her go. There was a gasp from the nearly suffocated bride, and the string ensemble began its recessional.

Guests filed out behind the newlyweds to crowd into the library, the dining room, and the small backyard. Quinn was just ahead of Stanley's parents.

"It's not legal without the glass," Mr. Markowitz complained.

"Sh, sh," pleaded Mrs. Markowitz.

"Listen, I've got a right. He's my son. Not even a *mazeltov*, for Christ's sake."

"Morrie, sh," said Mrs. Markowitz. "It was nice. Very nice."

Quinn turned around to smile at them. "It all went very well, don't you think?"

"What's not to go well? Two minutes and it's all over," Stanley's father grumbled. Mrs. Markowitz had turned red.

"Don't you think we ought to talk Stanley into breaking a wineglass or something," Quinn suggested. "Just to make it official?"

Mr. Markowitz gave his wife a bruising pinch on the arm. "See? Sharp as a matzoh, this one. So he doesn't break it under the *chupah*. The thought is what counts."

"Right," Quinn agreed, wondering how a matzoh could be sharp. Mr. Markowitz had Stanley's eyes. She enjoyed looking into them—soft, dark, affectionate eyes.

They formed a reception line in the garden outside. Stanley's uncle was talking with Mrs. Huntington at Quinn's elbow.

"What's that accent you got?"

"Accent?" Mrs. Huntington said.

"Yeah, where you from?" the uncle persisted.

"New York City." Her voice filtered up the back of her throat and out through her nose like an impersonation of William F. Buckley, Jr.

"Hey! Me, too! Small world!" he exclaimed. "Brooklyn, Ocean Parkway. Where'd you go to school?"

"Chapin," said Mrs. Huntington through narrow nostrils.

"Don't know it." The uncle lost interest. He moved on, and a moment later Quinn heard him ask Dr. Huntington if he knew a cardiologist in Borough Park by the name of Irwin Finkelstein.

Quinn spied Will's shoulder protruding from behind a tree trunk in the only secluded corner of the garden. She called to him, and he approached wearing the expression of a sacrificial lamb. She introduced him to Vanessa's teen-age cousin as Henry Thoreau.

Soon *Tales from the Vienna Woods* drifted out from the living room, where the ensemble had gathered beside the fireplace. The music gradually drew everyone indoors, but Quinn and Will lingered in the doorway, watching Stanley and Van come together in their first dance. Stanley was a little stiff with his carefully rehearsed *one*-two-three, *one*-two-three. Vanessa swayed like a calla lily in the breeze. Will watched the eyes in the faces that ringed the floor, eyes that enclosed the couple in a poignant circle of hopes.

Then Dr. Huntington cut in. He gazed down into his daughter's face and held her gingerly. Things would never be the same between them again, and both of them knew it.

Stanley, meanwhile, was having a hard go of it with Myra Huntington. Despite her lovely clothes and graceful figure, the woman could not dance. She moved her feet in tiny panicked shuffles. Stanley, with his lurching triangles, was practically dragging her across the floor. They struggled like strangers colliding and rebounding in a crowd.

At the urging of Vanessa, Dr. Huntington drew the Markowitzes onto the dance floor. Stanley's mother was bashful, but she danced easily in the arms of her son. Van and Mr. Markowitz paraded across the room, more walking than dancing. Quinn strained to hear the conversation as they came near.

". . . on marriage it's very tough," Mr. Markowitz was saying. "The hospital, all the time, the studying . . . good you and Stan got this thing, this strong thing . . ."

They moved out of earshot, with Van listening attentively. Then suddenly she looked weary, and glanced toward Stanley's back with yearning. Will could see that Stanley's expression was identically exhausted and wistful. Will and Quinn marched out onto the dance floor, Quinn to Mr. Markowitz, Will to his wife. Stanley and Van slipped into each other's arms like matching pieces of a jigsaw puzzle.

Mr. Markowitz huffed and puffed with Quinn and then, breathless, led her to the sidelines where Myra Huntington stood chatting with her bridge partner. The women wore simple raw-silk shifts, one almost gray, one almost beige.

"Hello, Myra . . ." gasped Mr. Markowitz. "Too much an old man for this business." He mopped his head with a handkerchief. "This young lady and me, we're talking about you take a look at those two dancing and Vanessa's more Jewish than our Stanley."

Myra's mouth twitched into a rigid arc. Her card partner gushed, "We have a woman in our bridge club who's the president of that organization, the one for . . . Judaic women."

"Hadassah," Mr. Markowitz said. The women escaped to the champagne bowl. Mr. Markowitz watched them go and muttered, "Why you think they wear such things to a *simchah*? Is it a funeral today?"

The air conditioning, vanquished by the June heat and the warmth of accumulated revelers, sighed and quit. The violinists could barely keep their slippery hands on their bows. Finally they quit too, and headed for refreshments. Will hunted for Quinn with Mrs. Markowitz in tow. The woman was flushed with heat and pleasure. Her face reflected the deep pink of her ensemble.

"My oh, my," she said to Quinn with a laugh. "Your young man has very long legs."

Quinn nodded. You're telling me, she thought, imagining the shape of his naked calves. She glanced at her watch, then up at Will, despairing. Her stomach shriveled into a small fist that lodged in her throat about larynx level.

"Gotta get ready, I guess." She forced the words past the lump.

"Yeah." Will hoped she would change into her jeans. He wanted to leave her that way, not resplendent and unfamiliar in a floor-length gown.

"You aren't leaving us?" Mrs. Markowitz said.

"I have a plane to catch," Will answered.

"You can walk out on such a good thing?" Mr. Markowitz protested. Will looked quickly at Quinn. She had heard it the same way. *Exactly*, her clear eyes accused him.

"I hate to do it," Will declared. The intensity of his response confused Mrs. Markowitz. She watched the exchange of glances between Will and Quinn. Mr. Markowitz started to speak, but his wife quietly drew him away. "Let's have something to drink," she said. "We'll say good-bye to the young people later on."

"A glass tea," Mr. Markowitz said.

"In this heat?"

Quinn fled upstairs.

They stood in the doorway and watched the festivities. The brightly colored clothing of the Markowitz contingent was sprinkled liberally among the muted garb of Vanessa's family like tropical birds chattering with barn swallows. Quinn spotted Stanley leaning against the mantelpiece talking to Dr. Huntington. The groom held a champagne glass in one hand and gestured expansively with the other. He looked a little drunk. Dr. Huntington wore his habitual expression of benevolent irony. Quinn waved to catch Stanley's attention. He set the champagne glass on the marble shelf and went to fetch Van.

Quinn took Stanley's arm. "I saw you doing your George Sanders routine over there," she chided him.

"Don't leave," Van pleaded.

"I'd rather not," Will said.

The two couples smiled at each other in silence for a moment.

"You two—" Stanley began.

"No!" Quinn exclaimed. "I won't get through it. Just say good-bye."

"Good night, Gracie," Stanley said.

"Will." Van stood on her tiptoes to kiss him. "It's hard to know what to say."

"Then don't say anything," Quinn begged. "I'm getting a terrible stomachache." She embraced Stanley, then Van. "Have a wonderful trip, Mr. and Mrs. Markowitz. Say hello to the Champs-Élysées for me, Tell 'em I'll get there some day. I love you."

"We're on the flight path," Stanley said to Will. "Dump some rice out the window when you fly over."

Will held out his hand and Stanley grasped it in both of his.

"Quick, Will," Quinn said in a strangled voice.

They bolted for the door.

Van watched them climb into the Huntington limousine, and leaned against her new husband. "I hope I live long enough to throw rice at *them*," she said.

"You'd better live to be a very old lady, Vanessa."

The ride to the airport was mostly silent, with Will holding her against him in a corner of the backseat. As they emerged from Callahan Tunnel into the sunshine, Quinn said, "Reincarnation, that's the answer."

"Grasping at straws, babe."

"Any straw will do. Why are we doing this?"

He didn't answer.

They walked stiffly through the airport. Their faces wore the expressions of children on their way to the principal's office to be punished. When they arrived at the gate, Will looked down at her.

"You shouldn't have come with me."

"Nope," she said.

He reached into the zipper pocket of his duffel bag and drew out an envelope. In the upper left-hand corner was the Arlington Copley logo. Quinn remembered the crumpled paper balls in the middle of the night. She started to open the envelope, but he put his hand over hers.

"No. Later."

A uniformed attendant said, "Sir, are you on Flight 305? Better get a move on."

Quinn forced a ghastly smile. "Well, it's been aces," she said.

Her freckles were like sand across the tops of her cheeks, eyes dark, deep blue now, like her mother's. *I love you, girl.* Out loud he said, "Okay, keep in touch. Take care of our little boy. And your mom."

"Oh, shit." She buried her face in his chest and held on hard. Then she released him. "No, don't kiss me." She gave him a little push and he started walking. She waited until he was through the door, just in case he glanced around at her. But he didn't, and when he disappeared, she gave way. Then she wiped her face with the back of her hand and marched down the long hallway toward the exit, clutching her envelope.

In the limousine she heard a plane take off. She craned her neck toward the back window and watched it arch out over the harbor and head due west. Then she opened the envelope, slowly, taking care not to rip its contents. The lines on the hotel stationery were scrawled in Will's bold, careless print:

Your soul brushes mine
So briefly—a butterfly kiss.
I look away for one moment
Feeling your warm breath
On my shoulder.
And when I turn back,
You are gone.

A butterfly. An airplane. She watched her hands grow shiny and wet, hands like her mother's, glistening as they'd stroked her grieving father's hair.

The limousine shot downtown toward the noisy crush of the city. She held Will's poem in an embrace and remembered the tall pines and rugged mountain ranges. So remote, so out of touch with the world's business. There was no reason why Boise, Idaho, shouldn't have a fine educational television station like New York or Boston, to bring political debate and culture into the boondocks. One of these days she'd check it out. You never know.